GIVING IT UP

A Novel

By

Alexandra Y. Caluen

GIVING IT UP

Copyright 2020 by Alexandra Y. Caluen

Cover design by RK Young

Cover photo by Alex Sheldon @slavewire *unsplash.com*

Author's note: The song ''Til There Was You' was written for the musical 'The Music Man' by Meredith Wilson.

GIVING IT UP
The Playlist:

California Dreamin'
Dana Owens a.k.a. Queen Latifah

When You Wish Upon A Star
Linda Ronstadt

Nowadays
Catherine Zeta-Jones and Renee Zellweger

The Land of Might-Have-Been
Jeremy Northam

Over the Rainbow
Harry Connick Jr.

A Dream Is a Wish Your Heart Makes
Steve Tyrell

Up On The Roof
The Drifters

Pure Imagination
Maroon 5

No Turning Back
Hooked Like Helen

GIVING IT UP

CHAPTER 1

November 2010

Liam thought he was doing pretty well. Being cool, being sociable. Chilling with his new friends over good food and a game and no expectations. He couldn't remember the last time he'd spent a holiday like this, with no expectations. Aside from the hosts, they were meeting each other for the first time. All the other guests were single, too. The chemistry was good. Liam was usually single on Thanksgiving, because taking a date to a family-hosted holiday thing was a recipe for disaster, or at least for endless hints and jokes and why-haven't-you-settled-down-yet. Why not with this one. To which the only honest answer was: well, because either he doesn't want to or I don't want to. And yes, it's great that there's been another wedding (or christening, or confirmation). Yes, I would have liked to get away for that. He never gave a hint of his true feelings: enough is enough. He didn't want his family to see the envy. The loneliness.

There was a moment, earlier this year, when he'd looked at one of his hosts and thought, maybe. A very brief moment, because their two dates hadn't led to anything, because Robert was already in love with Jade. It was, he decided, a much less damaging way to be rejected than the usual. 'I really like you but I'm in love with someone else' – said almost anxiously, with a clear desire not to hurt – was so much easier to take than 'this isn't going to work.'

It was still hard to take. He was forty-two; something should have worked by now. He'd been sort-of trying for ten years, ever since he got his head above

1

water with the student loans, and seriously trying for four. The business was solidly profitable, and since he hadn't bothered buying a house he was in great shape financially. Had a partner in the dermatology office, a physician assistant to help with the injectables, two aestheticians and a nurse. The suite rental was screamingly expensive, of course, but getting established in Beverly Hills was its own reward. He'd have loved to steal Robert's assistant Emily to run the front desk. The medical-office routine was important, but there was more to it than simply knowing how to set up the files, submit the claims, and manage appointments. Emily was adorable. She was attractive in the way that made other people feel good, without making them feel as if they couldn't measure up. A great smile, a ready laugh, and a pleasant voice. Robert would probably put out a hit on him if he actually stole her.

He was laughing to himself over that thought, refilling his plate from the buffet in the kitchen, when he heard the commotion of some new arrival. Everybody had been great, so he went back out to the living room prepared to be charmed. He wasn't prepared for Mark Valance. *I know that guy*, he thought blankly. Of course he didn't actually know him. He watched the show, that was all. Well, he could be cool around a celebrity. After all, he'd managed to be cool around his celebrity clients, and around Robert's client the wrestler, who'd wrapped his first movie role that summer.

Mark was hugging Jade. Shaking hands with Robert. Meeting and greeting, saying something to Robert's friend and fellow agent Parker. Giving Jonathan the wrestler a congratulatory comment with the handshake, doing a little light flirting with Emily and then with Jade's friend and fellow stylist Shaya.

2

Saying something about how when he was finally done on the show he was coming to her for a new look. Shaking back his nearly-shoulder-length auburn hair with an exasperated look that didn't fool anybody.

After a fake-insulted comment about why Mark should come to him instead, Jade said, "Mark, this is our friend Liam Byrne. He's a dermatologist."

Mark turned to the last person, the tall guy standing there with a plate in his left hand, and was deeply grateful he was an actor. *Holy shit he's got eyes like Elizabeth Taylor.* "Dr. Byrne, nice to meet you." They shook hands. "Mark Valance."

"Yes, I know. I watch your show. Nice to meet you too." Liam made that sound casually friendly. It was possible that Valance was here for the same reason Liam was, because he was single and didn't want to do the family holiday yet again. It was also possible he was only doing a drive-by. And it was irrelevant because he was surely not here to pick up a date, and even if he were, he was straight. At least Liam thought he was. Though the handshake went on that nanosecond too long, and the eye contact stayed with it. Then there was a small smile, the faintest shrug, and Valance let go of his hand. Liam felt bereft. He indicated the plate he was holding, saying something about the treats in store, and headed for the club chair in the den. Set the plate down next to his glass of pink champagne (he wouldn't have thought of serving brut rosé with Thanksgiving dinner and a football game, but it was perfect) and took a seat. He watched without watching while Valance chatted with everyone. Noticed when he went into the kitchen for his own plate, heard Jade laughing with him in there.

He was concentrating on the food – Robert and Jade were apparently both good cooks, because of course they were – when Emily plopped down on the loveseat.

"I hope you don't mind," she said. "I thought I'd make room for Mr. Valance to sit down out there." She waved at the living room.

"I don't mind. I should probably warn you I'm trying to think up a strategy to steal you from Robert."

"Oh are you?" Emily was delighted. "I've never worked in a medical office though." So he asked her about her history, and how she ended up working at the agency. It was pleasant. Got him through that plate full of food. She brought them both a refill of champagne after a while, asked him some questions about his business, and showed no sign of wanting to go into the adjacent room where the celebrities were. Then they heard a burst of laughter and turned their heads, looking past the wet bar to the living room.

"I literally have to sing for my supper?" Mark was trying to look offended. It wasn't coming off; he wasn't that good of an actor, at least not when he was halfway down his second glass of champagne and being showered with flattery.

Jade said, "Robert loved you in 'Chicago.' I was trying to give him some inspiration for the pageant." He glanced at his lover, who was waving that off. Robert's first foray into drag had been for a fundraiser in September.

Liam glanced at Emily. "He was awfully good in that."

"Yes he was." She looked proud. "I don't know what Jade is talking about, though."

"Neither do I." They both returned their attention to the nonsense in the other room. Mark was complaining about having no accompaniment, about not being a soloist, whatever. Jade wasn't having it.

"Fine, whatever." Again the fake-exasperated thing. Was there an ex-gypsy anywhere who didn't like being asked to perform? Well, maybe his 'Chicago' co-star. It seemed Andy Martin was serious about never again. His Velma Kelly had been a revelation, but that was four years ago, and not a thing since. Time to focus now, though. Mark handed his empty glass to Jade. The game was already muted. His shoes were by the door with everyone else's, neatly out of the way. There was plenty of space. He did the indefinable thing that turned a living room into a stage. Everyone was watching. He struck a pose and started to sing. "'It's good, isn't it grand, isn't it great, isn't it swell, isn't it fun? Isn't it, nowadays.'"

His voice was in good working order, even though he hardly ever got to do a singing part. It was one of the many things he kept up with for 'someday.' Someday he could be himself. Someday his prince would come. He let himself melt into the Roxie Hart character, body language going female, ignoring the fact that everyone here but Jade (and possibly Shaya) thought he was straight. Most of the world thought he was straight, or close enough to it. He'd never have that part if they didn't. Playing the boyfriend to a female lead character on a show that had zero non-straight characters. They didn't even have any non-white characters, which – given the show was set in California – was ludicrous. *Why am I on that fucking show.* Not a helpful thought, especially since he was trying to put on a show of his own. The temptation to change up the lyrics was strong. But if he changed 'Harry' to Robert, or Jonathan, or Liam, this would change from a party game to something else. He wasn't ready for that.

At least he thought he wasn't, except for some reason the line 'nothing stays' kind of stuck in his throat.

And then he finished the song, taking a really grand and overblown bow, and saw the way Jade and Robert were sitting, crammed together in a corner of the couch as if they couldn't be close enough. They'd been holding hands until they started applauding. Mark was thirty-eight, older than they were, and he didn't have that. All he had was a long-ago divorce, a twelve-year-old son he got to see less often than he wanted, and a desert of loneliness stretching out in front of him until he died. '*But oh it's heaven, nowadays.*' The thought was bitter. He turned the end of his bow into a dash to the kitchen for some water. That was the excuse, anyway, communicated with a few gestures. He leaned on the counter, trying to control his breath. It wasn't until he felt a hand on his back that he straightened up. Sniffing, blinking, swallowing. Ready to try to play off the fact that he'd nearly broken down in tears in a friend's kitchen. He expected the hand to belong to Jade. It didn't.

"Are you all right?" Liam spoke quietly. He didn't even know how he'd gotten to the kitchen so fast, didn't know if Valance wanted anyone with him, didn't know if everyone else was now happily watching the game again. The sound was back on. There was chatter out there. It didn't matter. Nobody was following them in here. His other hand was setting his plate in the sink.

Mark turned around, away from the hand, though all he wanted to do was roll into it. Stay with the comfort offered by this person he didn't even know. He leaned against the counter, staring at the doctor, trying to decide which lie to tell. Decided not to lie at all. But instead of answering the question, he asked one. "Why are you here instead of at home with your wife and family?"

It sounded kind of confrontational. Assuming that was because the guy didn't want to look weak, Liam held up his ringless left hand. "Not married. Can't get married. I'm gay."

Oh. Mark almost said that out loud. It took a second to close his mouth. The second sentence said a lot. It said, among other things, that Liam wished he could get married. "If you went to New England you could get married." That was a diversion. It was also really revealing, because it told this six-foot-whatever, black-haired, violet-eyed hunk that Mark paid attention to marriage equality. And the most likely reason for him to do that was if he were gay, too.

Liam blinked. Started to say something, closed his mouth. Tried again. "You're a great singer."

"I was on Broadway for a while," Mark said, back on solid ground. "It's a tough life and you don't make much money. So when Hollywood called I decided to answer."

Liam would swear this was the guy's natural hair color. The eyebrows matched, a rich reddish brown. Brown eyelashes, brown eyes, freckles. Not quite Robert's five foot eleven, a comfortable height to be kissed by someone who was six foot two. Handsome, talented, successful, and desolate. Was it even remotely possible that Mark Valance wanted the same things Liam did? What made a man almost cry in a kitchen on Thanksgiving? Maybe the same things that made Liam almost cry every time he turned over another month on the calendar, another month alone. "I'd love to hear more about it sometime."

"I'm not called again till January." That was not the same as saying 'ask me for a date' but it had the same effect.

"Would you like to get together for a drink? Next week, maybe?"

He would, oh he would, but he never did and if Liam didn't already know the reason Mark had to tell him. "I don't go on dates with men," he said very softly. "Not where people can see me." It wasn't a hundred percent true. He'd gone out for dinner with Jade that summer. But Jade was a well-known stylist, the kind of man Mark could be seen with because there was a business reason. There was a good back-story, about how they'd met when Mark did that all-male 'Chicago' with Jade's then-boyfriend Robbie Campbell. The kind of story that was easily diverted to a different track, the one about the Broadway legend and the benefit to pay his bills when he was dying from cancer. Very few people, even people in the press, would fail to latch on to that story. 'Robbie and I worked together on Broadway' was the kind of answer that led to linkable stories. Since Robbie was openly with Jade, and the other openly-gay men in the cast were clearly not dating Mark, the question had never been hard to deflect. That project was the most gay-adjacent thing he'd done since coming to Hollywood. Eighteen months later, he got the part on the dramedy, and since then the closet door had been bolted shut.

Liam heard Mark and thought, *Oh*. Of course. He was in the closet, because if he wasn't he might never get another acting job. Liam knew this. Everyone knew this. And Mark clearly knew Liam was asking for a date, not simply a get-together to chat about their careers. But he had not said 'I don't want to see you.' So, very carefully, as if picking his way through a minefield (which it kind of was because Liam had never dated anyone closeted), he said, "But you do come to dinner at a friend's house once in a while."

Oh God, was there hope? Was it possible this man understood? Mark sucked in a breath. "Yes, I do."

"My building has a secure garage. I have a tandem parking space." Subtext: you wouldn't be seen to be visiting me, the openly gay dermatologist.

Mark almost cried again. Even if this didn't go any further than one dinner, with maybe some sex (please, God, it had been so long), he wanted it. "Do you have your phone with you?"

Liam nodded. Pulled the phone out of his pocket and waited. They exchanged contact information. Put their phones away. And then it was a little awkward. How long had they been in here? Liam had no idea. "I'm going to see if there's anything left on the dessert table."

A grateful nod. "There's always room for pie." They both left the kitchen. Nobody seemed to have missed them. Pie plates in hand, they went to sit in the den with Emily. Liam returned to the subject of stealing her from Robert. He was overheard this time, which meant Robert was in there a few seconds later.

Much to Liam's surprise, he was in favor. "I would absolutely hate to lose you," he told Emily, "but the agency's a dead-end job if there ever was one and maybe Liam's gig wouldn't be. Or would it?" That was directed at Liam.

"An experienced medical office administrator has a lot of mobility," he said cautiously. "And we might pay more."

Emily snorted out a laugh. "I'll bet. Anything entertainment-adjacent, they pay you less because they think you think the possibility of brushing up against a celebrity in the elevator is worth more than money." She belatedly remembered she was sitting next to a celebrity. "Oh my God, I'm sorry. Too much champagne." Robert was laughing his ass off over by the bar.

9

Mark wasn't offended. "I would be the first to say follow the money. That's exactly what I did. And besides, you don't need that job to brush up against a celebrity. You have celebrity friends now." She gave him a comically starry-eyed look. "Speaking of which." He raised his voice a little. "Mr. Morris, I meant to ask if you plan to make any more movies."

Jonathan might have been watching the game, but he didn't seem to mind being interrupted. He even came to join them instead of talking across the living room. "I don't know about plan," he said, leaning on the bar beside Robert. "This guy tells me his friend over there sees a lot of scripts that might have room for an oversized goofball like me."

"You're not oversized," Parker said from the couch, momentarily distracted from some minor flirting (disguised as football commentary) with Shaya. "The doctor is taller than you are."

"Yeah, but he's like thirty pounds lighter."

"You have to be big," Robert reminded him. "So you can realistically slaughter people in the ring."

Now Jade chimed in. "Besides, you looked like a legit killer on set. All the reviews say so." Robert was splitting attention between his gorgeous boyfriend and his incredible hulk of a client. Liam liked the way his hosts were building the guy up.

Jonathan waved that off, though he looked pleased. "If anybody noticed me it's because of that makeup design you did."

"Well, thanks, but that's bullshit. He stole every scene, you guys." The wrestler was the first of Robert's sports clients to get a movie, and he'd requested Jade for his on-set stylist. Also Jade's first real date with Robert was a dinner with Jonathan. For these and several other

10

reasons, Jade was a fan. Emily, who was a fan because Jonathan brought her a box of See's chocolates every time he came to meet with Robert, said something about not being surprised he was a scene-stealer.

Liam and Mark exchanged a glance, as if they'd each thought of something they wanted to say but wanted to check in with the other first. It was a strange but compelling moment. Liam opened his mouth, then shut it again, shaking his head, half-laughing. Mark turned his head a few degrees away, slanting a sideways look at Liam. This was almost certainly a safe place, but it wasn't fair to ask other people to keep your secrets. Instead he made a comment about expecting Jonathan to put in a good word for him the next time he was in a room with a casting director. The conversation got very silly after that. Only a couple of people (Robert and Shaya, who had a bet) even cared what the result of the football game was. The rest of them started batting around ideas for a movie that could star both of them. It was Emily who said something about matching up veterans of Broadway and WWE.

Mark said, "Don't call me a veteran, it makes me feel old." Then Emily said age was just a number, Parker threw in a mention of Stockard Channing getting cast to play a high-school student at the age of thirty-three, and there was another round of nonsense. Mark would happily have stayed all night. But after the game, he made his excuses, saying he hadn't meant to stay quite so long. "I had a great time. Thanks for the invitation."

"You were very welcome. It was great to get caught up again. And thanks for that beautiful song." Jade had an expression that said 'I know something was up with you' but also 'later for that.' They shook hands after Mark got his shoes on. "Tell Jenny hi for me."

11

"I'll do that." He didn't try to say a separate goodbye to Liam. Couldn't decide if he wanted to send a text later, or maybe call. They made eye contact across the room, lifted a hand to each other, and then Mark was gone.

He thought about the TV show all the way home. Every time he had one of those moments, one of those 'I can't do this anymore' moments, he talked himself down. They were coming a lot more frequently these days. Maybe it was his age, maybe it was his growing irritation with the lack of diversity. He'd known going in that the network didn't hire gay people. He'd known it was an all-white cast. Only an idiot would call it out. On the rare occasions that social media made an issue of it – most recently a blog post titled NOT EVEN THE GARDENERS ARE LATINO – the show runners brushed it off. The show was built around a high-dollar real-estate office. Plenty of high-dollar residences were sold to non-white people in California, but elsewhere in the country was a different story. People wanted to see real life on screen, they said, with breathtaking cluelessness.

The person who sold Mark his townhouse was Mexican-American. The other owners in his eight-unit block were all employed at UCLA, its teaching hospital, or two nearby private schools; only one of them was white. Before moving to California, Mark hadn't really been conscious of diversity (or the lack of it) in TV casting. He'd lived in New York City all his life up to then, had gone to an ethnically-diverse university, and worked in the theater, which was still not the greatest place to be openly gay but had opened up to non-white performers in a big way since 'In The Heights.'

If he went back there, would things be better? He might be able to get a part on one of the series that shot in New York. There were a lot of parts for men that weren't overtly gendered. Maybe he could be out, and still get work. If casting directors didn't look at how he'd played this straight role and write him off as the opportunistic coward he was. He didn't know if he was ready to risk it.

It was a fair distance from Robert and Jade's apartment (Beverly Hills-adjacent, south of Olympic) to Mark's place in Brentwood, but traffic was light once he got past Century City. Tomorrow the city would be a madhouse of Black Friday shopping. He had no plans to go out at all for the rest of the holiday weekend. And for some reason that made him think of the doctor.

There was plenty of time to decide when (or if) he would contact Liam. Plenty of time to wonder if Liam would decide an undercover relationship – even if it only amounted to a one-night stand – wasn't worth having. That guy could not possibly be starved for companionship. All he'd have to do is walk into a club and he'd be mobbed. "He won't call," Mark told himself out loud, as if it would help him get used to the idea. And then his phone rang.

CHAPTER 2

Liam waited for the actor to pick up. Wondered if he was going to. Three rings. Would it go to voice mail? Four rings. Finally, "Hello?"

"Mark. Is this a bad time?"

"I thought you'd still be hanging out with the gang." That didn't answer the question. "No, it's fine. I got in a little bit ago and have been thanking all the gods I don't have to go out in Black Friday traffic. Are you working tomorrow?"

"Actually yes. My partner is on vacation so I'm covering the office. My business partner," he clarified, because being unmarried was not the same as being unpartnered. "The only kind of partner I have."

Mark was unexpectedly charmed by the over-explainy follow-up. "I was thinking, that is not the kind of guy who should be willing to consider what we seem to be considering."

"What do you mean?"

"Well, you're gorgeous, and I can't believe you couldn't walk into a bar anywhere in California and not walk out again with somebody to spend time with."

Liam couldn't believe what he was hearing. That tone of voice was exactly the same tone he heard from women who came to the office looking for something that would make them feel desirable again. "You're gorgeous too. Do you." He hesitated. "Look. Permission to speak freely?"

"Sure." Mark was nervous now. That phrase sounded military. Was this guy ex-military? He wasn't going to want somebody like Mark. This was probably going to be, you're gorgeous but you're right, this isn't what I want. He started to say something, to cut Liam off before he had to hear that. He was too late.

Liam let everything he'd been thinking since that moment in the kitchen spill out, more or less unedited. "I spent time with a lot of guys through college and medical school. Then it was five years of no strings because I was up to my ass in debt and trying to get my career rolling. I didn't have time to be a good partner and I didn't want someone asking for that much time. So I've done the whole walk into a bar and walk out with somebody thing, a whole lot of times. And in the past ten years, I've tried over and over again to find someone who wants what I want. I'm forty-two years old." He stopped talking, hoping Mark could fill in the blank.

After a pause, "I'm thirty-eight." Another pause. "Are you saying you're looking for a long-term commitment? Because wouldn't I be just about the last person in the world you should be talking to about that?"

"Yes. And I don't know. We haven't even had a real conversation face to face. I'm sorry. I shouldn't be saying these things. I should be saying, come over for dinner next week and let's see if we get along." He stalled again.

Mark thought for a few seconds. "Well, I could do that so we could do that. This conversation is not a substitute for that. There's another whole conversation to be had, too."

"About your career. I get it."

"I don't know if you do." Mark was letting the old rage and rebellion well up. Rage at being stifled, at having to lie, for no reason except that so many straight people couldn't seem to tolerate anything else. "I want

15

to tell you about the job I have now. Could we do that over dinner at your place?"

"Of course." Liam was relieved. He'd been expecting to hear that Mark was only interested in a one-night thing. A no-strings thing, a scratch-the-itch thing. That was not what he was hearing. "Who's Jenny?"

Mark smiled. "Jenny Wilson. Plays my girlfriend on the show. Or rather, I play her boyfriend. We're running a book on how my character gets booted off. But I could tell you about that next week."

"Or tomorrow." Liam couldn't believe he said that. "No, then you'd have to go out in Black Friday traffic."

Mark suddenly couldn't care less about traffic. "What time?"

Really?! "Seven-thirty?"

"Send me the address."

"Okay. What don't you eat? I have to warn you, I'm not a chef like Robert and Jade. This is going to be delivery."

"I can eat anything as long as it's in moderation. Not a fan of Chinese food except kung pao."

"Oh, so you're not afraid of a little spice." Liam let the tiniest bit of suggestiveness into his tone.

Mark gave it right back. "Mmm, I like a little spice." There was a long list of things he liked, and so far Liam was ticking a lot of boxes. Please, please let this not be an immediate disappointment. Please let what Liam wanted not be something that involved whips or chains. Mark hadn't had nearly enough vanilla sex in his life; not even for six-feet-whatever of gorgeous dermatologist would he abandon his boundaries. "I'm going to sign off now, Dr. Byrne. But I'll see you tomorrow."

16

"Tomorrow," Liam echoed. He disconnected still unsure if what he was feeling was hope or fear. It wasn't only the closeted thing. It was the being-an-actor thing. The last time Liam tried one of those it was a complete disaster, because that actor never stopped acting. He didn't exactly lie. He just never told the truth. Please, please let this man not be like that man. Please let him answer the question, why were you about to cry, in a way that was true.

"The number of people who want Botox or collagen or a mole check on Black Friday never ceases to amaze me," Liam said to his aesthetician Wei at the end of the day. He should have been saying it to his front-desk person, but that person had called in sick. It was a pattern, one of many reasons why he sincerely hoped Emily would decide to ditch Robert and the others at the agency.

Wei looked completely frazzled. She knew how to handle the phones and the scheduling book, but covering that on a day she should have been off was above and beyond. Of course, she was new; she wasn't around the year before to see what it was like. "It's always this way?"

"Mmm." Liam locked the suite door behind them. "Thanks again for coming in. We would have been screwed without you. Let me know what two days you want off in December to make up for this. With pay," he added, in case she didn't believe what she'd heard from the others. "And have a great rest of your weekend."

"Thank you," she said faintly, as if still processing. Then she shook herself and frowned. "Are you going to fire Erica?"

He couldn't answer that question. Instead he countered with, "Do you think we should?"

She made an are-you-crazy face. "Of course! I've only been here five months and she's called in sick on eight Fridays! It's ridiculous!"

He couldn't openly agree with that, either. So he only thanked her again and watched her start toward the public parking garage. Looked up at the sky, already dark; thought about driving down Rodeo so he could enjoy the holiday lights; and suddenly remembered he had a date. It was the first thing on his mind this morning, but got wiped by the scramble to find coverage, and then by the twenty patients. He pulled out his phone, scrolled to the number for Natalee Thai, and placed an order. By the time he got home, the delivery would be only a few minutes out. He'd done this so many times before. At least this time he wouldn't be eating alone.

Liam hadn't been on a date since September. Not so long, in the big scheme of things, except it was only the second date he'd been on since Robert. Also the last one was a truly bad date. The guy showed up late, drank too much, played with his phone incessantly, bitched about his ex, and then tried to grope Liam on the way out of the restaurant. He'd made the story funny when he told Robert about it later. At the time – and now – it wasn't funny at all. He told himself not to think about it. Not to think about any of the failures of the past ten years. This was a new chance, with a new man, and he was pretty sure he already knew the worst thing about this one.

He was home, in his jeans, and wondering if he should set the scene a little when his phone rang. He picked it up, saw Mark's name, and thought *oh fuck he's cancelling*. It felt like a kick in the gut. He took a deep breath and connected. "Hi Mark."

"Hi. Look, I'm sorry – "

"It's okay. I understand."

On the other end, hearing the depth of disappointment, Mark realized Liam thought he was cancelling. "No no no I'm here. I'm totally early. That's why I'm apologizing. You probably just got home or something. Can you let me into the garage? Or would you rather I go away for a while?"

"No. I mean don't go away. Yes. I'll be down in a second to open the gate. Don't go away."

"I'm waiting." Mark was smiling, because that reaction soothed a whole day's worth of anxiety. Even if the guy had whips and chains this might be a good night.

"I'll be right down." Liam disconnected, made sure he had his keys with the gate-controller fob, bolted out his door. Ran down the hall, down the stairs, through the lobby. Stepped onto the outdoor landing, saw a nondescript gray compact sedan, saw a flash of dark-red hair and a smile's worth of teeth behind a waving hand, and pressed the button to open the gate. He followed the car in, jogging along to indicate which space Mark should use. Waited nervously, only then noticing that he was barefoot.

Mark parked, switched off the engine, got out of the car. Reached back in for a bottle of prosecco. "I think this goes with everything, but if you hate it I can toss it back on the seat." He was hoping his nerves didn't show. Then he noticed Liam's bare feet and thought *he's nervous too*.

"I like pretty much everything with bubbles," Liam confessed. "That'll be perfect with Thai food. Though I have some beer that's pretty good with it too." He took a step toward the elevator, one hand extended back toward Mark.

The body language was definitely 'come with me,' and that was all Mark wanted to do. They didn't speak in the elevator, or walking down the hall toward Liam's open door. Then the door was closed. "Shall I put this in the fridge? Or is the food already here?"

"It'll be here any minute. The fridge is good. God, I'm glad you're here." He didn't mean to say that. "You look amazing." Or that. He thought *shut up* very hard at himself. The man was wearing jeans and a sweater, same as Liam. It wasn't the clothes that were amazing.

There was something Mark wanted to do. He needed both hands free. "Just a second." He went past Liam to the kitchen – this open-plan living space might be half the apartment, with an eat-in kitchen and a sort of den/office combo – and put the wine in the sparkling-clean and well-stocked refrigerator. Noted the uncluttered counters. The high-end coffeemaker, and the storage at the end of the kitchen island. A shelf of high-end booze there, over a honeycomb wine rack. So much like his own kitchen it was startling. He wanted to see what else the place had to say about his host, but first, this. He returned to Liam, who hadn't moved. Reached for one of his hands. "I'm glad I'm here, too." They were standing mere inches apart.

Liam slowly lifted his free hand. Brushed his fingertips over Mark's cheek, then into that mahogany hair. Made some kind of sound, and leaned in. Mark closed the distance and kissed him.

It wasn't one of those movie-style kisses where people go from zero to sixty, from first contact to consummation, in three frenzied minutes. It wasn't moaning, grabbing and devouring, tearing at clothes. It was silent and soft, gentle, *oh* and *hello* and *it's you.* Then it was, briefly, *yes*. And *what a relief.*

The front-door buzzer sounded. Liam stepped back, filled his lungs, stared at Mark. Opened his mouth, couldn't speak, gestured to the intercom. Mark squeezed his hand, then let go. He was feeling somewhat lightheaded but he could handle this. He was an actor, after all. He held down the button. "Hello?"

From the speaker: "Natalee Thai!"

"Be right there."

Liam stepped past his guest, able to think again. Picked up the keys he didn't remember dropping on the vintage console by his door, and went to get their dinner. Mark leaned on the wall, waiting.

There was a dreamlike quality to the meal. It was so prosaic. Takeout, eaten side by side at the kitchen island. Served on simple stoneware, with prosecco in mismatched souvenir glasses from national parks. They picked from each other's plates, using lacquered Japanese-style chopsticks or their fingers, talking mostly about the last time they ate Thai food, or the last time they ate with chopsticks, or the last time they'd been to a national park. Liam went to Western parks, on vacations. Mark went to Eastern parks, with his son. The only national park they'd both been to was Yosemite.

"I went in the spring a few years ago," Mark said, when it seemed they were done eating. "Early in the season. It was cold as hell. There was good snow and they said the waterfalls would be epic later. But I wasn't going to be able to get away then. The best part about it was there was hardly anybody else there. Half the park was still closed."

"Were you there by yourself?"

"I'm always by myself." It was matter-of-fact, not self-pitying. Not even bitter. They were turned toward each other, the takeout containers visible on the main counter and their plates pushed away. So not fancy. So intimate. Mark gazed at Liam, seeing understanding. He wanted to tell the man why, even though that understanding probably meant he didn't have to. "I had an opportunity to do what very few people get to do, which is have a career as an entertainer. This was the price. Even if I stayed in New York, stayed on the stage, I couldn't be who I am. Hardly anybody comes out while they're working. A stage production is different, nobody expects open-mouthed kisses, obvious tongue, or nudity. Hardly any parts even call for that. But most male roles are assumed to be straight, and there are so few productions that will consider casting an openly gay man to play a straight role."

"The other way around, more often," Liam said. "I've noticed. And then they get all this credit for being brave."

"Right. Things are changing now, but it's still a risk." A moment of silence. "I got married right out of college. My college sweetheart. She knew I was gay. Since our divorce I've dated women for appearances' sake, without wanting to. I've even had sex with women, because I was well-enough known that they might have outed me to the press. Or tried to extort me. My wife and I had a pre-nup, and part of that was a nondisclosure agreement."

"Right out of college?"

"Mmm. My senior year I was cast in a fairly high-profile off-Broadway thing. I had an agent, an attorney, and parents. They all said do this. If she balks, don't marry her. And she agreed, which meant when the marriage fell apart the way it was bound to she did a lot of screaming but only in private."

"Why did it fall apart?" Liam felt a little bit like they were doing a therapy session. He wasn't sure if Mark was telling him all this because it was essential for him to say, or because it was going to be essential for Liam to know.

"Well, I didn't hold up my end of the unwritten bargain. What we left out of the pre-nup was stuff like do we have kids. Do we keep having sex when one of us doesn't want to anymore. My son is precious to me, but I did not want more than one child. To be honest, I wasn't happy when Kerry got pregnant the first time. And I felt like, ugh." He paused, trying to think of a way to say this that didn't make him sound completely monstrous. "When we got married, I knew I could be looking at an entire lifetime of living a lie. In an abstract way. Since I didn't know what the truth even felt like I figured I wouldn't know what I was missing. Then there was a good six months toward the end of the pregnancy and after when she didn't want to have sex, and I didn't miss it. I caught myself looking at men, thinking about men. Wanting men. I didn't cheat, but I wanted to. By the time Chris was a year old Kerry and I were having the most awful fights, but staying married felt like the worst lie I could possibly tell."

Liam thought about that. Went to get the wine bottle, refilled their glasses, set the empty bottle aside. Stayed on his feet, leaning on the island facing Mark, instead of hitching back up on his barstool. "It was too much of a lie. To keep having sex with her."

"Mmm. In the beginning she said, okay, I know this isn't all you want but as long as we can have a full marriage I can deal with it. If I wasn't going to have sex with her, it was totally unfair to stay married to her."

Another moment. Mark could feel himself shivering with tension. It was so hard to say these things. He tried to relax, tried to breathe. "And the reason I'm telling you this is so you'll know what lengths I've gone to for my career. What depths. I'm probably one of the five worst people you've ever met."

"The guy I went out with in September was worse, I promise." Liam wasn't sure he even needed to ask; this level of soul-baring was beyond imagining, much less expectations. But if there was ever a time to ask, the time was now. All the filters were off. "Why were you so close to breaking down after singing yesterday? It got to me, too. And Robert, we talked about it for a minute before I left. I'm assuming you know the Robert and Jade story, since you guys are friends."

"Yes, I know the story. And that's why. I was doing my Roxie thing there and heard myself sing those words, nothing stays. Then I was looking at them, sitting together." His voice broke. Liam put a hand on his back again. "And I couldn't stand it." Tears coming now. "I can't stand it anymore."

Liam moved in, letting his arm slide all the way around Mark. Putting his other hand on the man's face, bringing his head to Liam's shoulder as he turned. Feeling Mark's arms go around him, holding on tight. Offering comfort, because he didn't know what else to do. This was not one of the ways he'd imagined this evening going. He held Mark until the shuddering breath evened out. Until the clutching hands on his sweater relaxed. "I think there's more you could tell me," he said softly. "Can we talk some more? Or is this enough for tonight."

"I want to tell you everything," Mark said to Liam's chest. "Tonight. I need to know what it feels like to tell the truth."

"Okay. Why don't you go wash your face. I'll clean this up and meet you on the couch."

Mark lifted his head. "In bed. I want to be naked with you." His eyes were red, lashes stuck together. Liam kissed him lightly and nodded.

He took his time tidying the kitchen, letting himself settle down. Thinking about the questions he should ask, since he had the opportunity. Wondering if Mark wanted sex, or if he simply wanted to be held. Liam wasn't usually passive in bed. This time he thought he should be. He had an uneasy feeling that the wrong move might actually break Mark Valance.

Then he walked into the bedroom and his job got a lot more difficult. Mark was lying there naked, face-down, with his head pillowed on his hands. He was almost as slender as Robert, but in a way that said he had to work for it. Long pale legs, heavily-freckled arms, and a swath of pigment on his back. Freckles were there, on his shoulders, but this was a patch of solid caramel brown beginning at his right scapula and meandering across and down to the top of his left buttock. Liam had never seen anything like it in the flesh, only in pictures during his internship. He wanted to study it. Wanted to kiss it. He detoured to the bathroom to freshen up. Then he undressed in the heavy silence, wondering if he should even ask any questions, or if he should simply wait for Mark to say the things he needed to say.

CHAPTER 3

Mark heard Liam come in, listened to the story told by all those sounds, felt the mattress give as the man joined him on the bed. *I am abusing this situation. He is not my therapist. What am I doing, and why am I doing it to him.* If it hadn't been for that kiss he might not have fallen apart in such a spectacular way. Or at all. He might have gotten through the evening like a normal person. He kept his eyes closed as that comforting hand went across his back. Slowly, the palm smoothing over his horrible skewbald skin with what felt for all the world like appreciation.

Liam lay close, his body in contact with Mark's from chest to feet. There was immediate involuntary arousal, his cock pushing against Mark's hip. "Ignore that," he suggested, and heard something like a laugh. "I won't do anything. Tell me about you and men."

Mark changed position, very slightly, so he could turn his head and look at Liam. His hair was somewhat wiry; when he was older, and the gray started coming in, it might curl. There were silver flecks in his five o'clock shadow, none yet in his straight black eyebrows. A symmetrical, strong-featured face framing those spectacular eyes. "I suppose you've been told you have eyes like Elizabeth Taylor's."

He couldn't help smiling. "Actually no. Do I?"

"Mmm. Really beautiful. Me and men." Mark thought back. "I've never been in what a normal person would call a relationship with a man. There were brief exploratory encounters in high school and college. Up to and including sex of the most tentative and uncommitted kind. It was always, we're just fooling around, this doesn't mean anything. Have another drink and forget all about it. I was well aware that coming out would do me no favors. All I ever wanted to do was be an entertainer. They say the ratio of gay to straight in the general population is, what, one out of ten? It seemed like every other man I met in the theater was gay. After the divorce I went to bed with some of them, people I'd come to know well enough that I trusted them to be discreet. Some of them were in the closet too, some of them were simply decent. The last was four years ago."

Liam was appalled. "Four *years*."

Mark laughed silently. "It's amazingly easy to do without when you're used to that. Or at least, it was."

"Who was the last? Or should I ask why he was the last?"

Brown eyes stared into violet. Mark didn't want to answer. *Tell the truth.* "My co-star in 'Chicago.' I don't know if Robert told you anything about that." Liam shook his head. "Well, it was a benefit for the man who played Billy Flynn, the lawyer in the show. He was a Broadway legend. Jade was his boyfriend at the time. We had an all-male cast and did a single performance as a fundraiser, because Robbie had cancer and his bills were out of control. Anyway, the man who played Velma Kelly," he checked for recognition, didn't see any, "the one who sings 'All That Jazz?'" A nod. "That man. He'd worked with Robbie before. He'd worked with me before. He knew I was gay. Never breathed a word. He's been out all his life and he advised me to stop doing what I'm still doing. That's why he was the last. Because he was right. And he was," a sigh, "great. He understood me, and he treated me well for a weekend, but he was not going to settle for an undercover relationship. He's five years older than me. Still single."

27

"Hard to please?"

Mark made an uncertain sound. "Not as such. He's uncompromising about some things. Drugs. Infidelity. And openness. He's a man who will kiss his lover in front of anyone, and damn the consequences."

"And you can't do that."

"I wouldn't do that," Mark corrected. "I've never done that. But it's slowly killing me not to do that."

They were quiet for a few minutes. Mark seemed to be lost in thought. After a while Liam said, "What are you going to do?"

Mark stirred. "I have to get off this show. I want to do it on my own terms if I can. My colleague Jenny and I, we've been tossing around the most-likely scenarios. We've only seen a couple of the scripts for the back half of this season. The first half, things changed for me."

"How so." Liam became aware that his thumb was caressing Mark's shoulder, the very edge of that caramel patch. There was a texture change, velvety-smooth brown skin to slightly-rougher white. He didn't stop.

"Well, my character has been a flake. Charming but unreliable. And this fall, I was less unreliable. More serious. They wrote me reasons for doing things, made the relationship a tiny bit deeper instead of being a source of one-liners. So Jenny and I think they're either going to have me propose, or they're going to kill me."

Liam's eyebrows shot up. "You mean on the show, right?"

Mark huffed out a laugh. "Yes. I mean, it's possible they'll do both. If what they have in mind is an Emmy push for Jenny, it would not be unprecedented for us to get engaged and for me to then die of some swift and horrible disease, or in an accident. It has some funny parts but this is primarily a drama, and Jenny hasn't had any good drama moments for a while."

"Do you have any power with the scripts?"

"Not really. Jenny has some pull. I need to talk to her and tell her I want out."

"Can you tell her why?"

"I think I can." He hoped so. "I should, even if it blows up on me. Of all the places to start, right? But I feel like she's not going to freak. We might be good enough friends that she'll understand." He felt Liam's hand stroke down his back, then return to his shoulder. It was so amazingly wonderful to be touched. That was the best part of working with Jenny: the hugs, the occasional kisses, holding hands. Giving each other a neck rub, or simply cuddling up close together on the couch in her trailer to run lines. Come to think of it, she might have already guessed, based on nothing more than the fact that Mark never made a pass. "Then maybe the two of us can go to the company and say, how about this. Because they've done that little shift already, as if they were setting something up. Your average audience member may not be consciously aware of how their expectations are managed, but they do have expectations. If a show does X, the audience expects Y."

Liam had never given it a moment's thought. Now he thought back over the fall season, realized that Mark was right, and said, "I do have expectations. I would have said, at the mid-season, that you were planning to propose. So would you come out then? Once you're off the show?"

"I think I have to, don't you? It might mean moving back East. Or, well. I don't know. I've never had a starring role. Never been on a syndicated series. The residuals I get won't pay the bills. I have to think about

29

what's next. How else I can make a living. This is all I've ever done." He moved, wriggling closer, shifting to his side. Liam adjusted, accommodating. They ended up front to front, Mark's head on Liam's arm, face pressed to his chest. His breathing was wrong again. He worked on settling it down. Couldn't help noticing that Liam's loose and undemanding hold was being contradicted by returning arousal. His own body said 'hey how about that' and 'what are you waiting for.' If he did something overt, Liam would probably go along with it. Would that be anything even slightly close to fair? No. He kept his eyes closed, kept breathing, didn't kiss Liam's chest. Waited for a question.

It finally came. "How long have you been thinking these things?"

"Forever, some of them. Others, since yesterday. Since I started telling you the truth. It hurt, but in a good way. I figured you probably wouldn't call, but then you did. And I thought, this is crazy, because I'm such a mess, but he knows I'm a mess and he called me anyway. So maybe I could tell you the rest. I didn't mean to fall apart on you. I meant to, you know. Show you a good time." God, the man smelled so good. The furry chest against Mark's lips felt so good. It was all he could do not to press into him, let his body ask for what it wanted. What they both seemed to want.

Liam pressed a kiss to Mark's forehead, doing his best to ignore the pair of erections. "It's fine. I'm glad you told me all this. I don't quite know what to do with you." Another silent laugh, a puff of breath against his chest. "I think you should stay here tonight. No one will know."

Mark was swamped with relief. The thought of getting up now, getting dressed, going home alone was nauseating. "You don't mind?"

30

"Ssshh. Go to sleep." They made a few minor adjustments, of the saving-circulation variety, both tacitly accepting they weren't going to have sex. It seemed that Mark did go to sleep almost at once, arousal abating fast. Liam lay there thinking of the ten thousand ways this was a unique first date until drowsiness finally pulled him under.

Mark woke up multiple times during the night. He was used to sleeping alone. It was as if every time Liam changed position, or if there was the slightest hint of a snore or a murmur, Mark's startle reflex went off. On the plus side, his wakefulness didn't seem to bother his host. After that pathetic performance after dinner, a good night's sleep was the least the man deserved.

Eventually there was enough light in the room to concede defeat. He was awake, he wasn't going back to sleep, and he didn't know what to do. He didn't want to leave. Especially not before speaking to Liam again. Would the guy want to talk any more? Would he think there was any real possibility here? Was he willing to wait for Mark to get himself out of the worst of his situation? It was going to be bad enough trying to reconfigure or rebuild his career as an out gay man, but at least they could openly see each other then. Until Mark exited the show, they really couldn't. Liam might say, you know, how about you call me when you're out of there. Why in the world would he want to sneak around, having the occasional night out with friends along for cover, or the occasional night together like this. One or the other of them could get away with it from time to time, but not as a regular thing. Neighbors noticed visitors, and everyone had a cell phone. Mark's car was nondescript, but he wasn't. Neither was Liam. Anyone would notice him. People would wonder about

31

the hunk going into Mark's townhouse, and about the extra car if he stayed overnight. They would wonder about the extra car at Liam's place, and how was he going to not be obvious? Wear a hoodie and sunglasses? Oh God, this would never work.

He got out of bed as quietly as possible, went to the bathroom, stared at himself in the mirror. From the front it wasn't too bad. He'd long since given up trying to keep the skin on his arms from freckling. Lavish applications of sunscreen kept the pigment from getting too hyper on his face and chest. It was the back view that always made him feel like a freak. He wondered if Liam's caresses the night before were automatic, or if he had a clinical interest. It probably didn't matter. This wasn't going to work.

But he couldn't leave without saying goodbye, so he sat on the bed. Stretched a little, slowly and carefully at first, trying to be quiet and not make the mattress bounce. Apparently he could have been dribbling a basketball; there wasn't a twitch from his host. He eventually sat up cross-legged and stared at Liam. The man was a champion sleeper. The thought made him smile.

Mark – beautiful, naked, smiling Mark – was the first thing Liam saw when he opened his eyes. "Mmph." That meant 'don't move' and maybe Mark understood, because he was in the exact same position after Liam rolled out of bed, stumbled to the bathroom, and eventually returned. "You look tired," Liam said, much more intelligibly, sitting an arm's-length from Mark. "Didn't sleep well?"

"A little edgy. I haven't slept with anyone for four years." Liam already heard about that. Mark didn't know why he even said it. "It was good to spend the night with you."

"Even though you didn't sleep."

"Well, I thought." Mark looked away, called himself a coward, and made eye contact again. "I thought you would probably want me to go, but I didn't want to sneak out while you were sleeping. Leave without saying goodbye, and thanking you."

"I don't want you to go." After nearly a minute of silence, he said, "I don't think we're done here." Slowly, his voice suddenly lower. Almost husky.

Mark swallowed. If that was Liam's bedroom voice, it was a very effective one. "Even though you know what a clusterfuck I would be?"

"You won't be a clusterfuck. The situation might be a clusterfuck. But that's temporary. Right?"

Now Mark had to remind himself to breathe. All that hope in Liam's tone, as if he thought this would totally be worth it. "Six months, max." It was a promise.

"Then kiss me." The only reason Liam hadn't already launched himself at Mark was because he needed to be sure the other man was choosing this. In the light of day, in this calm quiet morning, with everything out on the table.

Mark moved in, wondering how this was possible, telling himself to simply trust that it was. He was on hands and knees, mouth almost touching Liam's. "I'm clean," he murmured. "You?"

"Mm-hmm." Liam wanted that mouth so much he was about to die. "Last tests were in the spring and I haven't been with anyone since."

"This might go kind of fast, then." Liam was smiling when Mark closed that tiny distance. At first it was almost tentative. Then their mouths were open, and then Liam was flat on his back, Mark stretched out on top of him. Now they were clutching at each other, rolling and tangling, growling and panting. Biting, licking, over and under and everywhere until Liam got his mouth on Mark's cock. "Oh holy *fuck*." He heard a stifled laugh from between his legs. He was on his back, with one hand dug into Liam's hair, propped on the other elbow so he could watch this. "Jesus Christ. Liam. God, you – *yes*. Fuck that's so good."

Liam listened to the stream of praise. He would have been amused if it hadn't been exactly what he wanted to hear. He was pinning Mark down with an arm on his hip, the other hand pushing a leg up, fondling and teasing. Hearing the words turn into desperate nonsense, tasting the oncoming climax, feeling the balls draw up and the cock swell even more. He made a triumphant sound as Mark convulsed, crying out, then falling back. Liam swallowed, felt Mark's body jerk again, slowly let go with his mouth. Followed it with a stroke of his hand, palming the head of that softening cock, shifting up to sink his teeth into Mark's flank. Heard a sound that was something between protest and encouragement. Moved up again, lavishing more kisses and bites on that pale torso, licking the nipples with their few coppery hairs, hearing a whimper. *I could have you twice*, he thought. *I could have you all day and not have enough*. His erection was hot and hard against Mark's hip as he went for another kiss. He lifted his head to make eye contact. Mark looked dazed. "Now?"

It was hard to think with Liam's weight on him, those beautiful eyes dark with passion, and no idea what the man wanted. He had to ask. "What do you want?"

"Everything. Anything. You."

Awfully non-specific. He seemed to be saying whatever Mark wanted was fine. Not doing what Mark had half-expected (based on nothing but a previous experience with a tall powerful man) which was diving for the nightstand where there would be something in the lube category. Pushing Mark over, pushing his legs open, holding him down. None of that was happening. He was simply waiting. "I want you in my mouth." It was almost a question, as if this were some kind of test and Mark wasn't sure he knew the answer.

"How."

Okay. Another test. He could take Liam lying on his back. Have him stand up, and do it on his knees. Have him on hands and knees over Mark. It was almost upsetting, having this much choice. He wanted to surrender. He didn't want to make the wrong choice. "Fuck my mouth."

Liam wasn't sure if there was a problem. Mark looked as if no one had ever asked him what he wanted. That couldn't be true, could it? Had every single partner simply taken what they wanted, even the last one? Because Mark spoke of him with fondness, affection, regret. Did he want to be overpowered? That was a kink Liam had encountered a few times. It might have been his size; people expected him to be dominant. And he was, but he wasn't a capital-D Dominant. That wasn't his jam at all. He kissed Mark again, long enough to get his dick back in the game. He really wanted that mouth. He wanted to come. But he wanted Mark back again, as often as possible, as long as possible. So they had to get this right. He pushed away, heard a bereft sound, and thought *okay, so yes. He does want me.* He shoved some pillows around, making a back-rest. Should have a headboard. Someday he'd get one. He'd get Mark to tie him up, make him take control. *Stop it you asshole that's your fantasy not his.* He'd lived without that for eons, because the one time he tried it the other guy misunderstood. Thought he wanted pain. "Sit up there,"

35

he said, voice slightly hoarse. He was kneeling up, showing Mark the height they had to work with. Mark wet his lips, eyes narrowed in a way that said he liked what he was seeing.

He scooted back, nestling into the pillows. He wanted that cock. That man. Liam. "Give me." Liam moved up, straddling Mark, cock temptingly close. Mark ran his hands up Liam's thighs, detouring to fondle his balls, stroking his erection with a slight tug to bring it close enough to lick. Liam made a stifled sound. "I'm just going to relax, so if you want your dick in my mouth, you'd better put it there."

That was all it took. Now Liam knew it was okay. He moved slowly, nudging Mark's mouth, pressing inside. The other man had a hand on him, managing the depth. Liam let himself stroke in and out. Giving Mark time to lick him, swirl his tongue around, close his lips around the head and very gently bite down. "Mmm."

Mark liked that sound. He could imagine the look on Liam's face, as if he wanted to close his eyes but couldn't stand not to watch. Someday he'd do this in front of a mirror, so he could see that. Or on video. He made his own sound then, imagining watching the two of them fuck. He'd never done that, it wasn't safe. But someday it would be safe. And this body, Jesus Christ, how many hours did the man spend in the gym? He was picking up speed. Mark was very conscious of the power behind the motion, but he wasn't worried. Liam had one forearm braced on the wall, holding his body away. The other hand cupped the back of Mark's head. Mark still had one hand wrapped around Liam's cock; the other was on his ass, pulling him in. They were both making some very porny sounds. Gasping, moaning, slurping. Mark was thoroughly turned on again. That was the problem with a long hiatus, once you got in bed with someone you were apt to be a nympho. Oh Jesus he was going, here it was.

Liam wasn't producing words. If he had been they wouldn't have amounted to much more than 'yes fuck yes now yes.' The sounds Mark was making seemed to mean the same thing. As the climax crested Liam had to put his other hand on the wall; as it broke, he shouted something. It felt like every orgasm he hadn't had in the past year was exploding up his shaft and down Mark's throat. He heard a stifled cough and tried to pull away, but Mark wouldn't let him. He straight-up snarled, hand clamped on Liam's ass, as if he meant to drink down every last drop of him. Liam leaned on the wall, forehead on his arm, quivering. Only when Mark's hands relaxed did he push back.

"Mmm." Mark swallowed again, adjusted his jaw. Put his hand on his own dick as Liam collapsed backwards. "Look where you left me." Liam turned his head, which was roughly aligned with Mark's ankles. His face was flushed, eyes sleepy. He smiled. "Going to watch me?" Liam nodded. Mark scooted down again. "Next time I think you stand at the end of the bed and I'll hang my head over. How's that sound."

'Next time' sounded good, but all Liam could manage was "Mmm." He was watching Mark's hand move. Letting his fantasy play while that happened. All he had to do was lift his head a little to go from seeing Mark's spangled hand moving on his straining cock, to seeing his intent face. Imagining that face bending over him, that hand bringing himself to climax again, spraying on Liam as he waited, bound. *Oh God there he goes. Oh Christ he's so beautiful.* He made a soft sound, echoing Mark's harsher one.

The bedroom reeked of sex. They were only inches apart. It was too far. Liam moved his hand, brushing the

37

back of it against Mark's thigh. It was an invitation, one that Mark apparently understood. He sat up with something like a groan, curled his body, tucked his legs. A moment later he was stretched out half on top of Liam, who gave a surprised half-laugh at the wet patch plastered to his side. "Yeah, I didn't catch it." Mark didn't sound apologetic. He rested his head on Liam's shoulder.

"'Sallright." Liam wrapped his arm around Mark. He thought they would get up in a few minutes, go have breakfast. Talk about what came next. Instead they both dozed off.

CHAPTER 4

Liam woke up not too much later, possibly because he'd had a good night's sleep, and possibly because his stomach was growling. He felt Mark laugh. "Sorry about that."

"Not a problem. I can catch up on sleep tonight."

"Unless you stay here again. Oh, shit, never mind. What's wrong with me." Liam was blushing. "I know you can't do that."

Mark was actually not at all sure that he couldn't. He sat up, regarded his host for a moment, and said, "When are people usually around?"

"I see everybody at going to work and getting home from work times. On the weekends, it's hard to guess. There's probably a lot of traffic right now." Mid-morning on a Saturday: people were running errands. Going to the mall. Meeting people for holiday things. It was not an exaggeration to say, "Your best bet, honestly, is tomorrow night after eight. And you're welcome to stay till then."

"What would you usually be doing?"

Liam sat up. "Paperwork. Watching TV. You?"

"The same. And feeling sorry for myself because I was alone. I'd be happy to leave that part out."

"Me too." A small smile. It really didn't feel like Mark wanted to go. "And if anybody gets snoopy on Monday, I'll tell them I had a friend visiting from out of town."

Mark leaned forward, kissed Liam, made a contented sound. "How do you feel about a barbecued-rib omelet?"

"Will you marry me?" They laughed softly, lips touching, eyes half-closed. Neither of them thought it was one hundred percent a joke. One more kiss, then they got out of bed, took turns freshening up, threw on some clothes. Liam offered to share, and Mark was perfectly happy to leave his jeans and sweater for the next day. The warm-ups were on the long side; the cuffs of the long-sleeved thermal shirt had to be turned up; but he was warm, and clean enough, and best of all he didn't have to leave.

Liam made coffee, then sat at the island to watch while Mark de-fleshed the leftover ribs from the night before. He put the bowl of meat in the microwave to warm up while he broke six eggs into another bowl, gave Liam a thoughtful glance, and added a seventh. A quick rummage through the cabinets turned up some garlic powder and ground ancho chili. Whipping the eggs together with the spices and a bit of salt. Butter into the big nonstick pan, watching it melt, adding the seasoned eggs. He sipped coffee, waiting patiently. Then lifting the edges, letting the uncooked egg flow underneath, until the top was almost set. Distributing the meat in an even layer on one side, then folding the omelet. A few more seconds, then sliding it onto a plate, dividing it, and putting both plates on the island. He carried his coffee around with a couple of forks in the other hand, and sat next to Liam. "Eat."

"You gave me twice as much."

"You're almost four inches taller than me, you're built, and you're hungry." Mark could have said something about how he had to watch his figure, but surely that went without saying. This was plenty of food. And if it wasn't, there was more in the refrigerator. There was an infinity of places they could call.

"God, this is good," Liam said with his mouth full. He was reasonably competent with eggs, but this was special. Being cooked for was special. He knew that was one of the ways Robert courted Jade. The thought made him take a breath. Mark was courting him. Mark Valance, about whom Liam knew so much and yet so little, was sitting beside him, having put his future in Liam's hands. He had to know it. Was he insane? How could he possibly trust Liam this much?

Mark didn't know why Liam stopped eating for a minute, frowning down at his plate with both forearms on the island. Maybe he only now grasped the full implications of this situation. There was a lot more to be said. It would be nice if they could … not talk, for a while. He went for a refill of coffee, offered the pot, collected a nod. By the time he sat down again, Liam was eating again. And they didn't talk. Not for close to an hour, by which time the kitchen was clean and Mark was curled up on the mini-sectional in the den. Liam was doing something at the desk behind it. He asked if Food Network was okay, and Mark said of course. He paid minimal attention to the program, studying the contents of the room instead. It was a lot like his own home office. Books on the shelves surrounding the TV, with framed pictures scattered everywhere. It wasn't a big space. Mark could see the faces in those pictures. An older couple who must be Liam's parents. Liam with three people who must be siblings. All six together. The siblings in separate pictures with what had to be their spouses and kids. Not one picture of Liam with a significant other. There had to have been someone, sometime. Was it possible he had found the second-loneliest man in Los Angeles? Maybe even *the* loneliest. At least Mark had Christopher. And, to be fair, Kerry. The marriage was a wipeout but they managed to be friends now. Why on earth was this man single? What was he missing?

Liam probably could have spent some time on paperwork, but he didn't really need to. Instead he used that quiet time after breakfast to cyber-stalk his guest. IMDb and Wikipedia told him a lot. The Obie award, the Tony nomination. An Emmy nomination, and a long list of credits. When Mark wasn't sitting right there he'd go to YouTube and look for clips. And then there was the personal stuff. Married for six years, divorced for ten, in L.A. for eight. Their son went to a private school in Manhattan, not a boarding school. The ex, Kerry Watson, was a lawyer. Her parents were a plumber and a teacher; that made Liam smile. Good blue-collar blood, like his own parents. Mark's parents were a lawyer and an executive. Kerry had a brother in the Navy, again like Liam; Mark was an only child.

He wondered what it was like to have so much of your life open to the public. Well, there was a good chance he would find out. He couldn't remember doing anything that would reflect badly on his family. That had always been a consideration, not because they were afraid of the media but because of community, church, and extended-family oversight. A lot of people cared about Liam. He never wanted to let them down. They might give him some crap about the number of men he'd been with, if that all blew open, but at least nobody could claim he was a drunk, or violent, or irresponsible.

There were so many articles. So many pictures. Mark with Kerry, with other women. With colleagues from various jobs. Never with his son; they must be very careful to keep him out of the public eye. Pictures of Mark in character, including – deep in the results page – a cast photo from that all-male 'Chicago' he was talking about. Which one of these was the one he slept with? Impossible to guess, except it couldn't have been the black guy in the prison-matron uniform. Even Liam knew that was the Queen Latifah part. And it couldn't have been the oldest guy, because he was wearing a suit, and had to be the one the benefit was for. He looked good, but he didn't look well.

"What are you doing back there, Dr. Byrne."

Might as well tell the truth. "Stalking you." Mark laughed, twisting around to look over his shoulder at Liam. Eyebrows up, inviting questions. "So which one of these guys was it?"

Mark stood up and went around to the desk. Pointed. "That one. His name is Andy Martin. He's a photographer."

"Here in L.A.?"

"Mm-hmm."

Liam studied the picture some more. Mark looked kind of amazing – and nearly unrecognizable – in that flapper costume with the platinum-blonde bobbed wig. He had one arm around their Queen Latifah, one around the older guy. Martin was on the other side of the older guy. He was slim, dark, and attractive in a way that said he might be a lot of fun but you wanted to stay on his good side. Of course, that might have been the character. They were all looking at the camera, not at each other. All smiling, even though this had to have been kind of heartbreaking. "There's a good chance I'm going to stalk him now."

Mark laughed again. "Go ahead. That show was the only stage thing he's done here in L.A. He was a gypsy for twenty years. Did every musical known to man and a few that nobody's heard of. Gave it up before something forced him to."

Liam turned his head, looking up, making eye contact. "I'm not down with drugs or infidelity either, so you know. That's part of the reason nothing ever worked. I don't have any major kinks."

So there might be some minor kinks. Well, Mark could deal with that, if the sex was mostly like what they'd had so far. "Do you want to talk some more?"

"We probably should. How about a drink to go with that." Mark seemed to think that was a good idea. They went to study the liquor shelf. Eventually, as a concession to how early in the day it was, they decided on vodka and cranberry juice. Liam fixed the drinks, handed one to Mark, and headed back to the den. He stretched out on the chaise part of the sectional. Mark settled beside him. Liam thought it was his turn to talk, so he said, "I kind of made it sound as if I've never had a good relationship. And you might have noticed there's no pictures of me with anybody."

"I did notice that."

"There are a few that aren't up on the shelf anymore. Anyway, my family's in San Diego. I went to school down there, did my residency in Chicago, and my first job was in Minneapolis. I moved here when I was thirty-three, basically as soon as I got a chance, to get away from that weather. Jesus." Mark was snickering. "Opened my own office six years ago. So from that you might guess why nothing stuck."

"Till you got here, you were moving around a lot. There wasn't anyone willing to move with you?"

"Well, they were all in the same place. Trying to get their careers established, looking at having to move to do it. Sometimes it hurt. Hurt a lot," he confessed. "Having to look at each other and say, if this, then that, but not."

"And then you had all the stress of opening your own business."

"Yeah. I didn't have a lot of time or energy to spare, and I think I ended up picking people who didn't *want* a lot of my time because of that. But the past few years, since my partner came into the business, it's been different. I've been looking around, and it's like I missed a lot of chances when I wasn't looking. People my age, the ones who would be good to be with, they're already with somebody. I had a couple of dates with Robert." He huffed out a laugh. "And he was already in love with Jade, so that wasn't going anywhere." He sipped some of his drink, staring at the bookcase, then turned his head. "Except they invited me to Thanksgiving, and you were there." His voice was soft.

Mark buried his nose in his glass, trying to hide the thrill that gave him. Except why hide it? He swallowed a tangy mouthful and said, "If my career implodes I'm not going to have much to offer. An ex-wife who doesn't hate me anymore, an almost-teenager who I miss like a lost limb, and a townhouse in Brentwood. I couldn't even have a place that's convenient to your office."

Liam tripped for a second over the implication. Tried to make a joke out of it. "Come on, Brentwood. That's not bad. Malibu, that would have been bad."

"Pasadena."

"Hermosa Beach." They were both almost laughing. "Is it that likely to implode?"

Mark sighed. "I have to expect it. There's only one Neil Patrick Harris. And he was already a star, with a lot of goodwill behind him. I'm just some guy who's mostly recognizable because there are not that many red-headed men working in Hollywood."

"You are not just some guy." That got him a warm look. The next thing he said was not what he meant to say. "If we get through next summer, would you want to live together?" *Oh FUCK do you have no fucking filters --*

But Mark was saying, "Jesus, yes. That is absolutely, positively, the whole point of this thing. To be free to live my life side by side with someone, twenty-four-seven. To walk down the street together, and go out to dinner, and who knows, if my career *doesn't* implode, to go to industry bullshit together. I'm going to have to find someone to take to the winter awards things, and I'm dreading it." He'd managed to avoid having a date for the Emmys thanks to having been out of town most of the summer.

Liam thought about that for a second. He didn't know why having a date was desirable but if Mark thought so, then that's what they had to work with. "What about Emily?"

Mark blinked at Liam. Opened his mouth to reflexively reject the suggestion, closed it again. Recalibrated and said, "Do you think we could trust her?"

Liam heard the 'we.' It felt like a kiss. "She's awfully fond of Robert. I ran into them once at the coffee shop, they were like a couple of puppies." Mark snorted out a laugh. "She has to be good at confidentiality, working at the agency. We know she doesn't have an issue with gay men being gay. But you might not have to give her the whole background. I'd be willing to bet she would get a large charge out of going to industry bullshit."

"Especially if I got her some good stuff to wear. Wow. You think?" The more Mark thought about it, the more he was wondering why he never thought of this before. Why not a friend, someone who was in on it, someone he could be at least mostly honest with. Well, he hadn't trusted anybody, and that was the bottom line. Maybe he needed to trust one person first, and then the rest could follow. He'd certainly handed his life to Liam. "God, I want to ask her right now."

Liam patted his leg, stood up, and went around to the desk for his phone. He sent a text to Robert: *There is a non-assistant-stealing reason I'd like to contact Emily. Could you give me her number?*

The reply came back fast; Liam was still on his feet. *LOL sure here you go.* No questions, only the digits. He sat down to show the reply to Mark. "This guy does friend pretty damn well."

"Mmm. So does Jade." Mark waited to see what happened next, watching while Liam sent the next message.

Hi Emily this is Dr Byrne only please call me Liam. A friend is going to need a date for a string of high-profile things. Hollywood stuff. If he got you the clothes etc would you be up for it?

Again, a fast response: *OMG I was just sitting here feeling sorry for myself because I made the mistake of going to the mall yesterday and there was this awesome dress and I had nowhere to wear it so I didn't get it. Srsly?*

Seriously but there is a catch, which is that the reasons for this cannot be explained, for about six months

Curiosity doesn't kill this cat. I'm assuming this is not some person I would loathe being seen with. Those kinds of guys hire escorts, don't they?

47

Mark cracked up. Liam debated writing back to the effect that they were sorta kinda doing that, but he didn't know her that well yet. *You wouldn't loathe him. He's a nice guy, only in a bit of a bind*

Sign me up

Liam looked at Mark. "You want to talk to her?"

It was scarily, seriously real all of a sudden. Mark consulted with himself and decided that this was worth the risk. Expanding their little circle of conspiracy, so he didn't have to involve anybody else under false pretenses. "Let me go get my phone." He went to find it.

Liam texted: *He's going to be in touch very shortly. Thanks Emily*

No problem

Mark sat down next to Liam again, crowding so close he was practically in the man's lap. Liam wrapped an arm over his shoulders. With his other hand he held his phone so Mark could see Emily's number. Mark added the contact and composed a text: *Hi Emily this is Mark Valance. We met at Robert's on Thursday. I have reasons for needing a Platonic companion for the next few months. Our mutual friend Dr Byrne told me you might be okay with the idea.* He sent the message and waited to see what she would say.

OMG Mr Valance really?! WTF do you need me for, anybody would go out with you! Okay you have reasons which are none of my business. I would love to be your Platonic companion

Hurdle one met. Mark thought for a second. Emily was quick-witted, but she might need to pre-think this situation. *People will ask how we met and what our relationship is. What will you tell them?*

48

Well we were introduced by my boss at a holiday party and now we're friends

The truth, which was always best. *Perfect. Feel free to Google me and if you need me to fill in any blanks feel free to ask. I'll be in touch soon about when, where, and how. And thank you.* She had no idea how much he meant that.

You're welcome. I'm about to live the Hollywood dream, are you kidding? Wait can I tell anybody about this now or would you prefer to show up and make a big who is she splash

Mark laughed out loud. "Jesus, she's perfect." One more text: *Tell whoever you want, just know people will start sniffing around immediately*

Eww gross okay I'll choose carefully

And seriously everyone will assume we're doing sex things. You might want to have a few answers ready

On it

One last thing. Call me Mark

There was a slight delay. Then: *Sorry I had to squeal for a minute. Yes OK will do. TTYL*

Mark disconnected, blowing out a breath. Turned his head to see Liam smiling at him. "Did you get all that?"

"Mm-hmm. What's the next thing you have to do?"

"Well, on Monday I'll contact Jenny. But right now, I think I have to kiss you." He set his phone on the desk behind them. The movement turned his body toward Liam's. The next thing he knew, he was on his back, Liam was pressing him down, and they were kissing. They spent most of the next hour that way, in a haze of kisses, touches, murmurs. Occasionally saying things about growing up – they had such different

49

experiences – or about things they'd appreciated in other people. Quietly, unobtrusively, and comprehensively answering the questions 'do we truly like each other' and 'is there a basis for moving forward.' They both had reason to distrust mere attraction. "What it comes down to," Mark said after a while, "at least I think so, is we were in a safe place to tell the truth, and I told you the truth, and you wanted to hear it."

"It helped that your truth was something I wanted to hear. Your truth might have been, I chose career over love and I'm not changing." Liam heard the word land and instantly wished he could call it back. It was too soon to use that word. Even though they'd already spoken of the future, of possibly moving in together.

Mark petted Liam's chest, aware of the sudden tension and one hundred percent positive he knew why it was there. "The thing is, though, I didn't choose career over love. I chose career *instead of* love. It wasn't as though love was standing there in front of me. It was abstract. A thing I might or might not ever find. Whereas career was right there."

"And you were twenty-two."

"Mmm." Mark pushed himself up on one elbow so he could make eye contact. "I am choosing differently now. I know you didn't mean to use that word. But I'm glad you did. I hope you can believe I'm capable of it. I love my parents. I love my son. I loved Kerry in all but one way; I still do. And I will give up my stupid, pointless career if I have to, because from here on out I would rather have love." He was, unsurprisingly, wet-eyed again. This time Liam was too.

It was quite some time before they pried themselves out of the sectional for another round of freshening-up, hydration, and consideration of the refrigerator. Liam suggested ordering in, something different, so they could use the leftover Thai fried rice and noodles for Sunday breakfast. Mark said something about running a tab. Liam said, "I'm going to move into your house, remember?" They stared at each other for a moment, smiling. Mark nodded. Liam opened a drawer and got the Bossa Nova menu out.

There was a certain unreality about the next twenty-eight hours. They were deliberately not engaging with the outside world, aside from the brief interaction with the delivery guy. Both of them abandoned all the things they might have done with the time on an ordinary weekend. No gym, no paperwork, no errands. They watched a movie on TV after dinner Saturday, then went to bed. Made love again, getting off with pressure and friction while they kissed. Mark slept for eight solid hours.

In the morning, they did a round of bodyweight exercises and much-needed stretches before showering together. Mark cooked again. They lounged around watching TV again. It was like being on vacation, except neither of them had been on vacation with a lover for years (Liam) or ever (Mark). Toward midday Liam pulled Mark up off the sectional and took him back to the bedroom. "We're probably going to regret this," he admitted, sitting on the edge of the bed. They both already had whisker burn, love bites, various bruises; their mouths were sore from kissing. "But God knows when we'll get another chance."

And that was the crux of the matter. The torpedo in the water, waiting to be armed. "We'll figure it out," Mark said, hoping that was true. "This will not be the last time till June. Not if I have to book us into the Madonna Inn under a couple of fake names." Liam stifled a laugh. Mark bent down to brush his mouth lightly over Liam's. "What do you want." Again, he expected a certain thing; again, Liam surprised him.

"I want your mouth. But first." Liam hesitated, then forged ahead. They both needed the truth. He pulled Mark down beside him, leaned close to murmur in his ear, "I want you to bind my hands. Then do … whatever."

Mark didn't buy it. "Mmm. You want something specific. Tell me."

Liam swallowed. "Come on me," he whispered. "I want to watch you."

"And not be able to touch me?" Mark's voice was almost as quiet. "Just that bit of restraint?"

"Mm-hmm." *Please don't be turned off.*

"I'd like that. I liked the way you watched me yesterday." Liam's face was in Mark's hair. After a moment, he moved enough for another almost-kiss. Mark stroked a hand through Liam's hair, down his neck to his chest. "I want to see you too." Liam nodded. That was perfect. He didn't want to be told to strip. It was such a weird little kink. He'd tried talking about it on a forum and everyone piled on with questions. Most of them went to such hard-core BDSM stuff that he ditched. At least he was smart enough to be there with a dupe email address and a username that never appeared anywhere else. He took his clothes off while Mark went to the closet. The man could wreck Liam's favorite tie and he wouldn't care. "Hmm, this one looks good." Mark came back out, tossed the knit tie on the bed.

"I didn't remember I even had that."

Mark moved in a little. "Want to sit down?" Liam sat, knees apart. Mark stood between them and slowly peeled off his shirt.

"Turn around for a second?" Liam's voice was husky. Mark turned. Liam kissed his back. Kissed that swath of caramel skin, with his hands roaming all over Mark's front. Lingering on the half-hard cock under those warm-ups. "You're so fucking beautiful."

"Jesus, Liam." Mark was breathless. This was worth any amount of paparazzi bullshit. He hooked his thumbs in the waistband of the pants, started pushing them down. Liam helped. Then that mouth was on the curve of his ass. He'd love to spend a little more time with that. But right now they had a different agenda. He got his feet free of the pants and turned around. "Lube's back in the drawer?"

"Mm-hmm." He'd dropped it in there this morning. Now he watched Mark get it out, tossing it on the bed. Then he was on his knees behind Liam, mouth on the back of his neck, stroking down his arms and bringing his hands together behind his back. Holding them together at the wrist for a suggestive moment. Then letting go, giving Liam the chance to get himself where he wanted to be, which was sitting in the middle of the bed with his legs stretched out in front and the pillows lined up behind him.

Mark moved in again, analyzing the position. "This way?" Liam nodded and put his hands in front of him. Mark straddled his thighs and slowly wrapped the tie around his wrists in a snug, simple loop, knotting it like a shoelace. Then he put his hand on Liam's chest, running his fingertips through the black hair there. Not pushing. Liam lay back, raising his hands over his head. Stretched out full-length on the king-size bed that had been so depressingly empty for so long, and was now going to hold memories of Mark. They were both already hard, and Mark hadn't even touched himself. "Looks like your not-a-major-kink is working for both

53

of us." Liam huffed out a laugh. "Don't forget to watch." Now he had the lube. Taking his time slicking himself, cock so close to Liam's he could feel the motion. He made a sound that was mortifyingly close to a whimper, eyes riveted to what was happening out of his reach. It was amazing how thoroughly pinned down he felt, though both of them knew he could easily get himself free. All he had to do was bring his wrists down to his mouth, get his teeth on the end of the tie, and pull his hands away. Instead he bent his elbows so his hands were behind his head, propping it up, so he could watch. Mark was in it now, eyes narrowed, lips parted, breath coming faster. He knelt up, giving Liam an even better view, then tapped the inside of a thigh. They moved as if this were prearranged, Liam opening his legs, Mark putting a knee down between them. He braced himself with one hand on the bed beside Liam's chest. "I'm going to remember this. Remember your face. Remember how you watched me come."

"Oh God. Do it. Jesus. Yes." Liam's erection was brushing the front of Mark's thigh, and that little bit of contact was killing him. That, and the scent of their arousal, the sounds of Mark's hand moving and of his breath, and the way this looked. "Oh *God.*" Those desperate words pushed Mark over the edge. The climax took him harder than he'd thought possible, given how many times he'd already come this weekend. His head drooped, hair brushing Liam's chest, while he caught his breath. He pushed back with quivering arms, folded one on Liam's hip, and got his mouth on that erection. "Oh *fuck!*" Liam surged up into Mark's mouth, barely aware that the man's hand was wrapped around him too. He was shoving into the bed with one foot, so close, God his mouth was so hot, Jesus those sounds he was making, it was too much, it was perfect.

Mark would not have thought Liam had this much left in him either. He was fairly sure he'd scraped the man with his teeth. He held on till the pulse faded. Slowly drew off, licking up one last drop. Liam made a faint sound. His chest was heaving. Mark crawled up to his hands, pulled the tie free and dropped it somewhere. Lifted those limp arms one at a time, kissing the inside of the wrists, dropping them gently along Liam's sides. "Sorry if I bit you."

Liam started laughing. "Worth it. Oh my Jesus. That was great."

Mark stretched out alongside him. "I remember back in high school, the popular locker graffiti said fuck me raw. I had no idea what that actually meant till now." Liam laughed again. They lay there, touching only at the hand, dozing a little. But eventually they had to get up. Mark considered another shower and decided not to bother. He put his own clothes back on while Liam rinsed off. They scrounged another meal, discussed things a little more. Mark would be talking to Jade; Liam would talk to Robert; they would take advantage of those friends as much as they could. Find ways to see each other that wouldn't set off flares.

When the kitchen was clean again and they hadn't heard any activity in the hall for a while, Liam said, "It's probably time."

"I wish I didn't have to go."

"Me too."

"Do you have to open the gate?"

"Yeah, I'll walk you down." Before they went out, they took the time for a long embrace. They didn't see anyone in the hall, or on the stairs, or in the garage. Liam brushed his hand through Mark's hair, as close to a kiss as either of them could bear.

55

Mark got into the car. Waited till he could see Liam standing by the elevator. Slowly drove out, half-watching the gate rise, blowing a kiss. The first thing he did when he got home was hook his phone up to its charger. The second thing was send a text: *I will never forget this weekend as long as I live*

Liam's reply was so fast he must have had his phone in his hand: *Neither will I. So glad we met. See you soon*

CHAPTER 5

If they hadn't already been in the habit of talking about what was happening on the show, Jenny might have been surprised by Mark's call. It was clear she wasn't surprised by his reason for wanting out. There was a moment of silence, though, so he said, "I promise that I have never put your health in danger."

"Oh Mark, for God's sake. They don't make a straight actor hand over a medical report before writing in a kiss, and some of those guys are whores." He stifled a laugh that was half relief. She said, "I'm not worried about that. I was just thinking, I hope you don't get crucified."

"It's probably career suicide, but I hit the wall. I shouldn't have to live like this."

"Well, it didn't kill Neil. So you never know."

"It's almost not even the workplace stuff I'm worried about," Mark said. He was lying on his couch, staring at the ceiling, resolutely not looking at the wall of posters, Playbills, awards, and other career memorabilia. "It's the women. If I'm not seen with someone between now and the end of the season, the media is going to be obnoxious. They were last time." One year when Mark tried going solo, the press put his most-recent companion through the wringer, prying into why he wasn't with her now. Trying to get her to say who dumped who, did he cheat, was it because she was holding out for marriage, on and on. It was awful.

This was, though she wouldn't say so out loud, one of the reasons Jenny was married. "Whereas if you're with someone, the worst of it is 'who are you wearing' and 'is that a baby bump.' Unless you appear to be actively miserable or filled with rage." Mark laughed. "They do get really intrusive when somebody shows up alone who isn't usually alone."

"So I might as well tell you there is a specific person who's kind of precipitated this. He suggested a woman we both recently met, and we've made a plan. She agreed to be my Platonic companion. She works in an agency and is very presentable." He heard Jenny laugh. "And she's all in, even though we didn't tell her exactly why I need this. I'm going to hook her up with Jade Derecha for whatever styling she wants."

"Oh, good choice. So how about I draft something for the production team and send it to you. You review, revise, whatever. We send it under both signatures and copy both our agents. Good?"

"Good. I really hope this works for you. I mean, I hope you get the big moment you deserve."

"Well, I hope so too. I'll miss working with you, though."

"Same goes. Make the most of it while we have it, I guess." Mark put a smile on his face to keep his tone warm. He was grateful Jenny was willing to work with him on this. They ended the call, and he lay there on the couch for another few minutes. The drive to hustle, to find a new project, was grinding away. But he had to resist. There was no point talking to his agent about what might be around for the summer hiatus. He could read for something now, get hired, and then find himself un-hired in a few months. That poor guy didn't know what was going to hit him.

On the other hand, Mark wasn't the only client to throw this particular curve ball. His agent also represented Dana Richardson, who came out three years ago. It was a little different, because a lot of people who were grossed out by gay men didn't have the same objection to gay women. Rumor had it Dana was perfectly happy to not be called for the endless mom roles. Instead she'd bagged two recurring roles, one as a lawyer and one as a casino pit boss. On top of the long-running sitcom she'd exited before going public, she was doing fine. Maybe the fact that Mark had never had a super-high-profile part would work to his advantage. Especially if his character was a good guy at the end. If they made him a cheater, he was screwed. *Worry about it later*. Bathroom, coffee, and then he had another call to make. Or rather, a text to send; it was very unlikely that Jade was free to pick up the phone at this exact moment.

The return call came after dinner, when Mark was feeling very sorry for himself because a day ago he was in Liam's arms and now he was alone again, and he hated it. He was telling himself "Don't be a baby" as he tapped to connect.

"What did you say?" Jade sounded like he was half-laughing.

"I was telling myself not to be a baby. I have a metric ton of news."

"Yeah, I got that idea from your text. What's up?"

Mark told him everything, at least everything on the outside of the bedroom door, and without saying Liam's name. Told him about Emily, and Jenny, and the plan. "So can I send my Platonic companion to you? I want to make sure she gets everything she needs. It's a little tricky because I can't exactly give her my credit card. Or can I?"

"I don't think you need to. Why don't I take her down to Kenji Matsumoto? He did Robert's Mary Russell costume for the pageant. The Amelia Peabody, too."

59

"Oh wow. That was a hell of a dress."

"It won't be as cheap as shopping at Nordstrom, but Kenji can bill you. As can I. Everything will be perfect. I'm glad you're doing this." Jade's sincerity came through. "I think you'll be a lot happier."

"And if I never work again, I can be the trophy husband." A laugh at the other end. Mark didn't add, if it's not all too much for him. If I don't get to the end of this and find he's decided I'm not worth it. He had to trust. He said something else, winding up the call. Jade promised there would be an invitation soon, a dinner for four, somewhere. Mark disconnected again, regulated his breathing again, wondered if he needed to see his shrink again. Probably. It was never a bad idea to talk through a big life change with someone whose only interest was 'are you okay.'

If he hadn't sent a text the night before, and received a heartening response, he might have been afraid to send one now. It was still possibly unwelcome, and possibly unwise; there might come a time when some tabloid was hacking his cell records. But he needed a moment of contact, so he wrote *Hi Liam, talked to Jade & Jenny, things are moving. Just wanted to* – he almost wrote 'kiss you' – *say goodnight*. He sent the message. Now he really ought to take one of those sleeping pills because he was exhausted.

Before he got in bed there was a reply: *I'm calling Robert tomorrow. Keep in touch. Goodnight*

Liam's call to Robert came in the form of a text, suggesting a rendezvous at the coffee shop. He expected that Robert would have been fully briefed by Jade, which turned out to be the case. They greeted each other, stood in line for their coffees, and then went outside to a corner of the patio that was otherwise deserted, thanks to the cool winter breeze. "So," Robert said, smiling. "We did not expect that, but we're really happy about it. And we want to do anything we can to help."

"You are good people." Liam sipped his coffee. "There's this feeling of inevitability. Like, of course. Like I've been waiting for him all my life. Which I know is kind of crazy, but you said pretty much the same thing. That you met Jade at a certain moment because he's the one you're supposed to be with. Is that crazy?"

"I don't think it is. I talked about it with my therapist. I was like, bear with me here. He was all, again with this?" Liam inhaled some of his coffee. Robert waited for him to stop cough-laughing. "My idea is that at different points in life, there are different people who might be the right person for us. In that moment. It just so happened that I didn't meet the right person for the person I was when I was, say, twenty-six. Or thirty, whatever. Then I met Sharon, who was very obviously not the right person despite how cute she is, and she knew she was not the right person because of her own reasons, so she bailed. Which left me really questioning everything right at the moment when Jade walked in and showed me what I really wanted. If he'd rolled up on me when I was twenty-six I wouldn't have recognized him, and he wouldn't have given me a second glance. So it's coincidence, but it's also a genuine *rightness*. And in your case it's coincidence that this guy was at our party on Thursday, and that he was in a moment of accepting that he was at a turning point, and that you were there to be recognized."

Robert sipped some more coffee while Liam thought about that. "But the reason he recognized me, or we recognized each other, is a confluence of right time and right person."

61

"Ooh, good word. Yes. So now you can flow on together, and if you want to flog the river metaphor you can say there are bound to be sandbars and rapids and maybe a cascade here and there, but if you can hang onto each other through all that you'll get to a nice calm place where all you have to do is float."

Liam blinked, momentarily lost in admiration. "I have to remember that so I can tell him. He's expecting some pretty gnarly rapids."

"Flotation devices required," Robert agreed. "That's where we come in, I guess. We do not have a problem being the hosts into whose master suite guests disappear for up to an hour." Liam laughed again, this time without inhaling coffee. "I mean, if we didn't have the powder room it might be a different story. So Jade is going to be the style guru, and he's going to hook Emily up with Kenji, who will probably turn her into front-page fashion news. I think we should send her to you, too. Get the whole facial, laser, Botox thing going if she wants. Do you use Botox? Because I noticed I'm getting a frown line and I'm like, fuck you."

Liam leaned on the wall, so awash with affection that it was hard to believe this wasn't the man he was in love with. *Oh shit I really am.* "I do use Botox. Or actually, a less-pricey equivalent which I will happily inject into your face. Or my partner can, or our physician assistant can. We sell a lot of that. And yes, definitely. Send Emily to me. It won't cost her a thing."

"You going to let me keep her for a little while?"

Liam smiled. "That's up to her." Robert made an annoyed sound and grumbled something about getting back to work.

Mark's first actual phone call to Emily lasted nearly an hour. It seemed they had already given each other as much of the 'why' as either needed. What she didn't know about awards season, though, was everything. Mark rambled on about the various events, what she might want to wear, how they could work the transportation. She was perfectly happy to be collected in a livery car. "It's not so much that I don't like to drive myself as that I like the extra security factor," he explained. "Having a bonded driver reduces the likelihood of anybody planting something in my car."

"Oh my God! Does that happen?!"

"Not to me, but it's happened to more than one friend. One was involved in a divorce and someone planted a surveillance device in her car. Another got stopped for a traffic violation, the cop asked to search the car. He said sure, and then oh what's this, they found cocaine." Emily made a disgusted sound. "Mmm. Completely set up."

"Why would someone do that?"

"It was another domestic thing. Custody fight. He got it straightened out eventually, but it took months. So I'm a little bit paranoid."

"You know what they say. It's not paranoia if they're really out to get you. Okay, so is there some low-demand way for me to get used to being out with you? I'm really afraid of being on the red carpet or something and glancing over at you and just, like, shrieking."

Mark laughed. "How about I take you out to dinner." They agreed on a place and time. Emily promised she would put herself in Jade's hands. Then she asked what he was doing until then. "Well." He hesitated. "Reimagining my professional life, I guess. Things may be very different at the end of this season."

"I hope all this is worth it." She sounded sincere. He told her he was sure it would be, re-confirmed their date, and disconnected. *Please let it be worth it.*

December 2010

They were not quite three weeks in, and the nightly text was not getting the job done. Liam was holding on to the invitation for dinner at Robert and Jade's place the week after New Year, wondering if he actually could survive that long. It wasn't that he needed sex. He was used to going without that for months at a stretch, and he had some very good material to think about during self-service. What he needed was reassurance that this wasn't going to dry up, evaporate, in the absence of some contact more meaningful than one of those brief, cautious messages. Of course Mark shouldn't write more, and neither should he, not that way. Not over email, either, because the idea of tabloid hacking was not some kind of egomaniacal paranoia. There was no reason for the tabs to be after Mark, but what if they were casually snooping around and found something to focus on? That was what they did. How they stayed in business. It would blow the whole operation, wreck Jenny Wilson's chances of a career boost, and piss off the show's production company. Maybe even the media conglomerate that owned the TV channel. There were homophobes everywhere, even in Hollywood, and nobody liked being deceived. It was possible (if not, Liam thought, entirely likely; optics were everything) that Mark would come out of this with some real enemies. Better to push that risk as far into the future as they could.

So he understood, but he didn't like it. And he missed the man. It shouldn't have been this way, after only one weekend. Two days. Barely fifty hours, thirty-three if you subtracted the hours he was asleep. Though he and Mark had learned more about each other in those thirty-three hours than he'd learned about other men in six months. *Suck it up. It's not forever.* Mark was trusting him, had trusted him with his entire life, and the least Liam could do was be patient.

All the same, he was frustrated. Edgy. Worried. It all escaped him sometimes, most often in the gym, but occasionally at work. He was less tolerant of chatter amongst the staff, more particular about the reception area and their tiny break room. Took his front-desk person into his office and told her she was being written up for absenteeism. Civil, but sufficiently harsh that she went out with a flushed face and wet eyes. And then he felt guilty about that, which was ridiculous, because of all the basic things you could expect of someone you were paying to do a job, it was that they would show up, as scheduled, to do the fucking job.

He was sorting through the usual pile of mail the week before Christmas, disinclined to read the professional journals, irritated by all the advertising material. The plain white envelope with its handwritten address looked like a solicitation; it almost went into the trash bin unopened. Then he realized what he was looking at. The return address was Brentwood, and the initials above it were MV.

A letter. Had Mark written an actual letter? Was he as anxious and lonely as Liam, and had he thought of this old-fashioned solution? Or was Liam projecting? Only one way to find out. He opened the envelope. There were several sheets of paper. The top one was typed.

> Dear Dr. Byrne,
>
> It was a pleasure to meet you at Thanksgiving. Was thinking about our conversation and

wondering if I could pick your brain a little about a project. I've never played a medical professional and could use some pointers.

I'm heading to NYC on the 22nd and won't be back in town until Jan 3. My schedule will be screwed immediately because my show will be back into production. Plus I have a lot of evening commitments through February. So I was hoping you wouldn't mind consulting at a distance, as it were. Maybe that would be easier for you, too – I know running a business isn't actually a 9-5 job.

Anyway, if you're willing, please drop me a line sometime. If you have too much going on I certainly understand. Thanks, either way.

Happy Holidays,

Mark Valance

The handwritten sheets underneath were everything Liam could have hoped for, if he'd ever thought about hoping for a letter.

Liam –

I feel like an idiot for doing this but I miss you. I miss you and miss you, and it's scary, and I hate not being able to see you and hold you. I hate that we can't actually be together while I get myself out of this mess.

Is it stupid? I've been wracking my brain trying to think of a business-related reason for us to correspond. I shouldn't know, for example, that Emily is coming to your office for this or that, not that she needs to be made more beautiful. It might make sense for her to tell me she gets her hair done by Jade Derecha, but what woman confesses

66

glycolic acid peels and laser hair removal to the guy who's taking her to Spago?

That was fun, by the way. She's kind of great. It's such a relief to have the this-isn't-really-a-date thing understood. She can flirt like a champ, with just a glint to let me know she knows we're conspirators. So I can flirt back and not worry about oh God what kind of expectations am I setting up. Thank you for making that suggestion. Thank you for everything.

I'm going to NY to see my parents, and Kerry & Christopher. Haven't decided what if anything to tell my folks. Probably nothing, it's not need-to-know, and they won't be pissed off or hurt. And they won't be scared. (Press people are more likely to be scared of them.) K & C, though, that's a different story. I have to tell them. No clue how it's going to go with Chris. I don't think he has any idea about me, so I'm terrified.

Every time I send you a text I want to say 'kiss you goodnight' instead of 'say goodnight.' I hate that I can't do that. I do want to kiss you goodnight. I'm living for dinner with R & J. Did Robert really say they don't mind if we hide in their master suite for up to an hour? I laughed so hard when Jade said that but then I thought, really? That's kind of above and beyond. Maybe we can get by with hugging in the kitchen. Five minutes in your arms would feel really good. I could live on that for a while.

In my head I see these scenes, like actual scenes in a play or a movie, where you and I are together in public and how it would play out. Like maybe we're all out at dinner and I go to the men's room, and you go a minute later. And we don't do anything, we don't even acknowledge each other aside from eye contact in the mirror while we're washing our hands. We don't take extra time, we don't touch, we don't say a word. Only that look, a look that any audience member could read, the one that says 'I want to kiss you.'

Anyway, while I'm in NY if Chris doesn't go sideways on me we'll spend some time together. This time I'm not going to hide away with him. He's going on thirteen, and if he actually wants to be seen in public with me after what I have to tell him then he deserves not to be hidden away like a child. I'll see some of my old theater friends, too. Play up the idea that the show might be writing me off, without admitting it's my idea, or why. Some of them will already know why. I wish I could tell them about you. I wish I could tell everybody about you.

Jan-Feb is going to be nuts. I hesitate to even mention it because it sounds so conceited but last year I did a movie and it came out this year, and there are a few things we're being nominated for. So I have to go to a lot of the film things I don't ordinarily go to. Emily is going to get a workout. Jesus that sounds wrong. As you can tell from all the scratching-out I'm not pre-writing this shit at all. Maybe I'll get a little more organized about it next time, if there is a next time. If you'd like me to keep doing this. You don't have to write back. I only wanted to talk to you, and this is the only way to do it. I would love it if you wrote back. Even if all you do is tell me stories about medical school and stuff. I'm honestly interested. Maybe I'll use my imminent unemployment to try my hand at writing a script about a doctor. A hot doctor.

There are so many things I want to say to you. I can't wait to see you again. I hate that I have to wait. Are you going to SD for Christmas?

XOX

Mark

Liam folded up the letter, feeling like he'd never been handed such a treasure in his life. Tonight when he texted he would drop a hint. And he'd write back, of course he would. But at the moment, he had a patient waiting.

At the end of the day – home, fed, and relaxed – Liam sat down at his computer to write the cover letter. Casual, businesslike, with a short and semi-humorous story about his last year of medical school, and an invitation to send specific questions. Ending with a comment about how long it had been since he saw a good movie about a doctor. He checked for typos, double-checked for too-intimate language, and printed it out. Then he dug around in a drawer for something to write on, settling for a pad of graph paper. He wrote slowly, so it would be legible.

Mark –

I miss you too, so much. And yes, it's scary. Pretty much every day I go back and forth from thinking we're both crazy to thinking this is the obvious way to make life worth living for the next forty-whatever years. Getting your text at the end of the day always swings me back to the second thing. We will get through it. It will be worth it.

Yes, I'm going to SD for Xmas. There is no chance any party I might go to here in LA would be as rewarding as my Thanksgiving was, so I might as well go and let the fam put me through the

69

wringer again about being single. I will cope with that a lot better this year, knowing there's you on the other side.

Let's make a date to hug in Robert & Jade's kitchen for at least five minutes. If that's not enough we can consider the master-suite option. I'm willing to deal with years of embarrassment and/or with gifting them a fresh set of sheets. You know a friend is true when he basically says go ahead and get busy in our bed. I can't believe I only met those guys this year.

I can't believe I only met you < 4 weeks ago. That whole Sunday, it felt like we'd been together for years. The way you trusted me knocks me out. You might have guessed I don't often ask for the thing I asked for. I would still think you're worth waiting six months for if you hadn't gone for it, but I'm glad you did. That's something that always made me feel a little off about myself. It really meant something to me that you took it in stride.

Obviously I want you to write again. Obviously I want to write back. I'm so glad you thought of it. It's a good ruse, isn't it? Nobody ever gets in trouble for writing actual letters these days. It's always emails, or phone calls that some sneaky bastard recorded, or a sex tape. We can make one of those at a later date.

And actually I appreciate the excuse to write about my experience. I haven't told anybody most of my stories since I was living them. Plus, the world could use a good movie about a doctor. There's always medical shows on TV (ER was the closest to real) but I don't watch much fiction. Funny how the one series I've been keeping up with is the one you're on. I don't even remember why I started watching it, or when. I remember noticing you when you started. I remember being kind of annoyed with the guy you play. Like, don't be such a flake. Which must mean that you're a great actor, right? I'm happy to give you all the credit, anyway.

Someday we'll sit down together and work through the other things you've done that I've never seen. I've been all over your YouTube channel. I found that clip of you from 'Chicago,' doing that song about having your name up in lights. It's freaky how sexy you were, acting like a woman, almost looking like one, and with that disconnect about your voice because you weren't even trying to sound like a woman, were you? Then I have to confess I went looking for the other guy and found a clip of him doing 'All That Jazz.' Which: same, same, and same. I will say there is no gay man on earth who would question your choice there. Can I be a selfish son of a bitch and say I'm glad he wasn't perfect for you? I wouldn't wish an extra four years of loneliness on anybody, but God I'm glad you and I were in the same place at the same time.

I liked your out-in-public scenario. You could put that in the movie you're writing about a hot doctor. I'm going to wrap this up now and get it ready to go, so I can get it in the mail first thing in the morning. There's a chance you'll get it before you leave town. But I'll text you tonight so you know it's coming. And, so you know, when I say goodnight I'm wishing I was kissing you goodnight.

XOX

Liam

71

Getting Liam's text made the rest of the week almost fun. Having a letter to anticipate, cherishing the knowledge that the other man craved connection as much as he did. Mark became hyper-aware of the sounds associated with the mail carrier, and hyper-vigilant about checking his box. His evening text became a status report; they turned it into a continuing joke about waiting till the last minute to do Christmas shopping. Then it was the day of his flight, and he was afraid the letter would have to sit there till January, but he checked the box one more time on his way out to the taxi. And there it was. He sent a text on the way to the airport: *Delivery in the nick of time. Happy Holidays*

The reply came back fast: *Hope it fits. Merry Christmas.*

Chapter 6

Mark read the letter on the way to LAX, and again on the plane. Now he wished he'd kept a copy of his own letter, but something told him the original was in a safe place. Someday they could put the whole correspondence together. Love letters, to look back on sometime in the future, when this was all behind them and things were easy, and maybe they needed a reminder of how and why they put themselves through it.

Mark still wasn't sure how he was going to handle the next almost-six months outside of L.A, even after halfway thinking it through while he was writing to Liam. He spent most of the flight to New York obsessing about it. There would be the usual get-together with his parents; probably nothing needed to be said there. They knew about him, after all. When they heard the news, once he was off the show, they might think 'it's about time.' Or they might think 'well so much for that.' Then they would wonder what the hell he was going to do with the next forty years of his life. He certainly didn't have much in the way of a clue.

Then there would be the get-together with Kerry and Christopher, and that was the one he was really worried about. He was not out to his son. Going-on-thirteen was a tricky age to deal with emotional weirdness from your parents. Possibly a bad age, but was there ever a good age? And could he possibly just drop that bomb out of nowhere? How grossly unfair would it be to let the news break without giving Chris any warning? He couldn't do that. And he couldn't wait till spring break, either, because that wouldn't leave enough time for them to talk through all the changes. All the consequences. They were good on the phone, but this conversation – these conversations – needed to start face to face. If the boy even wanted to have them. If he didn't hate the very idea, and therefore his father. *Breathe*. Eyes closed, consciously relaxing his hands, trying to force calm on his body. He could pretend this would be like his first night with Liam. That everything he said would be understood, and everything he did would be welcome. It was possible. Not likely, but possible.

It was almost a relief to get to Kerry's apartment two days later and find himself in the middle of a holiday cocktail party. A dozen of her friends, most of whom he'd met before, because she was good like that. Lawyers, a judge, a semi-famous pastry chef, and the one mutual friend from the theater whose bond with both of them had survived the divorce. Christopher was there, of course, being his usual snarky, precocious self. Doing the fake-interview thing he'd started when he was nine, at Kerry's suggestion, when he'd complained about not knowing how to talk to grown-ups. Only maybe it wasn't fake now. There was something very intentional about it this time. After mingling for a while, putting on his best charming-celebrity act, doing his best to seem like he was worthy of Kerry at some point, Mark washed up beside his son. Whisky and ginger ale in hand, nervous, and not at all sure what to say. He couldn't start the important conversation while all these people were here. He settled for, "You remind me of a journalist tonight, Christopher."

"I started writing a book." The tone was slightly defiant.

Mark blinked, then stared at his son. "Really? That's fantastic! Want to tell me what it's about?"

"It's a murder mystery." Now the tone was cautious.

"You always loved reading those." He'd started plowing through Dick Francis, Agatha Christie, and Ngaio Marsh when he was ten. Lately it was Donald E. Westlake and Rex Stout. Mark was equal parts delighted and proud. Of all the ways for a super-smart tween *oh God don't even breathe that word, Chris would have a justified fit* to cope with being super-smart, this had to be one of the most constructive. "Did you have the idea because there was someone you wanted to kill?"

Christopher laughed for probably longer than that joke was worth. Some of it had to be relief. "Sort of, yeah. It's set in a prep school."

"Well, they do say write what you know. I'd love to read what you have so far, or when you're ready to show it to someone."

"I'm only about a third of the way in. I got the murder out of the way but now I have to figure out how the hero's going to solve it."

"Oh, so the murder was easy?" That made Chris laugh again. Mark suggested taking over a couple of the armchairs on the far side of the room. They were still talking – like father and son, but also like friends – when Kerry came over, looking somewhat tired and also nervous. That was so out of character that Mark instantly went on alert. He looked past her and noticed that almost everyone else was gone. Kerry must have made his excuses, told people that he didn't get to see his son very often, assured them that he wouldn't be offended if they left without saying goodbye. Possibly apologized for him, because a couple of those people were higher-profile than he was and might have expected a salute as they sailed away. The only other person there was the lawyer he hadn't met before. If he'd seen that person on the street he would have done a double take, thinking he'd spotted Don Cheadle. What was his name … Walter? No, Warren. "Kerry? Is everything okay?" Mark stood up. "I'm sorry I lost track of your guests."

"It's fine. There's something I need to tell you."

Mark glanced at Christopher, who clearly knew what was going on. Was this when he should say what he needed to say? Not in front of Warren, surely. "Here and now?"

"Yes, please. Come over to the couch."

The main conversation group was a pair of loveseats flanking a couch, with a big, low, oval table which was currently covered with empty glasses and the wreckage of hors-d'oeuvres plates. Christopher led the way. He sat on one loveseat, right in the middle, which told Mark to sit on the other one, facing him. Kerry sat beside Warren on the couch. She took his hand. *Oh my Lord.* Mark didn't even try to hide the comprehension, or the smile. He was truly happy about this. "Kerry. Are you and Warren …?"

"We're getting married."

"That's great! Congratulations!"

Something about his expression and tone must have reassured Warren. He visibly relaxed, though he didn't let go of Kerry's hand. Now he dug in his jacket pocket with the other one, pulling out a ring box. "Kerry said she wouldn't wear this until you knew."

"Well, let's see it." Mark was still smiling. He watched as Kerry and Warren opened the box together. She held it while Warren removed the ring – a really nice ring, with a sizable marquise diamond set horizontally on a gold band – and slid it onto Kerry's ring finger. Her hand looked pale and delicate in his two dark ones. A good-looking man, and clearly in love with her. Mark was so glad she'd found someone. "How did you two meet?"

"On opposite sides of a deposition table." Kerry's tone was somewhat dry.

"Thank the Lord we weren't actually opponents," Warren added. "That could have been awkward." Mark laughed. He got them talking about their romance, because he was interested and because he could see they were dying to talk about it. Christopher was curled up on the other loveseat, watching his mother with a faint smile on his face. He obviously didn't have a problem with this. He must like Warren. Well, the guy was likable. *Please let him cope with me this well.*

After a while there seemed to be a movement toward wrapping things up. Mark almost bailed out. It would be so much easier to call it a night on this good note. Instead he made himself say, "There's something I need to tell you, too. Well, Kerry, you already know. But Christopher. And Warren, because you'll all be a family now."

"You're family too," Christopher said, face suddenly neutral. God only knew what he was thinking.

Mark realized his hands were shaking. He wound them together tightly, glanced around at three cautiously-curious faces, and forgot everything he'd planned to say. Instead what fell out of his mouth was, "I'm in love and I'm leaving the show and it probably means my career is over because I'm gay." Breath quick and shallow now, and he felt a little bit light-headed. *You're hyperventilating, get a grip.* He squeezed his eyes shut, stopped breathing entirely for half a minute, listened to the silence.

"Mark, are you breathing?" Kerry's voice, soft and concerned.

He sucked in a breath, nodded, didn't speak.

"You knew about this." Warren's voice, calm, clearly addressed to Kerry. "Christopher?"

The boy cleared his throat. "No." Everyone was silent for another few seconds. Then Christopher said, "Dad, it's no big deal. My best friend is gay. It kind of makes sense. I mean, a lot of things make sense now." Mark covered his face with his hands. He should have known he would cry. Either way, he was bound to. *Oh, God, thank you.* He felt the cushion beside him sink, felt a tentative hand on his back. "Dad. Did you think I would mind?"

Mark sniffed. "I hoped you wouldn't. But so many people do." He wiped his face, sniffed again, coughed. Finally turned to look at his son. Heaved a breath through his mouth. Sniffed once more, shook his head, half-laughing with embarrassment. Eyes still wet. "I could not love you more. You know that, right?"

"Jeez, Dad." Christopher squirmed uncomfortably, blushing. "I love you too." He mumbled it, with a sideways look at Kerry and Warren. Then he threw them under the bus. "They're going to have a baby."

"Chris!"

Kerry's outraged squawk made Mark laugh. Warren laughed too. And suddenly everything was all right. They didn't talk much more that night; everyone seemed to agree they all needed time to settle down. The only other thing Mark said about his situation was, "Please don't tell anybody else yet." Everybody seemed to understand why.

Mark spent Christmas day with his parents, and most of the following day doing tourist things with

Christopher. When the boy needed a break from adult conversation, they both got on their phones to text their BFFs. Mark brought Jade up to date on the better-than-hoped-for reaction, and Kerry's news, asking him to pass it on to Liam. They signed off before Chris was done with his friend Ben. He sat on a bench watching people skate on the rink outside 30 Rock. It was cold as hell, but he didn't mind. Chris was leaning against him, the tiniest bit, and there was a place they could get some hot chocolate whenever he put his phone away. That eventually happened; Mark made the suggestion; it met with approval. They didn't talk about heavy stuff. Mark asked a million questions about how school was going, and what kind of research Chris was doing for his book. They got on Amazon together and ordered some things for Christopher to read. It was a good day.

That night, there was a family dinner. Warren and Kerry talked about how they were planning to merge households. Mark talked about his strategy for dealing with the show. "And this is going to be tough for all of you, because I really have to ask you not to say anything until it's over. I'm going to be seen out with a woman. She's a friend, and it's kind of a don't ask, don't tell thing. She knows we're not really dating. It hasn't always been that way. I've lied to a lot of people for a lot of years. There is going to be a backlash, and people are going to blame you for no other reason than that you know me. You're going to be insulted just for acknowledging me, never mind helping me keep a secret. It is not going to be pleasant."

"If we need to talk about things with anyone, we'll talk about them together," Kerry said. "Here, just the three of us, or with your folks. It's good you have some friends who know."

"Six people." Mark half-smiled. "Plus you, plus my parents. Twelve of us altogether. It's ridiculously unfair to ask that many people to keep a secret. There are others, men I've … been with. They always understood or it would never have happened. They're going to be glad I'm finally doing this."

"I'm glad you're doing it." Christopher looked so grown-up all of a sudden. His face wasn't a child's anymore. His voice was starting to change. Mark studied him, conscious of pride that his son was so clearly his. Same eyes, same mouth, and promise of the same nose. Darker hair, a smattering of freckles. Someday he'd be a handsome man. The author photo on the back of the best-seller would be great. "What?"

Mark blinked. "Sorry, I didn't mean to stare at you. I was just thinking your publisher's marketing department is going to have an easy job. Good-looking kid."

"Dad!"

Kerry laughed. Warren made a snorting sound. Mark was grinning. Then he sobered again. "Anyway, you might want to consider getting a publicist. Mine is going to have her work cut out for her, because I have to keep lying to her right up to the end." There was one possibility that was so far-out that he almost didn't think it was worth mentioning. But this was the time to say everything. "If Jenny and I can get the writers to go the way we want, it could finally mean an Emmy nomination for her. Those come out in July. The gossip about me should be mostly over by then, but if she gets nominated it's going to kick back up again, and it won't be over till after the awards in September. So I'm really sorry. It could be a shitty summer."

"What if you're wrong, though?" Christopher again. Totally blasé about being at a table where the grown-ups were cussing, even though Mark never had before and Kerry surely didn't. "What if nothing bad happens?"

Mark sighed. "We can hope. Look, it's not so much the people I've worked with. It's the women I've been out with in the past decade. The press will track them all down, and it's going to get really sordid. There's no reason for those women not to take the money and give the interview. I'm going to try to talk to everybody. If my publicist suggests a press conference I'll do that. But even if not one of those women says anything hateful about me, the world in general will. I have been a liar, Chris," he said plainly. "I'm not proud of it. I did deceive people, and abuse their trust. Being taken to a red-carpet event is not a fair exchange for being lied to on this scale. An argument can be made that I deserve whatever's coming to me. You guys don't, though. So protect yourselves however you can."

"We were planning to go out of town next summer," Warren said. "Kerry's due in May." Their joined hands rested on the table.

"I'm taking parental leave," she told Mark. "We'll rent a place up-state. It'll be our honeymoon, because neither of us can get away before then."

"I'd love to be out of town," he said. "I haven't had a chance to talk about what's next yet with the person I am doing this for, but, well. Chris, what would you think about Denali?" It was an impulse.

The boy's eyes lit up. "Really?! I'd love to go to Alaska."

"He's never been there either. Would you be okay with that, or would you rather it was just the two of us? Because that's fine with me."

Christopher didn't immediately respond; he was obviously thinking this over. Having a gay best friend who was also going-on-thirteen meant there might have been a few conversations about what gay men did together. He was not a sheltered child. And he had to know that Mark would not be blatant about anything in front of him. After a moment he said, "I'd like to meet him. Could we stay in the park? Without, like, camping?"

Kerry smothered a laugh. All previous expeditions had involved accommodations no more rustic than a cabin with indoor plumbing.

"I'll look into it," Mark promised. "There's bound to be a lodge, the park is too far away from any cities. I'll let you know as soon as I have some good information."

"And around that trip, Christopher can spend some time bouncing to grandparents," Kerry said. "My folks, your folks, Warren's folks. So he doesn't get stuck in the country with a baby." The boy couldn't quite hide his relief. "Maybe you could go up to the Hamptons with Ben for a while," she suggested. "Pretend to work on your summer projects."

"Mom, we will totally work on our summer projects." Then, craftily, "I could get so much more done if I had a laptop."

Warren and Kerry looked at each other. "That was foreseeable," he said after a moment.

"And yet, once again, our child is out ahead of me. We'll take that under advisement, Christopher."

Mark and his son exchanged a glance. It probably shouldn't have been quite so obvious that Mark was trying not to laugh.

The rest of his time in New York was almost entirely enjoyable. If Liam had been there with him, it would have been the best vacation that he'd had in years. He paid more attention than usual to the city since Liam mentioned, in one of their goodnight messages, that he'd never been there. Even if Mark's career blew up he'd be able to afford trips like this from time to time. They could stay here with his parents, in their ridiculously oversized apartment close to Central Park. Go out and do classic tourist shit, like see a show at Radio City Music Hall. The night before his flight back to L.A., Mark raided his father's home office for some writing paper. After dinner, he wrote down all those ideas in a letter beginning Dear Liam and ending Love, Mark. Stashed it away in his carry-on. When he got in, he'd type up a cover letter asking about what, exactly, a medical internship was. And he would let that revealing salutation and closing stand, because 'Love, Mark' was the least of what he wanted to say.

Mark hinted at an incoming letter, but Liam hadn't received it before their rendezvous at Robert and Jade's place. He arrived at seven-fifteen, tribute bottle in hand, to find Emily was there too. She asked him about his front-desk situation. "It's better," he admitted. "My person let something slip to one of the aestheticians. It seems she had a boyfriend with certain expectations. But hanging onto a good job seems to have won out. I don't know what the deal is with the boyfriend and I don't really care, but she hasn't missed any days since Thanksgiving."

"It's kind of sad that one month without calling in sick is noteworthy," Emily said. "That's good though. Because I have too much on my mind to be setting up a cage fight between you and Robert."

"Everything okay?"

"Are you kidding?" She went off on a riff about her glam Hollywood makeover, and the first few things Mark was going to take her to. Jade contributed helpful details about her new look, which was still a work in progress. Then the buzzer went off.

"That'll be Mark," Robert said, as if they didn't all know. He went to take care of letting the new arrival in.

When they got back, Mark was congratulating himself for not driving. "I remembered all those no parking except between eleven and four on a Tuesday signs and thought, I do not need to start the new year with a parking ticket. The downside is you guys will have to give me some advance warning about when you want me out of here, so I can whistle up the jet."

"No problem," Jade said. "What did you bring us?"

"Little something from La Provence."

"Oh my God is it the chocolate strawberry thing?" Emily looked pre-orgasmic.

"Might be. I'll just put this in the fridge for later." He hadn't said anything overt, didn't make a sign that went beyond a sideways look, but Liam was in the kitchen with him before Mark closed the refrigerator door. "Liam," he said, so softly. "Happy New Year."

"Happy New Year." Holding Mark close, wrapped as tightly around each other as they could possibly be. That was all they said. They didn't even kiss. They didn't hear Emily come in.

"Oh, excuse me." She sounded mortified.

Mark didn't move. His face stayed where it was, tucked against the curve of Liam's neck. Liam turned his head enough to glance at Emily. He raised his eyebrows over a rueful smile. There was no way he was going to jump away from Mark and try to play this off. What was the point, anyway. Her face said I Get It, and also That's Cool. She refilled her water glass and left them alone. It was close to ten minutes before they finally let go of each other. Mark lifted his head, they made eye contact, they kissed. Lightly, briefly, because anything more than that and they would have to address how much they both wanted to do everything else. Maybe after dinner. Or maybe they would take this simple, quiet moment and cherish it till next time.

Nobody said a word about it during dinner. Their hosts made no suggestive references to the master suite. At the end of the evening, because now everybody knew, they took a moment apart by the door while Mark waited for his car to arrive. "I feel like that hug stitched me together again," he said quietly. "There were places that were unraveling."

"I know what you mean." Liam ran a hand through Mark's hair. "Not going to lie and say I wasn't tempted." A soft laugh. "But that was enough. When I finally get you in bed again I'm not going to want a time limit."

"For real. Let's see how we're holding up in another month." They made eye contact, both smiling. Kissed again, lightly but lingeringly. Held each other, foreheads tipped together, until Mark's phone pinged. He used his normal voice to say, "There's my ride. Thanks so much for this."

Jade came over to walk him out. "Our pleasure." When he came back in Liam was leaning on the bar, chatting with Robert and Emily. Jade patted him on the back. "Enough?"

"Thank you so, so much. You guys are unbelievably great. As are you," he said to Emily. "We didn't mean to let the cat out of the bag so soon."

"Hey." She shrugged. "I won't lie, it's the first thing I thought of when I found out who was asking for a Platonic companion. I mean it was not necessarily because of you but, you know. I remembered how you teleported into the kitchen after he did that song, on Thanksgiving." All three men laughed. "Was that really the first time you met?"

"It really was. Crazy, right?"

"No." It seemed as though she was about to say something, then changed her mind. "Not crazy at all."

CHAPTER 7

Liam got Mark's New York letter the next day. At the first opportunity, he sat down to write about his internship experience. That he could do on his office computer, and saw no reason why he shouldn't. Before going down to his car, he walked to the drugstore for letter-sized envelopes and some better writing paper. He had a lot to say about 'Love, Mark.' It might have been too soon, but he didn't actually care. The way to get through this was to admit they were lonely and scared. Admit to the frayed places, and the rust spots left by things that went wrong before. Above all, to give each other that honesty. To say 'I'm in love with you' if that's what they felt, because why the hell else do this? Mark was trying to get to a point of living his whole life honestly, and Liam needed to show him why that was worth doing. Show him that he wasn't doing it alone.

Dear Mark,

You may think this is a little over the top. If so, apologies in advance. I'm going to answer the question you didn't ask.

Love, Liam

That's only for starters. There's this, too: I'm in love with you. I thought that last month. I was talking to Robert, he was being cute, and I was thinking: I like him so much, it's kind of amazing he's not the one I'm in love with. And I was like, oh shit, but not in a bad way. It was oh shit, really? Finally?

We were talking about a thing I said, about confluence. You read a lot so I'm sure you know what that is. He told me way back last summer that he thought he and Jade were meant to be together, because they were the right people but also because they met at the right time. Which is what I said to him about you. Then he ran with the river metaphor and said, from here on out we can flow on together. There will be sandbars and rapids and maybe a cascade or two. But if we can hang onto each other through all that, we'll come to a place where all we have to do is float.

I'm going to hang onto you, Mark. I don't know why you're the one I want, but you are. Yes you're gorgeous, and smart, and talented. I've known other guys like that. But they didn't come into my life at the right time, or I didn't come into theirs. None of them ever stood in front of me and reminded me I can get married now. Granted I haven't been with anyone in a serious way since it's been legal anywhere. The point is you're the one who heard 'can't get married' and realized that meant I wanted to. And also, you're the one I said that to. I don't know if I ever said it to anyone before. And I don't know if you want that. It doesn't matter. All that matters is getting through this, together. Getting to 'together.'

One thing I've been thinking about is the people who used to be important. The men. I told you there were a lot who were only convenient. There were six who meant more. Four I said 'I love you' to. I started dating when I was sixteen, so that averages out to six point five years per significant man. But the fact is none of those things lasted that long. One guy graduated and moved away. Then I finished medical school and moved away. Then there was a guy in Chicago, and I eventually did move away, but it was already over by then because we got tired. Trying to be together was too hard. And finally Minneapolis, the one that really hurt to leave. That wasn't all about the weather. I had to leave because he wasn't going to say what I needed to hear, which was 'don't leave.'

I'm telling you now, Mark, don't leave. Even when we're lonely and scared, we can be there for each other. If we get frustrated and start wondering if this is worth it, we can remind each other, it absolutely is. There was nothing missing from your life except someone to love you, and that's me. There's nothing missing from my life except you. I love you.

Reading back over this, thinking yep: over the top. We've known each other for six weeks, and we can't be really together for nearly five more months. But we made it through that first month, and I don't want anyone else. I can't imagine wanting anyone else. The next time I see you (and with any luck hold you again) I'm pretty sure I won't be thinking why did I miss him. I'll be thinking, no wonder I missed him.

Love, Liam

Mark was a little distracted when he emptied his mailbox. The day before, he sat through an ego-bruising conference with the head writer, the show runner, and Jenny. It was one thing to know you were expendable. To know you weren't essential to the book of a show. It was a different and much worse thing to have somebody say that to your face. They might have been harsh because he was basically saying 'I don't want to work here anymore.' They could have pulled up their big boy pants and been decent about it anyway, instead of sending him back to his trailer feeling like a dog dumped at a shelter.

He told Jenny later that he almost wished he never said anything. He could have called his publicist and said, you know what, set up a press conference. Let the show deal with it however they wanted to. Instead he tried to be fair, give them plenty of notice, enable an exit that could be optimized for all the regulars, and look what he got. *Breathe.*

He flipped through the stack. So much junk mail. The trades, full of other people's successes, and notices for jobs there was no point going after. Bills.

And a letter.

He took the mail in, dumped the rest of it on his desk, and opened the letter. Such a letter. He didn't keep a box of Kleenex on his desk, so he had to wipe his face with his shirt. He'd done more crying the past six weeks then he could remember doing in the preceding twelve years. Maybe that was part of being honest. Or maybe he hadn't let himself feel anything too much, because what was the point. There was no one to share it with till now.

He needed to let the real letter sit for a while. There was a lot to say about that. While it was simmering he dealt with the business mail, called his agent to report on the meeting, texted Emily to see if she was geared up for their next night out. Then he spent some time writing a scene, pretending he was really trying his hand at a screenplay. Using some of what Liam said in his cover letter, and some of what he said in the real one. It went to three pages, about three minutes of screen time. He'd mention that in the cover letter. This envelope was going to need an extra stamp.

Then it was time to do something about dinner. While he did that, he thought about how long he'd been doing it alone. How tired he was of doing everything alone. How much he was looking forward to repeating those hours in the kitchen at Liam's, putting something together for them to share.

That was definitely something he could say to his lover, though maybe not this time. This letter was going to be long enough as it was, and there was no chance there wouldn't be more letters. It was not the same as being in the same room, but infinitely better than nothing.

Dear Liam,

Your letter was exactly what I needed. Had a meeting yesterday, it was awful, and I was feeling bitter about trying to take the high road instead of dumping Jenny and the others in the shit. Now you've reminded me that I'm doing the right thing for the right reasons. And, in case you had any doubt, I'm in love with you too.

I said so to Kerry and Chris in NYC. I had this really composed speech ready, and instead what I led with was 'I'm in love.' Maybe that's part of why Chris didn't freak out. We talked a little more about it before I left. He came over to my parents' apartment and we sat in front of the fireplace and talked, and this is what he said (essentially):

You know a lot of my friends have divorced parents. You're the only divorced dad who never got married again. I always thought that must mean you still loved Mom, but then I couldn't figure out why you didn't just get back together. Because she never settled on anyone either, until Warren. When they started dating, I thought gee I hope this isn't

91

too hard on Dad. Then she sat me down and said Chris you know Warren and I have gotten really close, and we've decided to have a baby. And I thought wow. I figured that was it, you would give up now. Then you looked so happy when she said they were getting married, and I thought what the?

(Liam, imagine me laughing there. I hope you like my kid as much as I do. Back to Chris:)

So it was only like a minute but my brain was in overdrive going why is he happy, which is why when you said what you said it was kind of like, of course. For the record you're not the first parent among my friends to do that. I figure you and Mom must have worked it out a long time ago, because I never remember you fighting. Did you fight?

Back to me (it's all about me. This is something I am a little ashamed of, but you were aware that I'm an actor etc so I'm hoping that's not a complete turnoff. Has not seemed to be so far). We talked about that for a while. I gave him what I hope is an age-appropriate summary of when Kerry knew, how she knew, why she married me anyway, and why we didn't stay married.

That is a clumsy segue, but better than none. You mentioned the whole 'can't get married' thing. I remember mentioning that in New England, you can. And I remember you asking a certain question when we were talking about breakfast. You may remember that I did not say No.

I feel like this isn't the time to talk about that in detail. Not because I don't want to talk about it, but because it's going to be tough to deal with the present day if we're both spinning dreams about the future. The present day will probably take all our brain power.

That said: I liked being married. I thought I would, which is really why I did it in the first place. I grew up in a stable home, and I liked it. The kind of career I was going into was going to be a lot less stressful if I had someone to come home to. And Kerry loved me, in spite of everything. It meant being able to throw myself into the jaws of rejection, over and over, knowing there was someone there to scoop up the shreds. Even though I only managed to keep it going for six years, those were such essential years.

I helped her too, or at least being with me helped her. My parents put her through law school. When she got pregnant, they made sure she had everything that I couldn't give her, that her own parents couldn't give her. I have already been phenomenally lucky, which is one reason I still can't believe my luck in meeting you.

I love you. I plan to hang onto you, Liam, for a lot longer than six point five years. So don't leave.

Love, Mark

February 2011

Liam was completely addicted to the celebrity news sites. He'd never really paid attention to them before, only followed the occasional interesting link. Now he had things to look for intentionally. Mark would mention, in his good-night message, that he and Emily were going somewhere; Liam would check it out. Most of the stories weren't about Mark, really. He was simply one of the people attending whichever event it was. But he and Emily looked great together, so they tended to get photographed. There were sound bites. And, always, speculation. What's next, any plans. For the first time,

Liam noticed what kinds of questions were put to the people who attended without dates. No wonder Mark didn't want to go alone. Not only did he have someone to help him field the inquiries (and Emily was good at it), he had a reason to move along. Something about how shoes like these aren't made for standing around, or it's a little chilly for this dress. Mark was great at drawing attention to what Emily was wearing, often right after somebody asked a personal question.

Then there were the events for that movie. Critics' awards, the SAG awards, the Golden Globes. Mark wasn't nominated, but as one of the top five names in the cast he got plenty of attention. Those exchanges were slightly more substantive. How was it working with X. How did you prepare for the part. Did you think the film was going to do this well. And then, to Emily, have you seen it. She had a standard reply: "Duh, of course. We certainly don't sit around and talk about *my* work." Which reminded people that she had an actual job, and sometimes provoked a question about it, which she then declined to answer because of client confidentiality. When she came to his office, Liam asked if that was fun; her answer made him laugh. "I never knew how fun it could be to absolutely frustrate people! They totally want me to say, oh this person came in to the agency for a meeting. I'm like, nope. Go dig through our trash if you want to know, and by the way good luck with that because we've got the cross-cut shredder."

They always took a few minutes before or after whatever appointment she had. The staff didn't wonder about it because he did the same thing with all his patients who came in for non-medical reasons. Officially, it was to remind people that they were in a doctor's office and not a salon. Ask the appropriate questions about medications, allergies, sunscreen, any concerns beyond the immediate reason for the appointment. Make the recommendation about a mole check, update the history. All part of the service. Neither of them mentioned Mark.

They were exchanging letters regularly. Without those, Liam really wasn't sure if either of them could have dealt with everything. The letter he received right before Valentine's Day was enough to make him pick up his phone and text Robert: *Hi buddy, remember what you said about flotation devices? If you and Jade have a minute, there's someone who really needs to get his head above water*

A quick four-way exchange led to a proposed rendezvous at Robert and Jade's place. Then there was a brief delay while Emily and Shaya got roped in. Finally there was a date and time confirmed, and Liam could get back to the letter. The real letter, not the cover letter with its remarks about his latest medical story, and a request to fact-check a scene.

Dear Liam,

I keep telling myself not to whine and complain about how hard this is. I've been doing it (or a version of it) for almost twenty years, it's no worse than it's been before, except it's awful because this time there's something I would so much rather be doing. It used to be kind of fun going to all these bullshit events; better than being at home alone, anyway. Now all I can think about is being at home with you. Imagining watching the Globes from the comfort of my couch, with you sitting beside me, and you to kiss during the boring parts.

And there's nobody but you I can whine and complain to. God knows you're the last person who should have to ~~listen to~~ see that. I am lying to absolutely everybody else, even my shrink. Even Jenny, even Jade.

See where I crossed out 'listen to'? That's because in my head I'm talking to you. Because I wish I were talking to you. It was great talking to you the week before the SAG thing. I wasn't expecting the guys to have us both over again so soon after the last time, especially when they both had stuff out of town. There is not actually a way to quantify how big the IOU is going to be. Infinite IOU. I really wanted you to take me back to the master suite. It's good that you didn't, because we probably wouldn't have come out of there till the next day. Either that or I would have cried all over you again. I am on an emotional roller-coaster and I hate it.

On the plus side we are six weeks away from being done taping my material. If I didn't have to keep representing the show till sweeps I would immediately be cutting my hair. Not to mention eating everything in sight. It's hard on the temper being hungry all the time. I remember the good old days before I turned 30 when I could eat whatever I wanted, because I was in the theater all day every day. Barely even needed to go to the gym. Now I'm sitting on my ass most of the time, so even though I have a gym in my damn house, I'm still getting the side-eye from the wardrobe people. So tempting to say, remember how when I got this part I weighed X? Was there some storytelling reason why I now have to weigh Y? Tempting, but a waste of time, and pointless anyway because it's almost over. Through sweeps, and then I'm going to be face-down in a plate of brioche bread pudding from

Musso & Frank. Have you ever been there? We have to go.

My rebellion will manifest solely in refusal to shave the week my last episode airs. It's not unprecedented. The only reason I mention it is I'm going to look terrible and I want you to know it's intentional. Not a sign of deep and intransigent mental-health issues. Really, it's not. Speaking of my shrink!

I am rambling, and probably making so little sense that you'll be positive it's a good thing I have a shrink. Liam, I miss you. I love you. Ten minutes every three to five weeks is enough to keep me sane, apparently not quite enough to keep me balanced.

I have to do a thing in March. I say that like I hate the idea. The irony is it's something I've wanted to do for years. The opportunity opened up, and I said sure, now's a great time, even though it's a lousy time. There's a jazz bar up on Beverly Glen called Vibrato. I'm going to do a set there. Here's the date. Emily said she can come. Jenny and her husband might come. If I had some other friends there that would be great, except once again I'll have to pretend we aren't friends, which I increasingly hate doing.

This got away from me a little. I'm not quite as much of a mess as you'd think. I'm going to send it all instead of re-writing, because I'm tired, and you deserve to know exactly how much of a mess I am so you can re-think this if you want to. It truly is not a chronic condition. No weed jokes please, except this one: Don't leave.

Love, Mark

Writing an answer to that took some time. First he had to write the cover letter. He honestly enjoyed the medical correspondence, especially reading whatever scene Mark had written and commenting on that. He asked how long a screenplay had to be, slotted in a story about a rotation in the burn unit that he'd written a few days earlier, and wrapped that up. Then he got down to the important business.

Dear Mark,

Before I started this I pinged Robert and yelled for help. So as I'm writing, we have a plan. I'll see you soon, hold you and kiss you and tell you it'll be okay. It really will be. You do sound a little messed up. Hang in there. It's worth it. I love you. We're halfway home, and pretty soon you won't have so many things where the press will be all over you, right?

Also, fuck the wardrobe department. If you're hungry, eat. I know you're vain enough not to let it go too far. Same as me. I do penance in the gym every time I have dessert, but dammit I'm having dessert once in a while.

FYI those two are heading to Vegas to see Robert's sister. She's the only one of his family who's reached out since he told them he was gay. Nobody even sent a Christmas card. I'm glad he's taking Jade for this meet-up.

What was it like for you? I came out to my parents when I was seventeen. They asked me who I was taking to prom and I said Francisco. They were like, uh, so you're going stag? I thought, you know, here goes nothing and said no, I'm taking him as my date. Then we all kind of stared at each other, I was dying inside, till Dad said well do you want to bring him along to the tux shop so you can get something that matches. And that was it. My brothers were a little weird about it for a minute. They were both already out of high school. My sister was two years behind me, and she didn't give a shit. Or more accurately, she was thrilled to have *two* good-looking guys dropping her off at whatever. (See, I'm vain too.)

Did your family do church? Ours was one of those kind of country-club Catholic churches. I knew the word would get around in about a minute, so I was dreading going. Next thing I knew the guy who ran the music program was saying, feel free to talk to me any time if you're wondering how to relate to your faith. I did go to talk to him a couple of times. Not so much about myself but for his take on the official Catholic line and how we practice in the real world. I've gotten away from the church recently, not a super fan of the leadership. Or maybe I just like to be lazy on Sunday mornings. I can't really imagine preferring church over lying in bed with you.

Reading back over that, can't really imagine preferring anything to lying in bed with you. Now I'm thinking about our Sunday. You were so perfect.

And now I have to stop writing because there's something else I need to do with my hand. I'll see you soon. Remember, this might feel like rapids, but we'll get to that place where we can float.

Love, Liam

The letter he received three days after their meetup at Robert and Jade's was brief, a single page behind an

99

equally-brief cover letter. No scene this time, only 'thanks for the inspiration, working on something.' Liam had no idea how all these various stories might come together into a single story, or if the whole thing was simply an exercise. It didn't matter. He set that page aside.

Dear Liam,

Thank God for you, for Robert and Jade, for Emily, for Jenny. I don't know what I've done to deserve such great friends. Have you promised them all free Botox for life?

We covered a lot during our kitchen moment. I forgot to tell you that the set I'm doing has the potential to sound tragic. Don't worry, it's a strategy not a statement. I will find you in the crowd (conceited enough to assume there will be at least a small crowd) and give you one of those looks that you know means 'I want to kiss you.' I always do.

Love, Mark

CHAPTER 8

March 2011

Liam sat at the table with Robert, Jade, Parker, and Shaya, filled with a mixture of genuine happiness and envy. They were all at Vibrato for Mark's concert. Emily was at a table with Jenny Wilson and her husband. Everyone there who mattered knew that he and Mark were connected, but they still had to hide it. As far as the world knew, they weren't even acquainted, so Liam didn't go talk to Emily. He stayed with his friends, drinking champagne with dinner to celebrate their big life change.

Robert and Jade had been engaged since Christmas. The idea was that they'd get married after the Supreme Court knocked down Prop 8, whenever that might be. Till then they were going to keep it unofficial. Something must have changed, because they registered their partnership soon after their trip to Las Vegas. Their happiness was contagious, but Liam wanted that so much for himself and Mark that he had to play the Good Friend in a very conscious way. Envious because they could. And they hadn't even been together for a year, had only been living together since Halloween. If Liam moved in with Mark someday, he could ask that question.

Or he could ask the other question again. Mark might be ready to go beyond not saying No, and say Yes. There were good reasons to make it official, one way or another, once they were sure their relationship worked in the real world. Liam would settle for being registered domestic partners, but he still wanted to be married. And Mark said he liked being married. There were good reasons to get married somewhere in New England. It might even be legal in New York by this summer. He let those thoughts keep him company while Mark sang another heartbreaking song.

This set was definitely music to cry in your drink to, from 'Over the Rainbow' to 'Pure Imagination' and 'Nowadays' to 'The Land of Might-Have-Been.' In between songs Mark talked about his history with them. The first time he heard the song, whose performance inspired him, why it was part of the set tonight. Liam was not generally a live-music guy; now he felt like he'd been missing something. Maybe in his next letter he'd look back at music that stuck with him, and why that might be.

And he'd mention how it felt to be across the crowded restaurant, watching the man he loved. Waiting for the moment when they made eye contact and it meant 'I want to kiss you.'

April 2011

Mark was done. He'd never been so happy to be done with a job. And his last two days of taping were so easy, because there was literally no acting involved. All he had to do was get made-up (he took a selfie at the end of that process, because he'd never looked quite so horrific and he thought it might be helpful for Christopher to see it in the same old reassuringly ordinary dressing room as the other selfies he sent from time to time) and lie around being dead. It would make a funny story someday. He did write a short letter – a real letter again, enclosed with Christopher's birthday card – to tell him what was going to be on-screen during sweeps. The kid was tough, and he understood the difference between fact and fiction, but still: father, looking dead, on screen. He sent a text to Kerry, asking how she was doing; she wrote back with a series of complaints about swollen ankles, backache, feeling like an elephant seal, etc. Her final text read: *Thanks for asking. I am not bitching to Warren so I needed an outlet. It is different doing this at thirty-eight vs twenty-five. Looking forward to seeing you when you come to get Chris for your big adventure*

And the great thing was, he knew that was true. They were married now; got that taken care of in February, a small ceremony with only their immediate family. Chris said it was really nice. The unspoken questions of how was Mark holding up, did he ever get to see his person (none of them knew who it was yet), was he still planning to go through with it: he could feel them. He talked about how much he was looking forward to taking a summer off, which was true. Everything else would simply have to wait. The only person he could say everything to was Liam. A week after he wrapped, he wrote again. This time his cover letter asked oh-so-casually if Liam had ever been through the kind of scenario that always turned up on the medical shows – someone needing emergency surgery in the field, or anything equally dramatic. He said he needed a climax for his script. Then he went on to write the real letter.

Dear Liam,

It might be cruel to even use the word 'climax' when we're still a few weeks away. Unless you want me to run up my tab and ask Jade about that master-suite offer? The closer we get the more I want to wait until we have all the time in the world. And the more I don't want to wait at all. I keep thinking about our weekend together and, my God.

The sweeps episode is going to be gnarly. Jenny was crying for real. I'm so lucky she was in this with me. If she doesn't get a nomination I'm going to be severely pissed. And I have to say, the show runner may have his panties in a bunch because I told him I wanted off before he had a chance to fire me, but the writing team has given me some good stuff too.

I've been thinking about June. So looking forward to that trip. When we're both back in L.A., once we get organized, I'd like to invite you over to my place for a weekend. Maybe the weekend before they announce the nominations? You'll get to see me at my anxiety-ridden worst again, maybe that's not such a great idea. I could stay at your place if you'd rather. Or I could stay out of your hair until that's over with.

My agent sent me a lot of stuff to consider for the summer. I told him another set of lies, this time about maybe staying in New York for a while after I take Christopher home from our trip. So then he asked if I wanted to see about picking up some work there, like maybe on one of the soaps that tapes in the city, and I was all, um, thanks but no. Implying that I might be talking to some of my theater contacts, or I might be open to another movie, but not another TV gig for a while, even as a guest. That poor guy. It's too late in the year for anything much to be open in film (unless somebody drops out of something). He's probably livid, dammit, won't get paid again this year.

I meant to lead with thanks for coming to my little gig. And thanks for your letter after that. As you can imagine, the only people truly important to me who have seen me perform live – up to now –

were my parents and Kerry. Now there is you, and you have no idea how nervous I was about singing in front of you. Even after Thanksgiving. It was kind of risky putting some of those songs in the set. Back when I first talked to the management about it my goal was to do something completely different from the last stage thing I did. 'The Music Man' in Sacramento =/= major credit. My only decent clip from it is 'The Sadder but Wiser Girl' which is fun but makes me cringe now. Anyway that's irrelevant. What's important is those songs all meant something to me, and they showed some range that I don't often get to show, and I'm really glad you could be there. If those songs mean something to you now, too, that's kind of amazing.

I am talking about myself as usual. Narcissist much? At the very least this correspondence has given you plenty of advance notice about my personality flaws. But then it's also given me the chance to say I love you. It seems so long since our last kiss. When we're finally together I'm going to kiss you so much. I love kissing you. I want to kiss you all over. I want to strip you naked and spend about an hour just looking at you ~~and then~~

Well this got away from me in a really embarrassing way, but I'm not going to rip it up and start over. You can't say you haven't been warned what's in store for you.

Love, Mark

Liam momentarily regretted reading Mark's letter at work. He always did read them right away, was the thing. The letters were delivered there, and he wasn't the guy who would wait until he got home to open the envelope. This time he had to fold it up and fan himself

105

with it for a few seconds, resolutely thinking about the consult that was next on his schedule and how he was going to present the patient's options. Once he was decent, he slid the letter into his messenger bag, zipped it up, chucked it under his desk, and got back to work.

He had a thing to go to in the evening, which meant he didn't get a chance to write back until the next night. He started with the cover letter, as usual. Telling a story from his ER rotation, which had definitely provided some drama moments. They were so close to the end, he couldn't resist adding an offer to meet in person sometime. Then he got to work on the real letter. It might be the last one; they were taking turns, as if both of them wanted to have a letter in hand before they wrote another one. If it was the last one, he wanted to make it good.

> Dear Mark,
>
> I was at the office when I read your letter, so I was kind of glad you didn't keep going with 'and then.' Now that I'm at home, I'm really wishing you kept going. The idea of standing naked in front of you, watching you look at me, let's say I found that unexpectedly arousing. I'm tempted to ask you to write down all the things you want to do. When we're together, I'll ask you to tell me. We can make a list. I can't wait to start working our way through that list.
>
> If you gave in to the wardrobe Nazis and didn't start eating when you're hungry, I'm going to feed you every time I see you. I hope that's every day. I'd love to spend a weekend at your place any time. I want to spend every weekend with you and I don't really care where. Once we get to the end (and the beginning) I hope we can take some time to talk

about what comes next. I love you. I want us to have a life together. That doesn't have to mean we live together but I hope we can. Be thinking about that, please. I'm hanging on but I believe the way we'll float best is if we're truly together.

I get anxious too. I'm not that much older than you, but it feels like I've been alone forever. I'm afraid of screwing up the being-together thing. At least I did live with someone a couple of times, so I've had a little bit of practice. And you had Kerry for a while. It's not easy living alone, even though I'm not up for rejection constantly like someone who has to go to auditions, or up for judgement like someone who performs. I guess you don't think there's anything particularly brave about that, but seriously? The idea of getting up on a stage and talking freaks me out. I've given talks a few times at conferences, with notes, a lectern, and slides to protect me. Singing? No. Just no.

Which reminds me, I went looking online for The Music Man, because it's yet another thing I've never seen. You could sing the hell out of that love song, the one the Beatles recorded. Till There Was You. I listened to it on YouTube. Those people in Sacramento should have given you that song instead of whoever was playing the girl.

Does Christopher like musical theater? What does he like to do besides write? You have to fill me in so we can talk up in AK. It's going to be a great trip no matter what – a place I've always wanted to see, with the man I love – but I really want to get along with him too. He sounds like a great kid, and I'm not just saying that because I'm in love with you. Kerry sounds great too. The whole family.

I hope you'll like my family. None of them know I'm in love yet. The minute the news gets out, they're going to be all over me.

I want you to be all over me. I want to be naked with you, holding you, kissing you. Making love with you until we're both exhausted. I want to go out with you, be seen with you, eat brioche bread pudding at Musso & Frank with you and then stand with my arm around you while the paparazzi do their thing. I'm hoping somebody asks me why I would agree to wait for six months and barely see you. I can't wait to tell them, because even though I fell in love with him, he had a job to do. He had co-workers he wanted to be fair to, and I was willing to wait because, well, who wouldn't?

I could go on like that until my hand gives out. We're almost home, honey. Hang on.

Love, Liam

May 2011

The proposal was so heavily foreshadowed that there wasn't a ton of media response to that episode. Speculation about what that meant for Mark's role in the future ranged from 'he'll be a permanent full-time cast member next season' to 'they're going to kill him.' If Liam hadn't already known what was going to happen during sweeps, he would have bet on 'permanent.' The way Mark and Jenny were together on the show, the warmth and reality of it, made him feel bad for the people who were trusting in a happy ending. At least the show didn't do what they did to Mekhi Phifer's character on 'ER' and kill Mark before he even got to propose. That one always stuck with Liam. And he suspected he would have a hard time watching Mark's final episode. Even though it was fiction, seeing someone you love die had to be wrenching.

Robert might have had the same idea. They were at the coffee shop talking about Liam's front-desk situation, which had improved so dramatically that he was glad Emily was too busy being celebrity arm candy to think about changing jobs. After getting to the end of that chat, Liam glanced at his watch and made a move to go. Robert said, "You should come over on Thursday and watch that thing with us. We usually watch from the DVR but it seemed like this was something we should be up to date on."

"I used to watch from the DVR, too. This season I've been watching when it airs." Liam tipped the last of his coffee down his throat and tossed the cup into the trash bin. "Yeah, I'd like to. What can I bring?"

"Mmm, how about something from Frida? Not tres leches. Do not bring tres leches." The look on his face said 'please bring tres leches.'

Liam tried not to laugh. "Mexican food it is. I can be there around seven-thirty."

"Perfect. Go get some work done."

"You too." Liam walked back to his office, suddenly realizing that this was it. This was the end. After this episode aired, the media would be all over Mark, and he was going to … do what, exactly? All those letters, and he hadn't told Liam his plan for the actual coming-out part of it. Only that he had one. How would he do it?

They hadn't seen each other for a month. The last time had been in public, so they couldn't speak freely. An event at the Getty Villa, a play; they arrived separately, of course. Mark was with Emily, of course.

A security person stood at the end of the row where they were seated, watching the people around the celebrity, ignoring the play. Liam had a hard time concentrating on it himself. He only got to speak to Mark because Emily made a show of introducing them. Oh hi Dr. Byrne, did you enjoy the play? Mark, this is my dermatologist. At the back of the long and slow-moving queue to exit the amphitheater, in full view of hundreds of people, and with quite a few hanging around to eavesdrop on the celebrity and take surreptitious pictures. Liam didn't know if that had been orchestrated. Mark had to know that people would take pictures, and some of those pictures would have Liam in them. At some point, someone would make the connection and say hey, I wonder if that was a coincidence.

So he needed to stop worrying about what Mark was about to tell the world, and start rehearsing what he was going to say for himself the first few times someone stuck a mic in his face.

He arrived at Robert and Jade's place with a bag of takeout and a case of nerves that made eating seem like a bad idea. His hosts took the bag out of his hand and put an open bottle of beer in it. By the time the show came on, he was closer to being relaxed. The burrito, beer, and tres leches were playing nicely together. By some telepathic agreement, he was seated in between Robert and Jade, which meant when the accident happened they could each put a hand on him.

It was horrible anyway. Mark and Jenny were crossing a street – on location, in downtown Ventura, where their characters went for a romantic engagement getaway – when a kid on a bike came flying at them. At the edge of the frame, an oncoming truck. They sprang apart to avoid the bike, Jenny forward onto the safety of the sidewalk, Mark backward. Jenny screaming his name, a cut to his startled reaction, a cut to the looming truck. A view through the windshield at Mark, the squeal of brakes. Then Jenny's point of view up at the cab of the truck, the driver's horrified face. A thud, people yelling. A crowd on the street, Jenny on her knees, and the sound of her sobbing. Commercial break.

Liam took a deep shaky breath, blew it out through his mouth. "That was a little too realistic." His phone buzzed. He pulled it out of his pocket. A text from Mark: *I don't know if you're watching tonight but I'm here. I'm fine. Emily and I will be out tomorrow and things will be said. Can I meet you at the Regent Beverly Wilshire on Saturday? Dinner, 7:30. XOX*

He texted back *Thanks so much for getting in touch. Yes. See you Saturday XOX*. Set the phone on the coffee table and watched the rest of the episode. Jade's hand stayed on his thigh, Robert's on the back of his neck. He felt profoundly comforted, watching the montage of aftermath with a little more distance. Only a TV show. The body on the gurney, the commotion in the emergency room, none of that was real. Mark was safe. In two days, he would walk into the restaurant at the Regent, and maybe that was the actual moment when they would stand together as two ordinary men who happened to be in love.

Mark watched the episode as he always did. Half to see how it looked cut together with effects and music, so he could be ready with an intelligent comment on it; half to assess his own performance. He thought he'd done good work in the back half of the season. All the way through, really, but he'd be the first to admit that knowing the end was in sight let him dig a little deeper. Find a little bit more than the writers gave him. His conspiracy with Jenny helped. The low-demand arrangement with Emily helped. And the letters: those helped a lot.

He turned off the TV, glanced again at the text from Liam, and sent one to Emily: *Ready for Musso & Frank tomorrow? We'll pick you up at seven*

I'll be ready. Fair warning I plan to say something and it may sound for a second like I'm talking about you but I'm not

Hmm very tantalizing Ms Lincoln. No hints?

Eh no I'm afraid if I talk about it in advance I'll chicken out. In case I haven't said so before, thanks for this. It's been a lot of fun

It has been fun. We'll stay friends?

OMG Yes. Get a good night's sleep, you're going to be on the phone all day tomorrow

Ugh okay. Hasta

Mañana. They disconnected. Mark put his phone on the charger after sending one more text to Liam. It was early to be saying goodnight, but he needed to take a sleeping pill. All the stress of the past six months felt like it was bouncing back to hit him again, now that the end was upon them. Tomorrow night was going to be rough. The night after that … well, he could only hope.

CHAPTER 9

On Friday night, Emily looked so appealing that Mark felt the tiniest regret that they weren't a real thing. She slid into the town car. "Oh hey! I like the beard." She leaned across to give him a light kiss, then buckled in with a sigh. "Also I want you to know that I finally understand why you never see celebrities actually eating. I barely got this dress zipped up."

"You look great. You always look great. My agent's going to be dropping by while we're at dinner."

"Did you talk today?"

And of course they had. That made a good topic of conversation on the way across town to the restaurant. Once they arrived, there was an endless stream of people cruising by their table to ask Mark about the show, say nice things, and try to find out what he was doing next. "I'm going to take some time off," he told everybody. It wasn't until they were leaving – in an intentionally slow way, chatting with more people, gathering the maximum amount of attention by the time they reached the sidewalk – that he answered by saying "I need a little time to deal with personal things."

Right on cue, a paparazzo said, "Is this where you make an announcement about you and Emily?"

"No," Emily said, before Mark could say anything. "Mark is one of my best friends in the world and I hope he always will be, but this was not a love affair. Not because he's not great, but because I don't swing that way. I'm gay." All of a sudden there were six more people with microphones and cameras. God only knew where they came from. Random people on the sidewalk had phones up, taking pictures or video. People were yelling questions at Emily. Mark put his arm around her and she leaned in. "Holy shit," she said under her breath.

"Okay?"

"Mmm. I've got this." She straightened up, though still within the protective shelter of his arm. Wrapping her own around him. "Yo! Stop yelling. That's so rude." She started picking less-obnoxious questions out of the babble. "There is someone very important to me who I haven't been with for reasons which are none of your business. She's not a Hollywood person any more than I am. No, she doesn't live in Los Angeles. Of course I'm not going to tell you her name, are you nuts?" That got a general laugh. "I'm never going to have a better L.A. experience than these past few months with Mark and it's time to get serious about my life. I'm hoping she'll give me another chance."

"Mark, what are your feelings?"

"Well." He took a deep breath, felt Emily give him an encouraging squeeze, and said, "I basically have all the same things to say, except my important person does live here in L.A." There was an explosion of noise. He picked out the most pertinent questions, half-aware that Emily had fished his phone out of his jacket pocket and was texting. "Yes, I'm gay. Yes, Emily knew. My family knows. I have a lot of people to apologize to. No, not Jenny, she knows. I don't know what will happen to my career. No, I don't have anything booked for this summer. I'm taking some time off for a trip with my son. We'll see. Yes, in a perfect world I would continue to work in film and TV, and in the theater. No. My important person is not public property any more than Emily's is. It's his choice whether he talks to the press. We met at Thanksgiving. Yes, that's why I'm doing this now." He saw their car pull up at the curb, hazard lights on, and started edging toward it. "My agent and my publicist have been briefed. Send follow-up questions to them. We're done." Another cacophony of questions. He said sharply, "I'm done. Good night." Pulled the car door open, let Emily scoot in ahead of him, dove in and slammed the door. The locks engaged immediately. "Get us out of here." He was trying not to hyperventilate. The car was moving.

"Put your head down. Slow and deep. Hold your breath. Count to four. Now breathe out. Four, three, two, one. Again. Okay. There you go, honey. Jesus fucking Christ." Emily had her hand on his back. Why did people always do that? Well, he probably looked like he was about to have a heart attack. Mark had never heard her use the F word before. "All the way through this I was wondering why you needed me."

"Now you know," he said. It sounded a little faint. He took another deep, slow breath. Didn't straighten up yet. He was shaking. Emily petted his back, made a soothing sound. After a few minutes, around the time the driver turned west on Sunset – he'd totally missed the turn onto Highland – he sat up, leaned back, and wrapped his arms around Emily. "Thank you." Neither of them was strapped in. The safety alert was beeping. They both continued to ignore it until approximately Fairfax. Then they separated, fastened their seatbelts, and rode in silence until they got to Emily's apartment complex.

"You've got to be kidding me," she said. There was a TV news van on the street outside. "God I'm glad there's a gate." The driver had her code. When his window went down, they could hear yelling from the press gathered on the sidewalk. Through the gate, around the loop, pulling up outside Emily's building. She unbuckled.

"Will you be all right?"

115

She looked at him. "I'm going to have a stiff drink and send an email to a certain person. You might want to do the same when you get home."

"I'm going straight to prescription drugs. Let me know how it goes with your important person."

A sudden smile. "I will. I have hopes. I might have to auction off all these dresses to get where I need to go."

"Anything you need," he said, hoping his sincerity came across.

"You're a sweetheart." She leaned across and kissed him again, like a sister. "Don't let anyone tell you different. I'll be in touch."

"Okay. Goodnight."

"Goodnight." The driver had her door open. She got out, the door was closed, the driver stood keeping watch as she walked up to her building. Then he was back in the car, the doors were locked, and they were leaving. Another wave of noise from the press as the car exited the complex. No doubt there would be another cluster like this at Mark's complex. Another gate to be grateful for.

It was even worse. Two satellite vans, a herd of people with cameras, one lane of the street completely blocked. People surged right up against the car during the seconds (it felt like hours) they were waiting for the gate to open. A few even stepped through the gate, then fell back, discouraged by the armed security guard moving toward them. Mark was doing his best not to freak out again. Nobody got through. There wouldn't be anybody at his townhouse, where another of the extra security people he'd hired would be keeping watch. He'd get in touch with Liam, let him know the news was breaking, confirm their date the following night. Warn him. Someone would be burning the midnight oil, scouring the footage and images from the past six months. Someone would see the recurring faces and start putting it together. He needed to give Robert and Jade a heads-up too. Robert seemed to be good with the press, and Jade was an expert. Would Liam even leave the house tomorrow? He wouldn't need to. He didn't work Saturdays. *Oh God let this not be too much.*

Pulling up outside. The security person opening the car door. "All right, Mr. Valance?"

"Holding it together. Thanks." Up to the door, unlocking it with a surprisingly steady hand. Inside, all the locks engaged, distracted by the message indicator flashing on his old-school answering machine. Fuck that. He pulled out his cell phone. A quick text to Emily, to thank her again for everything up to and including summoning the car. Then a text to Liam: *Sweetheart it's done. Shitstorm. Research will happen overnight. Watch yourself if you go out tomorrow. Can't wait to see you. About to shut down with chemical assistance. I love you*

First time he'd put that in a text, obviously. It felt ridiculously significant, even though they'd said it to each other in so many letters. He set the phone on its charger, stripped, and went to wash up. It was amazing how tired he felt, when all he'd done today was talk on the phone and go out to dinner.

He was in his pajamas, on the bed, stretching, when the phone buzzed. He snatched it up. *You're all over the internet. Did you know Emily was going to do that? Now I'm dying to hear what happens with her person. In case you're wondering, you are my important person too. See you tomorrow. I love you*

117

Mark had an unbelievable number of texts, voice messages, and emails in the morning. The temptation was to simply delete everything unread and unheard, but he slowly worked his way through them. Many could be discarded. No way was he talking directly to anybody in the press. If they wanted him, they could go through his publicist. Checking in with the family. Reading Emily's text with genuine pleasure: *Looking good here. Quote are you getting your own ass to Spokane or do I have to come and get you unquote. Give Liam a kiss for me!*

Only when he was at inbox zero did he consider getting online. That was probably one hundred percent of a bad idea, so he resisted. The only thing he really needed to do online was already done. Plans for the trip to Alaska were finalized way back in March. All that was left was a call to the lodge to confirm their reservations. With that mission accomplished, he went into his home gym. He'd lost some weight in the past month, more than he could really spare. That couldn't be remedied in the few hours remaining before he saw Liam again. Now that he wasn't on TV, he could eat normally. Work out the way he wanted to. Get back to a point of feeling healthy, instead of always slightly fatigued. Not to mention getting back to a point where he was sleeping without chemical assistance. He had a feeling he was a little too dependent on those pills.

Feeling shaky after thirty minutes with the weights, he fixed himself lunch instead of going straight into the shower. Fed, rested, and clean, he stared at himself in the mirror. It was time for that new look. This haircut did not go with a week's growth of beard; it made him look like John Ritter, circa 'Three's Company,' after going on a bender. He would ask Jade for a favor. Another favor. A changing-my-life-emergency favor.

Liam was too curious to stay offline. He didn't see much yet that was overtly hostile to Mark. If it happened, he'd have to school himself not to overreact. None of it was really important. The whole 'never work again' worst-case-scenario would only be a problem if Mark changed his mind about Liam moving in. He'd checked with a realtor friend and was positive he could cover the mortgage by himself if necessary. If Mark would let him. It made more sense than giving up the townhouse, though, and Mark was a practical guy. They would cross that bridge when – if – they came to it.

The images and video from the night before were a little troubling. The facial hair was like a bad disguise. Mark looked thin. In fact, he looked unwell. Liam hoped it was only stress. And he really hoped none of the tabloids decided to make up a story about all the things it might be, including the thing they loved to speculate about when it came to gay men. Something else to worry about when and if it was a real thing. Tonight he needed to be steady, solid, unflappable, the man who could reassure a new patient about her failed collagen or an old one about his melanoma. He did not need to walk into the Regent giving off anxiety vibes. From now on, they were together. Whatever they needed to deal with, they could handle together.

He groomed himself with greater than usual attention to detail, dressed carefully, aware that someone sometime tonight was bound to take a picture. Took a look outside from the apartment lobby before heading down to the garage. There were cars parked along the street that he didn't recognize, but nothing like a TV van. If those cars held paparazzi, they could follow him to the Regent if they wanted. The valets and doormen were not going to let anyone hassle someone coming in.

It was a short drive, and in the typically heavy L.A. traffic he couldn't be bothered trying to keep an eye out for pursuit. But either someone was following, or someone was waiting; as he sat in the queue for the valet – well outside hotel property on El Camino – a group of people with cameras came down the sidewalk toward his car. He made sure the locks were engaged, kept his eyes forward and his face expressionless, and ignored the activity around him. The yelled questions, the camera lenses. Gradually he inched over the sidewalk and into the no-trespassing zone. Pulled up to the valet stand and got out of the car. Stepped away from it immediately, tipping his head toward the stand to redirect the valet heading his way. They made the exchange of key and claim ticket as far out of sight from the sidewalk as possible. Liam took a moment to speak to the guy running things back there. "I'm going to be leaving with Mark Valance. Can I call from inside to have the car brought around?"

"Absolutely, sir." The guy handed over a card. "I believe Mr. Valance has already arrived."

"Great. Thanks." Liam was relieved, even though he suspected that tip might get passed on. Earlier that day, his name wasn't in the news. Now it was. Well, it had to break sometime, and at least this was a semi-controllable situation. He'd have to be careful driving home. "Catch you later." He turned and went inside. Walking through the palatial hall toward the restaurant, feeling extremely conspicuous as he approached the host stand.

"Dr. Byrne," the host said with a pleasant smile, as if they were longtime acquaintances. "Mr. Valance is expecting you."

Wow. That was easy. Liam followed without a word. All the way through the restaurant, to a table in a corner. Had to be intentional. Giving everyone in the place a chance to notice him, a chance to see who he was there to meet.

Mark stood up as Liam approached. Wearing dark jeans, an open-collared silk shirt, and a linen blazer: almost the same outfit Liam had on. The beard was trimmed. The hair was short. The unkempt eyebrows that made him look approachable were groomed and shaped to a peak toward the outside, like a raptor's wing. He looked sharp, sexy, and sensational. Best of all, he was smiling. "Liam."

"Mark."

"Your server will be with you in a moment." The host might have said something else, but neither man heard her. Mark's hands rose, palms up. Liam read it as an invitation, and stepped into his arms. They hugged hard for a brief, sweet moment, then separated. Took their seats. Gazed at each other.

Liam spoke first. Not loud, but not like he was trying to avoid attention, either. "I sure hope you were planning to come home with me tonight, because that's what I told the valet guy." Mark laughed. "How was it last night, really? The clip I saw looked pretty gnarly."

"It was kind of gnarly," Mark agreed. "Emily took care of things. She was texting the car while they were chewing on me." A brief interruption for service. "And I heard from her this morning, her person's been in touch."

"Oh, that's great. Was that out of nowhere, or did you know?"

"I had no idea! We'll have to get together and pry the whole story out of her before she leaves town. All I know for sure is Spokane."

"I went there for a conference once. Nice city."
They talked about travel in between dealing with menus
and servers. Managed not to say the words 'Alaska' or
'Denali.' The trip would be tough to pull off without any
kind of media attention. Nobody was likely to go easy
on Mark just because he was with his kid. The plan was
for him to fly to New York, collect Christopher, and fly
to Fairbanks. Liam would fly to Anchorage, and they
would meet at the park. Christopher predictably said he
could travel alone, and if his father wasn't expecting to
be a little too famous they might have let him. Kerry,
Warren, and Mark all said no, not this time. Liam
decided to hope they wouldn't run into any problems up
there. It wasn't exactly prime paparazzi territory. He
watched Mark eat, observed how even over the course
of this meal the man was relaxing, and decided he was
fine. A little run down, a little stressed out. And no
wonder. After a few weeks with nothing to do but be in
love, he'd probably feel like a new man. He certainly
looked like one. "So I'm guessing you ran up your tab a
little for this haircut. It's really fantastic."

"I look a little older." Mark shrugged. "But that's
not necessarily a bad thing. I've been playing under my
real age for most of my life."

"What do you want for your birthday?"

His thirty-ninth was rapidly approaching. Mark sat
back in his chair, holding eye contact with Liam, letting
his peripheral vision take in all the small movements
around the room that meant they were being observed.
"You mentioned going home with you." He said it in his
smoothest, most seductive tone of voice, pitched to the
range scientifically proven to appeal to all genders, and
projected as if he were on stage. Not loud at all. Simply
… very clear. Liam looked as though he couldn't decide

between laughing, or launching himself at Mark. He nodded. Mark said, "That's what I want."

"It's been a long six months." Liam's voice was low, a little bit husky. His bedroom voice. Someone at the table nearest them shifted in his or her seat. "Might take a while to satisfy me."

"Me too. Do we want coffee?"

"Not here."

"Mmm." Mark tore his gaze from Liam's and took a breath. Caught their server's attention, then laid his napkin beside his plate. Liam did the same. There might have been something good on the dessert menu, but neither of them cared. Liam called the valet boss while Mark dealt with the check. They detoured to the restroom near the bar on their way out. Didn't touch each other, didn't speak, only made eye contact in the mirror as they washed their hands. There was no doubt the second they were through Liam's door they were going to be all over each other. The car was ready when they went out. A mob of press jostled on the sidewalk at the El Camino driveway, already in full cry. Mark said, "What do you think."

Liam looked at him. This was not at all a bad place or time to be photographed. He nodded and slid his arm around Mark, who did the same. They walked out to the back of the car. Turned toward the waiting photographers, stood still for a few seconds. He felt Mark squeeze him, a signal: that's enough. They turned back to the valet. Liam tipped lavishly. "Thanks."

In the car, buckled in, rolling slowly toward the exit, waiting for a signal from one of the valets telling them Rodeo was clear. Liam turned left, defying the signage, and made it through the neighborhood in less time than was careful. Then they were on Olympic, another slightly illegal left turn, heading for his apartment.

Mark was laughing. "Do not get a ticket." Liam didn't get stopped. He had his thumb on the gate remote as soon as they turned onto his block. It was nearly open by the time he rolled up. They were inside with only a brief delay, so quickly that the whoever-it-was running toward them on the sidewalk missed his chance.

Liam pulled into his space, turned off the car, and turned his head. "Jesus, you're beautiful." He pulled out his phone and took a picture. In the dim light, Mark's eyes were very dark; with the beard and the haircut, he looked almost sinister. "Check you out."

"Wow. Send that to me for my portfolio?"

"Definitely. Let's get upstairs."

"God, yes." They got out of the car. Liam waved to a neighbor who was heading to the laundry room. No one on the stairs. Another neighbor in the hall, an exchange of distracted greetings that did not extend to introductions. Through the door. Dropping his keys on the console, hearing Mark lock them in. Shoes were kicked off, and then they were moving toward the bedroom, stripping off jackets on the way. In less than two minutes they were on the bed, skin to skin, kissing like there was no tomorrow.

CHAPTER 10

It was nearly noon on Sunday before they exited the bedroom, mostly due to the enticing aroma of coffee. "I set it up before I left last night," Liam said, pulling on his summer robe. "Something told me I wouldn't want to mess around with that this morning." He handed a robe to Mark. "Got one for you."

Mark took it. A simple waffle-weave robe in natural cotton, and it felt like ermine. Setting up the coffee on a timer was thoughtful; the robe said 'you have a place here.' He was looking forward to seeing Liam's reaction to the new thing at Mark's place. "For the record, you are already racking up points for this whole being-together thing." Liam laughed under his breath. Brushed his lips across Mark's mouth, then headed for the coffee.

Liam got online after breakfast, and they went through some of the coverage. The fact that Liam's name was out meant a round of phone calls with his family. He put Mark on speaker for all of them, feeling both relieved and proud that all of his people said, in effect, welcome to the family. Of course they also said when do we get to meet you, which meant some artful dodging because he and Mark hadn't even talked about that yet. Then there was a round of calls to the East Coast. "Maybe we could figure out a trip to SD while we're up in Alaska," he suggested once they were finally off the phone.

"That's fine, sweetheart. We can go anytime, you know."

"Yeah. The great thing is they're all in one place, so we could see everybody on a weekend. It doesn't have to be a big thing."

"Are you kidding?" Mark was smiling. "It's going to be huge. I haven't done the meet-the-family thing since I was in college. You've already told me so much about them, though. I feel like all I need to know is, was there a boyfriend of yours they wanted you to stay with."

"Ah." Liam considered that. He knew Mark was really asking, am I going to be an also-ran for anybody. "The person they knew best was Francisco, my high-school boyfriend. The most important guy before you was the one in Minneapolis, and they never met him. Look, they've been waiting a long time for me to settle down. You could hear how happy they are."

"Mmm." That was true. Mark let himself lean on Liam again. He was so comfortable. So warm, so solid, so *there*. "I don't suppose," he began, then stalled.

Liam gave it a few seconds. "What, honey."

"Could I stay here tonight? I know you have to work tomorrow."

Liam looked at the top of Mark's head, resting on his shoulder, and got a hand on his face to enable some eye contact. "Hey. As far as I'm concerned you can stay forever. Come and go whenever. There's a key in the drawer with the delivery menus, and you probably noticed what the password is for my computer."

Mark nodded. Five letters, all caps: ROXIE. "When did you change it to that?"

"I never even had one before. I only put a password on it after we started writing letters. I was kind of mocking myself for doing that. The idea of having someone break in here to snoop around seemed pretty far-fetched. But it wouldn't be all that hard to do. I mean, the locks are nothing special. So I figured at least make them work for it."

"And it was never an issue, thank God. We were lucky."

"We were careful," Liam amended. "Robert said we could have come over a lot more often than we did. And we never arrived or left at the same time. Even if someone saw you, that same person didn't see me."

"I think it was only one time that I met someone going in or out. And the two times we were in the same place out in the world, we had buffers." Mark smiled. "Speaking of which, Emily said to give you a kiss."

"I'll take it." Liam leaned in, put his mouth on Mark's, instantly forgot about the many kisses they'd already shared since the night before. A minute later they were stretched out together, the robes were unbelted, and they had their hands on each other. Some time after that, Liam said "Jesus," and put a little space between them.

"Liam." It was a protest.

"I should have put the lube in my pocket. If we keep doing this we're going to regret it."

That was, regrettably, true. Mark pushed his erection against Liam's again anyway. The heat, the friction, the scent of their arousal: he didn't want to stop. Liam bit his lip, smiling, and shook his head. Mark made an irritated sound and Liam laughed. Mark ran his fingertips through all that black chest hair and said, "Go get it then." A quick kiss and Liam was on his way to the bedroom.

Mark was starting to wonder when Liam would initiate something beyond hands, mouths, and frotting. Those were the things Mark had always preferred – if his experience was extensive enough to even have a preference, which he sometimes doubted. The only man aside from Liam that Mark had been with for more than

127

a single encounter was Andy Martin. His total experience with men amounted to barely two dozen encounters. Six in high school and college, the rest since his divorce. It was kind of amazing he'd been skilled enough to please Liam. And it was surely too soon to be worrying about this kind of thing. He was still lying in the same position when Liam returned a minute later. "Weren't you thinking about me?" He dropped the lube and a hand towel on the coffee table. Sat on the edge of the sectional, running a hand down Mark's body to his cock. "Lost interest already?" Petting, fondling, stroking.

"Well, you were gone for hours," Mark said. Liam laughed softly, bent down for a kiss, kept doing things with his hand. Made a happy sound at the result.

"Get your knees up." Mark obliged, wondering if his question was about to be answered. Liam changed position, kneeling on the cushion, facing Mark. "Legs around me." He knee-walked in, so Mark's hips were up on his thighs, his own erection nudging Mark's balls. He reached over for the lube. "I want to stroke you off. Is that okay?"

"Mm-hmm." Mark hoped the nervousness didn't come through in that non-word. Or in the words that followed. "And then what?"

"And then I want to fuck your mouth." The night before, Mark went down on Liam and he lay there passively, moaning, gripping the bed to hold himself back. There was something uniquely wonderful about Mark's mouth. He didn't use a lot of tricks. It was single-minded focused intention, which somehow conveyed a sincere appreciation of Liam's body. Thinking about that now while he worked Mark with his hand, watching those gorgeous eyes go hazy, Liam felt his own cock drooling. He bent forward a little so Mark

128

could feel that too, the precome running down Liam's shaft to Mark's balls. Jesus, he was beautiful. Lips parted, breathing fast, one hand clutching the cushion and the other clamped on Liam's thigh. "God, Mark, you feel so good. Give it to me. I want to feel it. I want to see you. Come on, baby, you're so hot." His free hand sweeping up Mark's thigh, across his hip, up to his chest. Teasing a nipple, hearing the breathy sound. "Oh yeah. More of that. Let me hear you." Mark's breathing vocal now, hips moving, pushing himself into Liam's hand. "You're so close. Come on. Now, baby. Jesus, all I want to do is watch you come. Now. *Now*. Yes, baby *yes*, oh *God*." He watched it happen, felt Mark's body spasm, heard the breathless cry. Sucked in a lungful of air and bore down against his own climax. "Fucking hell. Can I." Mark was still catching his breath, but he nodded. Liam wiped his hand on his own chest as he knelt up, then got one foot on the floor. Mark scooted down, reaching for Liam's cock. Liam straddled his chest, braced his hands on the side of the sectional, and felt that mouth close on him. This was not going to take any time at all. "Jesus Christ." A stifled laugh. Mark's hand on the front of his hip, the other holding his dick, managing the depth and the force. Liam let himself go, fast and shallow, right up until he peaked.

Mark felt it coming. He shut his eyes, let Liam shove all the way in, controlling his gag reflex somehow. He forgot how to breathe for a few seconds, then remembered his nose. This was going to be funny later. Right now he was trying not to choke on come. He could hardly even taste it, Liam was so deep. Not like before, when Mark kept a hand on him. How many waves was it? He'd lost count. Starting to soften now, starting to pull back. Mark swallowed and let him go. Couldn't quite stifle a cough. Felt Liam's hand in his hair, then on his face. Eyes were watering. Lip definitely bruised. Well, that was something. He blinked, looked up, saw Liam bending down for a kiss.

"You okay? I didn't mean to go so deep."

"I'm fine." Mark let Liam tug him up to a seated position. "There was a second where I forgot how to breathe. It's a problem I have. Not necessarily related to having your dick in my mouth." They both snickered.

"You need to be careful, honey. I never want to hurt you." Arm around Mark, both of them wriggling around to get into a comfortable semi-reclined position.

"Mmm." How to say he was still learning how to do this? How to say, I'm not confident I'm giving you what you want? He certainly couldn't say, I'm a little afraid of everything you might want. It was safer to say nothing. To turn in and hide his face against Liam's neck, relax into his embrace, and pretend to doze off. Except that was a lie, and he was through with lying to people. "I trust you not to hurt me. It's just, I don't really have a lot of experience so I might not do things the way you want and I want you to love it."

Liam stroked his hair. "I do love it. But I hear you. Sex is," he paused to collect his thoughts. "It is not the most important thing in the world to me. Being close like this is. Having you to talk to and *be* with." How to say this so it didn't sound patronizing. "If I want something that we haven't done before, I'll be clear about it, okay? And if you don't want to do that, you have to tell me. Please. With words." He felt a silent laugh from Mark, gave him a squeeze, and went on. "Other way around, too. I want to hear what you want, and if I don't want to do that I'll say so. There's a difference between consent and participation. I don't want you just yielding to whatever I'm doing. We're in this for the long term, so a lot of things have to be negotiated. I mean, from two percent to half and half. Not a metaphor."

Mark was laughing again. It sounded so simple: ask for what you want, tell me what you don't want. He'd never felt like he was in a position to ask for what he wanted. Had hardly even *known* what he wanted, aside from 'some kind of sex.' Some amount of bare skin, a kiss, someone else's hand on him. This was going to take some getting used to. He reached over for that hand towel and wiped both of them, tossed it back on the coffee table. Still a little damp and sticky, but more comfortable for cuddling. He let himself do that, listening to the strong beat of Liam's heart. "We need to negotiate when you'll move in with me."

Liam dropped a kiss on his forehead and held him close. They were both quiet for a few minutes, thinking about that negotiation. Liam wanted to say something needy and greedy, like 'tomorrow.' But there were logistics, things to manage, things to plan. Notice to be given, movers to be hired, and oh yes a ten-day trip to Alaska to fit in. Mark felt so relaxed in his arms. They needed a few weeks of this. Settling in, getting used to each other, relaxing. Dealing with whatever needed to be dealt with on the outside. Giving themselves time to be sure this was really what they both wanted. "When are the Emmy nominations?"

"Sometime in July."

"How about the end of July, then?"

It sounded like forever away, but they both had a lot to get done in the next couple of months. Mark wriggled down to rest his head on that broad, hairy chest and said, "Perfect."

It was somewhat strange to leave Mark in his apartment and go to work on Monday. Strange, but wonderful. Two nights together felt like not-nearly-enough; a single night would have been completely unsatisfactory. And this way, Liam could bring home something for dinner. Possibly convince Mark to stay one more night. He would ask, anyway, because surely it made more sense to call for a car Tuesday morning than to haul out after dark. They didn't have to hide anymore.

For now, he needed to get his head in the game. It was a bit earlier than he usually went to work. He was fully expecting some kind of media presence around the office building. For him (and his partner) it wouldn't be too bad; they had parking on site. The rest of the staff parked in the public deck, a block away. Liam's plan was to go up to the suite and get into his lab coat, then go down to street level and face whatever music there was. With any luck, that would satisfy, and the staff wouldn't get hassled.

He was ready for it. Two nights and a day of Mark, up to date on what was being said so far, and full of an excellent breakfast. Being with a guy who liked to cook was going to be a true luxury. Turning onto Bedford … and yes, there they were. Not a mob, only a few people. Should be manageable. He made the turn into the driveway and was down the ramp before anyone spotted him. Up to the suite, into his coat, checking himself in the mirror. Grinning at the love bite under his collar, Mark's revenge for the lip bruise. Keys in pocket, back down to the street. He walked out through the open-air lobby to the sidewalk. It took about three seconds for the media people to notice him.

He cut through the gabble of questions – starting with an amazing number of repetitions of his name; how many times did they need to say Dr. Byrne? – and said, "I'm here to talk, so calm down and let's talk." Responding to one question at a time. "Yes, Mr. Valance was talking about me. Yes, we met at Thanksgiving, at the home of mutual friends. I've been out all my life. We did not go public right away because Mark was working for a show that airs on a channel not known to foster diversity. Well, what I mean by that is the CEO of the company is on record with a number of bigoted statements. The sportscasters and newscasters are notorious for racist, sexist, homophobic comments. Not one of the channel's prime-time shows has an LGBT character or an openly-gay cast member. Mark had every reason to believe that coming out while he was still on the show would be damaging for his co-workers. Did I mind?" He couldn't help laughing. "No. I missed him, and I wished we didn't have to wait six months to be together, but I didn't mind. He was trying to be fair to everybody else on the show, and I respect that. I can be out in my job. I support the Los Angeles LGBT Center and AIDS Project Los Angeles. There's material about those organizations in our reception area. During the Pride Festival we do rainbow scrubs. If there are patients who don't want to consult a gay doctor, they can see my partner, or they can go to a different office. It's not equivalent to Mark's situation at all. I'm glad he chose to come out now." He saw his physician assistant and front-desk person sidling past behind the media people. Deliberately didn't acknowledge them. He'd sort that out later. Listened to a few more questions without answering; they were either repetitive, or way out of bounds. Finally heard another one he was willing to address. "I want to be with Mark because I believe he's the man I can be with for the rest of my life. That's what we told our families yesterday. And now I have to go to work. If you submit a civil inquiry through the office portal there's a fair chance I'll answer it. Only today, though. This is my place of business and I expect you to respect that. Have a good day." He turned away from another flurry of questions, held up a hand to signal he was done, and walked unhurriedly to the elevators.

Back up to the suite. His front-desk person was at her station. "Hi Erica. Cheryl, are you back there?" The physician assistant came to the reception area. "In case you were wondering what that was about, I've been seeing someone sort of famous and he came out on Friday. I'm hoping the media will leave you alone. If you have any trouble let me know. And, well." He didn't know what else to say. Settled for, "If anyone has any questions, feel free to ask." He stepped past Cheryl and went to his office to check the schedule. From that point on it was a perfectly ordinary day. Except he and Mark texted several times, they spoke on the phone before he left the office, and he picked up dinner for two on his way home. It was an amazing day.

For the first hour or so after Liam went to work, Mark dithered. This – being left alone in someone else's home, someone who wasn't Kerry or his parents – was so new he didn't know how to handle it. He displaced the anxiety by cleaning the kitchen. Then he prowled through the place finding out where absolutely everything was, and figuring out how Liam preferred to organize things. That led to taking the spare key and a load of laundry down to the basement. It was a long time since he'd used coin machines, which prompted some self-mockery for being a member of the one percent (however transient that status might be). Somebody's housekeeper was down there putting a load in the dryers. She didn't seem to recognize Mark, which was fine with him.

There was a chair, and a stack of magazines, so he stayed downstairs to supervise the wash. Told himself he wasn't trying to establish his bona fides as a housewife, simply doing Liam (and himself) a favor. Once the load was transferred to the dryer, he went upstairs and got online to see what was new. About himself: follow-ups galore from Jenny, others involved with the show, his parents, Kerry, his agent and publicist (repeating the statement they'd issued on Saturday), an array of former co-workers and women he'd dated, and 'Mr. Valance can't be reached for comment.' About Liam: sound bites and short 'what we've learned' pieces following a morning skirmish with the media. He'd handled them well. No one had dug up any details of Liam's history yet. Maybe they wouldn't bother; nothing about him said this was a guy with a scandalous past. Mark took a minute or five to cherish 'I believe he's the man I can be with for the rest of my life.' He so wanted that to be true.

Once he knew the status, he finished handling the laundry, taking his time with it. Then he called his agent, who picked up immediately. "Mr. Valance. Any more surprises for me?"

It was impossible not to wince at that. He hadn't been Mr. Valance for years. "Hi Brian. No, nothing today. I don't think there are any surprises left, actually. I'm really sorry."

A moment of silence, as if the guy didn't know how to respond to that. Or maybe couldn't think of a polite response. "I can't say it hasn't put a lot of things in the maybe-not column. All we can do is submit you and see what kind of feedback we get. Was the nothing this

135

summer bit for real, or was that in expectation of nobody wanting you to come in?"

"Both. I'm taking a trip with my son next month, and if all goes well Liam will be moving in with me at the end of July. So I'm going to be … not very available."

"Got it. What about after July?"

Mark didn't want to speculate about the Emmys, or what kind of effect a nomination for the show (or Jenny) might have on the industry's view of things. "We should definitely talk in August. See what the landscape looks like then. I'm not," he began, then hesitated. "Like I said on Friday. I hope to continue working. But like you say, all we can do is wait for feedback. If it comes down to a choice between 'Big Brother' or nothing," he stalled again. Didn't want to say he'd prefer nothing to being some desperate-looking D-lister.

"What about 'Dancing with the Stars'?"

Mark blinked. That almost sounded serious. "Are you serious?"

"Well, they haven't contacted me. But it's only been a minute. Just trying to get some sense of your boundaries."

"If I were single and doing this, I might not have any boundaries. But I have Liam to consider. The press hasn't really gotten to work on him yet. I think," yet another hesitation. It was good to be pushed on these things, even though they were making him uncomfortable. "There's a lot of people I haven't talked to yet. I'm not even forty. I've got some time to recover. I'm not going to go broke if I don't work for a while. So I'm sorry because it's going to affect you, and I'll understand if you don't want to continue representing me."

136

"Whoa, slow down. Not going there. You're saying you'd rather wait for a career-enhancing project. Even if it takes a year or two."

"Right." God, he could feel the damned cortisol spike. Conscious breathing. "I'm happy to look at anything you think is worth sending me, but the whole point of doing this is to build a life with someone. I can't do that if I'm off shooting in Vancouver or wherever. He committed to me and I don't take that lightly. His life is here."

"I get it. Maybe you could run down your credits and send me a markup with things that would be in the No column now. That way we won't waste each other's time."

"I can do that," Mark said with relief that was probably audible. "I appreciate it."

"No problem. Oh, just so I know, if nothing else is on the line when pilot season rolls around, are you going to be up for that?"

Shooting a single episode didn't sound like a way to re-launch a career, but once in a while someone got into a great new job that way. And it was low commitment on both sides, so he had a good chance of getting cast. Plus, if a show got picked up, even if the company wanted to re-cast the part, it wouldn't look like a total personal failure because that happened so often. "Probably, yeah. Why not."

"Okay, good. You send me that thing, and we'll talk in August."

"Great. Thanks, Brian."

"You're welcome. Stay in shape." He disconnected on Mark's surprised laugh. That had gone a lot better than he expected. Or maybe it wasn't expectation, only

137

fear. Being dumped by your agent was never a good thing.

By the end of the day he was feeling considerably more relaxed. Liam had checked in, hinting that he'd be glad if Mark spent the night again. There was no reason not to, and several reasons he'd like to. Such as finishing what they started before Liam had to get ready for work.

CHAPTER 11

Liam could already tell he was going to like the living-together thing when it finally happened. When he tried it before, both parties were so swamped with work that they were more like roommates with benefits than lovers. He kissed Mark goodbye Tuesday morning, securing a promise that they'd see each other again on Friday, and went to the office.

Mark tidied up the apartment, got himself groomed and dressed, then called for a car. He wasn't going straight home. It was three days since he'd been seen in this outfit, and if anybody wanted to comment on it he'd be happy to tell them he'd been with Liam the entire time. Today he was heading into Beverly Hills for a rendezvous with Emily. Apparently she'd seen one of the pictures from Saturday night. "That looks familiar," she said when she arrived.

Mark rolled his eyes as he stood up to hug her. Then he hugged Robert, who'd come with her. "Went home with Liam Saturday, heading back to my place now. Laundry was done in between." Robert snorted. "Nice to see you both! I was hoping Emily might have some news for me."

"I do! Boss, you want to get us some coffee while I gossip?"

Robert gave her a 'really?!' look, but obediently went inside and got in line. There weren't many people in the coffee shop; most of them were pretending to ignore the celebrity. Mark pretended to ignore them right back as he sat down with Emily. "I'm giving myself an hour a day to get online and see what's happening. Are you heading up north immediately, or

139

are you going to be around long enough to go out with me and Liam?"

"Ooh, that sounds great. Where are you taking him first?"

"Musso and Frank, I think."

"Then I am definitely going out with you, we barely got to eat last time. Um, the plan, to the extent there is a plan? I'm cleaning house and purging my junk. The agency is looking for someone to replace me. When they're covered, I'll pack up my car and start driving. I'm so excited and so scared, it's like," she made an 'eek' face. "I guess you know all about that."

"Yeah, kind of. Why didn't you go north when she did?"

Emily winced. "Eh. We hadn't been together all that long. She had a job, I didn't, all my friends are here. I've never even been to Seattle much less Spokane. It was one too many insecurities. But I missed her."

"Well, I'm glad you're going and I hope it works out. I'll talk to Liam and we'll figure out a date. Maybe Robert and Jade could come with us too." He said that as Robert joined them.

"Come with you where?"

"Musso and Frank."

"Ooh, that sounds great."

Emily laughed. Mark tried not to. "I owe you and Jade so much."

"No you don't. We were glad to help. Oh crap."

Mark and Emily simultaneously said, "What?" Then Mark looked over his shoulder and spotted a person with a camera. "Better run for it unless you feel like being quoted."

"Maybe not today," Emily said with a slight grimace. "I am not camera-ready today."

"You're always camera-ready. Give me a kiss." She stood up, leaned in and did that, then hustled away with Robert. Mark waited for the inevitable sound of his name.

"Mr. Valance!"

"Yes?"

"May I ask you a few questions? I'm with Pop Quiz."

That was a fairly new, locally-based entertainment-news site. Mark didn't know anybody there yet. This could be a good chance to get off on the right foot with them. "Sure, have a seat."

"Wow! Really? Thanks!" The young woman sat down somewhat gingerly on the chair vacated by Emily. "Hi, my name is Sherry Martinez. I'm a court reporter in real life but I fooled Pop Quiz into taking a thing recently and they issued me a camera. Thank you for talking to me."

Mark was fairly close to cracking up. "Welcome to the rumor mill. How did you find me today?"

"Well, I was reading up on Dr. Byrne and noticed he was friendly with Mr. Anderson, who I noticed walking away just now with Ms. Lincoln. Is Mr. Anderson the person who introduced you?"

"Yes, he is. He and his partner Jade Derecha."

"Oh my goodness, Mr. Derecha, I would die to have him cut my hair. Did he cut your hair?"

Stifling laughter again. "Yes, he did. I left it long till I was officially off the show, but it was time for a new look."

"If you don't mind my saying so, the current look is very hot. Does Dr. Byrne like it?"

"Mm-hmm." He couldn't help it if that sounded a bit sultry, could he?

"So." Sherry composed herself. "Is it true you and Dr. Byrne didn't see each other for six months after you met?"

He could either tell the truth here, or tell her a story. If he went with option B and she took it the right way, this could be the beginning of a beautiful friendship. "Actually, no. I used to do this kind of minor disguise and have a car drop me off, after dark, up the block from his office. Then I'd walk down to his building and go up to the suite, and we'd go up on the roof. Hang out there on a couple of patio loungers, you know. Have a drink, catch up with each other, make out. It was romantic."

The reporter's face was a picture of WTF. "I feel like one percent of that *might* be true."

Mark laughed. "Yeah, no. I never did that. We did see each other, but not often, and not alone."

"It's a good story though. Should I run it?" She was grinning.

"Be my guest."

"Mmm, no, thanks. So was Dr. Byrne able to see you at Vibrato?"

"Yes, he was there with Robert and Jade. There was one other time we saw each other in public, at the Getty Villa."

"I'm going to look for that," she promised. "You guys really kept it quiet. Jenny Wilson told me how much she appreciated having the whole season to work out your arc."

Mark produced half a smile to go with half a shrug. "I really didn't want my co-workers to have to deal with drama about me in the middle of the season. A year ago,

142

when I got another recurring contract instead of a full-time contract, I was expecting to be written off. There were a couple of ways that could go. And after I met Liam, I was fine with it. But I wanted to go out as a good guy if I possibly could, because people remember the last thing they saw. So we talked to the team right before taping started for the back half of the season. And they still could have positioned me as a bad guy. I'm very grateful that they didn't."

"You mean the character could have degenerated into some kind of scumbag, instead of the sweet but flaky guy. It seemed to me, looking back, that they already had you positioned for the proposal at mid-season."

Mark gave her an interested look. "Keep paying attention like that and you'll be the next Barbara Walters."

"Oh em gee squee! Thank you! But didn't they?"

"That's what we thought. At that point, Jenny and I were betting the show would be killing off my character, it was only a question of how and when. When we talked to them, I told them when I was off the show I would be coming out."

"Oh," she said, looking enlightened. "Which meant they said, uh, we'll keep you on till sweeps. That was some brilliant strategy."

"Well, only if they cared about keeping the focus on the regular cast," he pointed out. "Which they apparently did. I wanted to give Jenny a crack at an Emmy."

"She did some great work this season. So did you," Sherry said. "I have taken up a lot of your time. Thank you so much. May I give you my card?"

"Yes, you may. And if I have any good news, I'll be sure to call you." He took the card, they shook hands, and she went away. Mark sent a text, then finished his lukewarm coffee while he waited for his driver to come around. Maybe he would add that imaginary rooftop scene to his imaginary screenplay when he got home. There was all kinds of rooftop stuff on 'ER;' people would almost expect it in a movie about a doctor.

And now that he thought about it, maybe he should stop pretending the thing was imaginary. It would be smart to sit down with Brian and say look, I wrote this thing. If there's nothing for me in front of the camera, maybe we could pivot. At least, it would be smart if all the scenes he'd written actually added up to something.

They had two more weekends before Mark flew to New York to collect Christopher. He spent them, in full, at Liam's. Arriving on Friday afternoon, going home on Tuesday morning. In between there were conversations, quiet hours watching TV, plenty of sex, and a whole lot of kissing.

By the second week, the tabloids were talking to women Mark had dated. Or escorted, or been seen with. There were only three he'd taken to bed. Oddly enough, none of those women had terrible things to say. One of them, a soap actress named Andrea, told an interviewer, "The thing is, nobody in Hollywood tells the whole truth. If I were telling the truth back then, I'd have said look, Mark, you're not my type at all. I'm going out with you for exposure. I need to be seen. And it worked, didn't it? I got hired based on the fact that I could ad-lib amusingly on the red carpet. The thing is, he knew that. I didn't have to say that. The only reason for *anyone* to be on the red carpet is to be seen. He didn't do anything wrong."

The interviewer looked skeptical. "You don't have a problem with him being gay?"

"All that matters to me with a guy is, does he treat me well, and Mark did. He was good company. We had safe sex. He didn't promise me anything, he didn't ask me to do anything I wasn't happy to do, nobody was harmed. I don't have a problem."

"Have there been people who didn't treat you well?"

Andrea laughed. "Of course there have. What business are we in?" And with that irresistible hint, the interview went a different direction.

Mark showed the clip to Liam after the fact. It wasn't quite representative; there were plenty of former co-workers who had unflattering things to say. One of those was a man he'd worked with in his early twenties, an out gay actor whose bitterness about parts he'd lost to straight actors overflowed onto Mark. When asked for comment, Mark said, "I don't blame him for feeling bitter. I know I've gotten work that I would not have gotten if I'd been out. It's always been this way. I'd like to think the work I've done might help casting directors think twice about dismissing a whole group of talented performers. But things didn't change when Rock Hudson was outed, so I don't expect they'll change because of me."

The reporter asked, "What will you do if you don't get hired again?"

"Learn to do something else." Mark was glad it was a telephone contact, so the reporter couldn't see his face. And he was glad it was a day when he was at his place, so he had some time to decide whether he would

145

mention it to Liam. The question of whether he still had a career wouldn't be answered for months. He was doing his best not to obsess about it. This time was better spent getting fit, getting organized, and getting as much out of being in love as he possibly could.

Liam knew Mark was putting off any serious thought about his career. Part of him wondered if they should start having that conversation now; the other part thought it made more sense to wait until they had more data. And while they waited, they could concentrate on this brand new wonderful thing they had. There might come a time when Liam needed to say 'I will take care of you no matter what;' there might come a time when Mark needed to hear it. But at the moment, they had a lot of other things to say.

It felt like it might be months before they even caught up with each other. Liam wanted to hear all about the years in New York. What it was like to audition, to rehearse, to perform a role over and over again for weeks or months. Mark turned it around by relating it to medical training. Learning and perfecting a technique, adapting it to each patient, always trying to improve the execution and the results. They spent one whole evening discussing Liam's surgical rotation. "Are you going to put that in the script?"

Mark shook his head. "I don't think so. It's great background and I want to be able to reference it correctly, but too much of that and the story would grind to a halt. This story is about something else."

"What is it about?" Liam was smiling. "I couldn't help wondering if it was only an exercise."

"It totally was! At first. But there's so much of it now. It's," he hesitated, because the truth was that the

146

damned thing had gotten personal. Maybe everybody's first try at storytelling was personal. Liam wasn't pushing, only giving him that 'tell me when you're ready' look. *I love him so much.* "It's a midlife crisis story. I figured they always say write what you know." Okay, Liam was laughing now, trying to stifle it. "Go ahead and laugh, I know it's funny."

"No, honey." Liam pulled him close for a kiss. "The fact that it's a midlife crisis story is not what's funny. It's that part about write what you know. You know all kinds of stuff. I'll bet you went with midlife crisis because the rest of the setting was so unfamiliar."

Mark blinked. That was a good point. And it raised a question. "This setting is awfully unfamiliar. For you. All this celebrity-adjacent bullshit." The staring, picture-taking, whispering attention when they went anywhere together. "I'm trusting you to tell me if it's ever too much."

"It's not even close to too much," Liam said promptly. "Compared to being an out gay teenager in a Catholic church, it's nothing. I do have one question, though."

"What's that, sweetheart."

"When do I get to see your place?" He was not going to admit that a few weeks of not-seeing it had him feeling a little insecure. It was only a few weeks. Plus his own place was a lot more convenient to work than Brentwood. There were plenty of good reasons for him not to have seen the townhouse yet.

"When I'm back from New York," Mark promised. "I got something new this spring and I'm hoping you'll like it enough to spend a few days with me. I felt like we were juggling a lot, and that would take some organizing. But if I'm wrong and you want to get a look

147

before we go to Alaska, that's fine." He was nervous now. Did Liam feel like he wasn't being given enough access to Mark's life? That really wasn't why he'd been holding off. It really was about the new thing. "We could go over there tonight."

Liam was about to say yes, he'd like to see it before their trip. Then he checked himself. After a second he thought of how to say this. "I keep tripping over where we're both coming from. Neither of us was ever at, we're going to try to make this last forever, were we?" Mark shook his head mutely. "That was always a possibility, but never the intention, right? Even for you and Kerry."

Mark cleared his throat. He would have liked to say he always intended for that to be forever, but the truth was, at twenty-two, his vision of the future didn't go much further than a decade. "Right."

"So this is different, and we have to give each other space. I have to give you space, the way I would if we were doing the normal dating thing and not coming off of these past few months. I want you to share things when you're ready, not just because I want them. Even if that means me moving in later."

Instant rejection of that, and inspiration for how to say so. "Not what it means. I was kind of imagining this as part of the process of you moving in."

"Okay." That made a big difference. Liam smiled. "That is totally okay. Kiss me." God, the way this man kissed him, as if he could never get enough. "I love you." Murmured against Mark's throat. One hand sunk into his hair; it felt so different now. Too short to grab onto, but now he had the whole man. Finally. And he was going to have a damned good try at making this last forever.

148

Mark let himself go flat on the couch. Liam was propped on one elbow, using the other hand to unbutton Mark's shirt. "I love you. Oh God." Liam's mouth on his chest. Licking, brushing across to a nipple, sucking it in. "Mmm. Yes."

In a hazy sort of way Liam seemed to recall saying something about how sex wasn't the most important thing. He would swear that was still true. But Mark's hand was on the back of his neck, pressing him in. He was arching up into Liam's mouth. Liam's hand slid into the small of his back, pulling that pliant body tight against his, feeling Mark's erection against his belly. His own was hot against Mark's thigh. They had way too many clothes on.

CHAPTER 12

June 2011

The flight in was a bit of a letdown; cloud conditions didn't let them see much. The train ride down from Fairbanks was another story. Neither Mark nor Christopher had ever seen a landscape like this; they were both glued to the windows. It was too much to even talk about. Once they'd arrived at the lodge, Mark got Chris settled into his room before heading for the cabin he'd be sharing with Liam, a couple hundred feet away.

His knock was answered by a door flung wide and a bear hug. After hauling in his bags, they both went into the tiny kitchenette to see what they had to work with. It took a while, because they kept taking breaks to kiss. "It felt like you were gone forever," Liam said after a while. "Three days. And I talked to you every day."

"I'm glad you missed me." Mark's voice was muffled against Liam's neck. "I missed you too." One more kiss. "Come on, we need to be able to answer the s'mores question." The cabin had a fire pit on its small, almost-private back deck. If necessary, Mark was poised to express-order some campfire supplies. As it happened, he didn't have to. "Oh." S'mores weren't the only option.

"Oh is right." Liam noticed the four metal toasting-fork things hung on the wall above the counter. Two were standard campfire forks. The other two weren't. He took one down and compared it to the printed instructions for campfire cannoli. "They must have had these custom-made." Wooden handles and sturdy metal arms, tipped with a cylindrical cage of fire screen. The instructions amounted to 'wrap toasting cylinder with

150

foil, wrap crescent roll dough over cylinder, seal the end, and bake over the fire until golden brown and delicious.' A variety of potential fillings were provided, along with the dough. Liam visualized one of these things full of marshmallows, melting from the hot bread. "Should we get all the dick jokes out of the way now?"

Mark snorted out a laugh. "Christopher's had these before at Ben's place. I'm pretty sure he's heard all the dick jokes."

"I'm wondering if my nephews have heard of this. Well, that's tonight's entertainment, I guess." He put the toasting fork back on the wall, grinning. Time to get unpacked. Then over to the lodge for dinner, and meeting Mark's son. He was hoping his experience with his siblings' kids would apply here.

"Don't worry," Mark said, reading his lover's mind. "He's really looking forward to meeting you. He might not say much at first, so just follow my lead."

"Okay." Liam blew out a breath. "How do I look?"

"Gorgeous. Perfect." God, those three days really did feel like forever. Mark needed another kiss. "Mmm."

Liam put some distance between them, not without difficulty. Waiting till after dinner, and after some entertainment with the fire pit, was the responsible thing to do. The adult thing. The almost-impossible thing. "Later." He said it with promise.

The first round of getting-to-know-you felt slightly formal, if not awkward. Christopher was so accustomed to dealing with random adults that he had an established methodology. He didn't go with the interview format that night, maybe because Mark led with the Thanksgiving story. Making fun of himself for being a show-boaty Broadway boy, singing for his supper. Turning his mini-meltdown in the kitchen into a much simpler moment. If Liam hadn't been there too, he would have believed it. When Mark invited him to tell his side, he followed that lead. Focused on the funny parts, about trying to steal Emily and about the Broadway-WWE movie discussion. Chris was, as advertised, fairly quiet, but not in a sulky way. Liam had spent plenty of time with kids of all ages, so 'quiet' didn't bother him. He wanted this kid to take his time. They had the whole week.

By the end of the evening, they had a plan. Mark would have breakfast with Chris the next couple of days, and they'd take a hike or two together. Liam would entertain himself while father and son had some alone time. Dinner would be all three of them every day. A number of activities were already on the schedule – it wouldn't have been smart to leave booking the helicopter or the Jeep till the last minute – but they'd all have plenty of time to simply chill out and enjoy the glorious landscape. This particular teenager was obviously not going to hunker down in his room, or demand his father's undivided attention. It was, Liam thought, probably the ideal situation for beginning to build this branch of the blended family. The after-dinner campfire nonsense didn't hurt.

Mark did not think it was only his imagination; he was fairly sure the other teenager in the lodge was about to boil over with something hateful. And he knew Chris could handle it. Needed to handle it. If nothing similar had happened yet in New York, it would surely happen later. Possibly over and over again for the rest of Christopher's life. At least he was here to lend support, if wanted. He told himself it would make for a good father-son talk later on.

Liam might have sensed it coming, too. He didn't go out for a walk after dinner the way he did the night before. Instead he sat in the lounge with Mark, side by side in armchairs not too far from the fireplace. Chris was across the room at one of the tables set up close to the power supply. Focused on his laptop, right up until that slightly-older teenager came in, walked up to the table, and all-too-audibly said "Your dad's a faggot."

Liam made a low, angry sound. Mark closed his eyes for a second and took a breath. Then they waited to see what would happen. The other adults in the room looked profoundly uncomfortable.

Chris leaned back in his chair, regarded the other teenager for a moment, and said, "That word means a bundle of sticks. Are you suggesting we should throw my dad in the fireplace?" The other kid was so confused, he forgot to look hostile. "Oh, you meant the other thing. Most people use the word gay. Personally, I prefer bent, because that's a better stylistic parallel to calling someone straight." Liam made a new sound, something an awful lot like a stifled laugh. Mark was watching his son with pure admiration. "I'm a writer," Chris said, with a modest shrug. "So I try to think about the words I use. Why do you care who my dad sleeps with?"

The other kid took a step back. "I don't!"

"Then why make that comment?"

"It's, it's – I don't know!"

Chris let that sit for a really praiseworthy second before saying, "If you don't know why you're saying something, maybe you shouldn't say it."

The other kid might have recovered if they'd been alone, or if he'd had other teenagers backing him up.

153

Finding himself the center of attention from a lot of adults who looked either openly disapproving or embarrassed, he muttered something and fled the scene. Chris made eye contact with Mark; took a visibly deep breath; and focused on his laptop again.

"I want to go hug the crap out of him right now," Mark said to Liam, very softly.

"Let him enjoy his victory."

"It sounded a little bit rehearsed." Mark got his phone out and sent a text: *You're amazing. Does garbage like that happen often? If so I'm sorry*

Christopher's phone was on the table next to the laptop. His eyes flicked to it; he picked it up; gazed across the room for a second as if deciding what to say. It took a couple of minutes for him to finish composing a reply, and for it to land. *First time about you. Someone in NY said something about Mom and Warren*

"Oh shit, I didn't even think of that. It's so, you know, nothing." He texted again: *We've really given you a lot to handle*

Lots of material

Mark laughed out loud. He was about to type something else when his phone buzzed again.

Going up to my room now to watch a movie

Okay kiddo. See you at breakfast. Mark watched while Chris collected his gear and headed out. He gave them a wave as he left the room. "I wish I could take more credit for how great he is."

"You've contributed plenty. Is this our cue?"

"Jesus, yes, let's get out of here." He was on his feet before Liam. They were out of the lounge a moment later, collecting their jackets from the coat-check, and crunching across the gravel to their cabin.

Liam closed the door behind them and said, "Thank God for that wood stove. Can you imagine actually camping up here?"

"No, I can't. I've never camped anywhere. Holds no appeal." Jackets hung up again, shoes off, swapping jeans for warm-ups and pouring a couple of glasses of whisky. "You cannot imagine how grateful I was, the first time I asked Chris if he wanted to camp, and he said No!" He gave it a full adolescent-horror spin. Liam laughed. "Mind you, he was six. I never asked him again."

Liam was grinning. "You were like, okay, that question was asked and answered, we're done here."

"Exactly." Mark curled up on their bed, which was the most comfortable place to sit. Also the place he wanted to be right now, especially since Liam was right there beside him in a few seconds. They leaned on each other, sipping whisky. The glow from the wood stove supplemented the nightlight in the bathroom. "I keep catching myself about to get online."

"Me too. Are you reading your publicist's emails?"

"Nope. Not till after I take Chris back to the city. I can spend the whole flight home reading those, and the ones from my agent. Whatever's out there, Jade and Emily are not passing it on."

"Mmm. Robert's keeping it to himself too. You'd think they discussed it or something." Mark huffed out a laugh. Liam finished his whisky and reached over to set the glass on his nightstand. "I'm really glad you wanted me along for this. I might not have sprung for the helicopter tour if I came by myself."

Mark gave him a sideways look. "Someday you can take me to Grand Canyon, and we'll do the helicopter there, too. Because I'm not rafting it."

"No Bright Angel trail, either, I guess."

"Hell no. I read that book when I was a kid, and there was a minute when I was looking at parks to take Chris to, and I saw what they said about that and thought, how about Acadia." Liam laughed again. "He's the only kid he knows who's been to Maine. We did a Stephen King tour."

"Oh, of course you did. Has he read all those books?"

"Nooooo. No no no. I told him, some of these will give you legit nightmares if you read them before you're ready for them. He wanted to read 'Carrie' when he was nine. I said, let me talk to your Mom. So we talked about it, and decided he could read it but only if he was in the room with her, and if he wanted to ask me about something he could call me, any time. I think it's an important book," he explained. "It's about intolerance and peer pressure and consequences. And the movie is good, but it's hard to get through the violence to the message."

"So what else." Liam's voice was soft. Mark was done with his whisky now too, leaning against Liam's chest, cuddled under his arm. These were the moments they'd both been craving – even more than sex – during the waiting game.

"'The Dead Zone.' I think that is actually the greatest American novel I've ever read. I mean, it's *about* America in this really deep way, about religion and violence and politics. And you connect to it because of this tragic love story. You really want that to work out, and it hurts that it doesn't. Chris loved it. The second one he read was 'The Shining,' which he didn't like as much – let's face it, Jack Torrance is a very unpleasant person to spend any time with – and then he asked what he should read next."

"You're a really good father."

Mark felt himself blush. He couldn't think of anything to say. Played that sentence over in his mind a few times, because it was awfully nice to hear, and started to think there was something about the tone of it. Something wistful. "Liam."

"Mmm?"

"Did you want kids? I can't believe I never asked." And Liam hadn't said anything, because right at the beginning Mark said he didn't want more than one.

Oh shit, Liam thought, realizing he'd given it away. "I, um. I did. I kind of put that away a few years ago." Mark didn't say anything. After a second, as if there had been another question, Liam went on. "You saw those pictures. My brothers have five kids between them. My sister has one. Watching them get married was bad enough. Watching them have kids was getting really painful. And now," he shrugged. "It's a little late in the game for that. Our parents are both retired. I'm going to be the one looking out for them, and it's fine. I can be the cool uncle in L.A."

"You are a cool uncle, I'll bet." He wanted to offer. Even though they weren't in a great place for it, and he was ambivalent at best, and Liam wasn't the only one who was going to be on call for aging parents. "We could do that, you know. There are ways."

"Oh, honey." Liam turned his head, kissed Mark, wrapped his other arm around. Stayed there with their heads tipped together. "I appreciate the offer. Four years ago, maybe even two, I would have been really tempted. I wanted a family. But I'm going to have one now, and I'm not hung up on passing on the name. There are plenty of Byrnes." Mark laughed softly. "I'll be cool uncle Liam. Dad's boyfriend Liam." Maybe even,

157

someday, Dad's husband Liam. He didn't think they were ready for that word yet. At least he could use the other one. "I love you."

"I love you, too. Scooch down." Liam made a querying sound, but complied. Mark resettled them so he had his arm around Liam's shoulders. "I brushed up a little something in New York." And why he was nervous, he would never know. The man said he wanted to hear this, after all. He started to sing, soft and low. "There were bells on a hill but I never heard them ringing." He felt Liam's breath hitch, then a sigh, then a hand reaching up to his. Not another move, even at the end of the song, "Till there was you." They sat quietly together as the fire burned down to embers.

When they went into the dining room the next morning, they saw Christopher and the other teenager, sitting together. Mark made a confused sound. "What the actual fuck," Liam murmured.

"I can't even imagine. But they're talking, so let's let them talk. Oh wow this means I can order a Bloody Mary." He felt Liam laughing silently beside him. They found seats and waited for the server. It was impossible not to keep an eye on the rapprochement that appeared to be happening, though they did their best not to stare. Midway through king crab eggs Benedict and sweet potato pancakes with reindeer sausage, the boys stood up. The stranger gave Chris a clumsy but clearly well-intended buffet on the shoulder, then went out. Chris made his way across the dining room and pulled a chair over to join them. Mark raised his eyebrows. "Okay. What."

"His name's Louis Turner. Found me in the lounge and apologized. So I said let's go get something to eat."

Chris picked a stray chunk of Hollandaise-covered crab meat off the plate and popped it in his mouth. "Oh yum."

"Did you actually eat? All I saw was muffins."

"Yeah, we kind of mostly talked."

Mark got the server's attention to deal with that, and to request a refill of coffee. Then, "Obviously you handled it perfectly. Did he tell you what his deal was?"

"Mmm. His parents are getting a divorce. His father left his mom for another woman. His mom took his sister to Palm Beach, where one set of grandparents live. He's here with his aunt and uncle, who sound like decent people even though they're from Texas." Liam choked back a laugh. Chris shot him a look. "Anyway, they were taking a break from each other last night. I guess Louis hasn't been the easiest person to get along with. They left him to have dinner by himself and went to their room."

"Oh. Feeling a little abandoned. A lot abandoned."

"Right. And here I am with my dad, who's a little bit famous and an easy target. Sorry."

"No apology required. I haven't been looking at the news. Is it pretty bad?"

"Not as bad as you thought it might be. Oh yeah." Another round of crab Benedict, this one with a side of bacon, and a mug of hot chocolate. Christopher dove in.

"Did you tell him we're here all week?"

"Mm-hmm."

"He could come with us for the flight tomorrow. The glacier landing. They said there were a few empty seats on the plane." Christopher's mouth was full; his eyes got big; he made a face that said 'really?!' Mark nodded. "Get around the rest of that. I'll go leave a note at the front desk, and we can track down his aunt and

159

uncle later. The Jeep people are picking us up in an hour."

Liam watched Mark go, well aware that his little-bit-famous boyfriend had booked the whole plane so they could have a private tour. He really was good at this father thing. It might not be the kind of trip he could afford in future years, but this year he could, so he was making sure his son got the trip of a lifetime. And sharing it with Liam, trying to make sure they had a chance to bond. The self-guided Jeep safari was going to be five hours of forced proximity. Liam hoped Christopher understood that he was there because he wanted them to be a family, not simply because he wanted to spend time with Mark after six months of forced separation.

"You really love him, don't you."

Liam turned his head, startled. Chris was gazing at him steadily. Liam cleared his throat. "Yes, I do. I'm probably going to ask him to marry me."

"Why probably?"

Jeez, this kid was sharp. Might as well have said he already *did* ask Mark to marry him. Would Mark be embarrassed? Better play it off a little, so it didn't seem like this was all moving too fast. "Okay. Definitely. Don't tell him, though, okay? I'd like to kind of have a plan for it."

"Warren took Mom to the Rainbow Room."

Liam was smiling. "Is that the most romantic place in New York City?" Chris shrugged; his mouth was full again. "I guess it got the job done." A stifled laugh from across the table. "I'm looking forward to meeting them, too."

A little over an hour later, they were heading out in their rented Jeep. Liam was driving; Christopher was in

160

the front passenger seat, navigating. Mark was in the back seat, taking pictures out the window and trying not to completely crack up over the interrogation happening in between map checks. Chris – who had mostly been communicating with Liam through Mark – was doing the interview thing. From time to time the two men exchanged a glance in the rear-view mirror. The first time, Mark was afraid it meant 'make it stop.' After that, he was sure all it meant was 'I'm about to die laughing.'

Well before they were halfway out, the interview was over and Chris was caught up in the scenery. They stopped several times along the way, for short walks or simply to stand around looking at the immensity of the landscape. "This is the coolest," Chris said as they got back in the car after one of those stops. "Every way we see it, it's different."

"Imagine hiking through here," Mark said. "We'll have to get you that book." There were copies of 'Into The Wild' at the tour company office.

"There's a couple of mystery series set in Alaska, too," Liam offered. "Our friend Robert is on this big mystery kick. He read one called 'Murder on the Iditarod Trail' and told me to read it before we came up here. You might like it."

Chris made a 'could be' face and jotted down a note on the edge of the map. "I read 'Call of the Wild' a few years ago. That book is awesome."

"Read it in high school." Liam's tone was the tiniest bit dry. Chris grinned at the map and didn't say anything. They were all quiet until the next stop, when they took the opportunity for another short hike.

Mark kept an eye on Chris, who was up ahead of them. "He likes you."

"I like him too. I was wondering."

"Mmm?"

"Would it be offensively obvious bribery to let him get behind the wheel for a minute? Just here in the pull-out," he added. "I started learning to drive when I was twelve. He's tall enough."

Mark's reflexive No died unspoken. "I got to drive a tractor when I was twelve. We were out in the country, at this model farm kind of resort. I thought I was the shit." They both snickered. "Sure, I guess. If you want to. I mean, you rented the Jeep." Another snicker. "We're not too far out to walk back now." Liam laughed out loud. Chris looked back at them. Mark patted his lover's ass and jogged ahead, catching up with his son.

A minute later Liam heard Chris say, "Are you *serious*?!" Not too long after that, Liam was giving the teenager a driving lesson. The pull-out was large enough for buses; there was plenty of room for Chris to practice. He was attentive, cautious, and a quick study. The adults were unsurprised. They were also not surprised that he spent most of their return to the lodge texting. Mark was expecting the text from Kerry right before dinner: *Driving a Jeep?? facepalm*

He laughed for a minute, showed the text to Liam (who also laughed), then replied: *Well we had a Jeep. Now Ben's dad is going to have to level up*

OMG Mark you instigator

Liam started it. How's the baby?

Baby is good TYVM being out of town is great. Our kid says you're landing on a glacier tomorrow and will have a spare teenager

Yes long story will report by email if Chris doesn't fill in all the blanks for you. Say Hi to Warren for us

Will do, watch out for moose or musk ox or whatever

162

Mosquitos honey it's mosquitos

LOL bye. Mark disconnected. He was still smiling as they walked over to the lodge. There might be bad news coming when he finally got back to looking at his business messages, but at the moment he couldn't remember being happier. The whole family was in a good place and Liam was here by his side, knitting it all together.

CHAPTER 13

A not-very-long conversation with the aunt and uncle from Texas resulted in a full flight to the glacier. The four adults and two teenagers kept the pilot busy answering questions on the way. He tried to keep their expectations low; sometimes the weather didn't permit landing, and they wouldn't know until they got there. "The mountains make their own weather," he reminded them. "It can be one way at the lodge, another way at our airstrip, and something completely different at our destination. So keep your fingers crossed." Fortunately, they arrived to hazily-blue skies and good wind conditions.

Chris was taking notes the entire time. Louis was clutching a sketchbook. When they touched down on the glacier, the boys were first out of the plane. Chris went one way, Louis another. None of the adults asked him about the sketchbook, but at the end of the day Mark asked Chris. After a contentedly conversation-free dinner, they distributed themselves around the fire pit behind the cabin with some decaf for the men and hot chocolate for Chris. Mark said, "So what's the deal with Louis and the sketchbook? He's an artist?"

Chris stifled a yawn. "Mmph. He tries to act like it's no big deal. I asked if I could see what he's doing and he said maybe after breakfast."

Mark glanced at Liam. They'd all be leaving the park after one more night. The Texas contingent were flying home out of Anchorage, like Liam. He said, "Have you guys exchanged numbers?"

"He doesn't have his own phone. And he's not sure where he'll be living for the school year."

Mark thought *assholes* at the parents. "Well, you could give him your number and maybe he could call you once he knows where he is."

"Maybe."

Mark didn't push it. The boys seemed friendly today, but it might not amount to anything. Chris already had a lot of friends. He was on the phone with Ben every day. And he was getting up, taking his mug to the sink, saying goodnight. "Good day today?"

"Great day. Thanks Dad. Thanks Liam." A hug for Mark, something between a salute and a wave for Liam. Shrugging into his jacket and saying, "See you in the morning."

The door closed behind him. Liam and Mark washed up and got in bed, enjoying the silence. Lying there lazily, settling into their favorite cuddle position, until both of them dozed off.

Christopher was already in the dining room when Liam and Mark sauntered in for breakfast. They spent most of the meal discussing whether they wanted to repeat any of the hikes near the lodge, or take a different bus tour, or simply hang around. When the plates were almost empty Chris admitted he'd like to spend some time alone. "I've got some stuff I want to write down while I have the landscape in front of me. But you guys can do whatever."

"I kind of want to spend as much time outside as possible," Liam said.

"Maybe one of the hikes. We'll check in with you when we get back and if you're still cool, we might go over to the cabin and sit on the deck there." They'd been doing plenty of that, at various times of day, but Mark wasn't tired of it. And if they got bored, there was the bed. His sidelong glance tipped Liam off. They both tried to look innocent.

Chris was oblivious, nibbling on the last piece of bacon. "That works. I'm going to go get my laptop."

"We'll see you in a bit, then." Mark watched his son go. "Is it my imagination or did he get taller this week?"

"I think it's your imagination. Let's see if we can get a muffin or two to go." Muffins accomplished and check signed, they made a detour to the cabin for camera, mosquito repellent, canteens, and sunscreen. Half an hour later they were a quarter-mile down a trail, comfortably silent. Liam would not have said that this trip was any kind of intentional test, but it had functioned that way. Spending this much time together, living in close quarters, dealing with the minor hassles of being away from their usual environment. Dealing with people, most of whom either truly didn't care that they were gay, or did a fair job acting as if they didn't care. Getting used to being open about who they were.

The first time Liam touched Mark in public in L.A., there was tension. Not the kind that said he didn't want to be touched; it was more that he was afraid of how other people would react. There were very few socially-acceptable ways for straight men to touch. Both of them had mastered those as teenagers. Since then, Liam had gotten plenty of practice being gay in public. Mark had next to none. It was good they had this interval, after the fairly-intense first couple of weeks in town. They'd confirmed not only that they really did like and enjoy each other as people, but also that they dealt well together with all those minor hassles. Plus, it was an enormous relief to Liam that he and Christopher got along. That would have been a deal-breaker, for sure.

166

About ninety minutes out, they started back. It was one of those decisions arrived at without discussion. All they did was stop at an overlook, take in the view for a few minutes, and then turn to make eye contact. Exchanging a smile that seemed to say *enough for you? Okay, me too.* Strolling away from the breezy clearing and into the woods. The ambient temperature was cooler. It was dim under the trees, and very quiet. They'd barely spoken. Mark breathed in the scent of evergreens, slowing his steps, not even sure why. In a few minutes they stopped again. Liam gave Mark a curious look. He took a step closer; Liam's arms came up by reflex, wrapping around him. They stood there without speaking. It was like one of their kitchen moments, with the same kind of temptations. They could kiss here. Maybe even make love here. They hadn't seen another person the entire time. Liam took a step back, bringing Mark with him. Resting his shoulders against a tree, letting his hands wander, mouth on Mark's neck. Mark had his hands under Liam's jacket. Then unbuttoning the flannel-lined corduroy shirt, exactly like the one he had on. Hands on bare skin, and Liam was kissing him. Pressed together at the hips, Liam's feet apart, one of Mark's in between them. Moving against him, Liam's hand on his ass, urging him.

Some kind of noise got through and they both froze. Cautiously turned their heads to look down the trail toward the voices, not close, but approaching. Mark made a soft frustrated sound; Liam huffed out a laugh. He retrieved his hands. Mark buttoned the shirt up again, took a step away, adjusted himself. Liam shoved a hand down his jeans to do the same. "That was close."

"For real. I'm so pissed."

Liam laughed as quietly as he could. "Could've been worse. Could've been a bear."

"Whatever. Let's get back to the cabin." By the time they passed the other hikers, they no longer looked like men who'd been making out. Mark had intended to go into the lodge to track down Christopher. Instead, when they finally got there, he sent a text: *Want company? If not we'll head to the cabin*

A minute later: *Kind of in the middle of something. Where did you guys go?! Had lunch already*

Then we'll get something to eat and ping you later

KK. Mark put the phone away. "We're not needed."

"Why don't you go and warm the place up. I'll bring back some sandwiches."

"Okay." A light kiss, then they parted.

Mark had a good fire going in the wood stove by the time Liam returned. "I half expected you to have your clothes off." He locked the door, set down the takeout box, and took off his outerwear, then accepted a bourbon and ginger ale from his lover.

"It was tempting, but I'm hungry. And we've got some time."

"We're going to need it." They wolfed down their food, then took their glasses over to the bed. Stripped eagerly, as if they hadn't made love at least once a day on this vacation. They knew each other's bodies pretty well by now. Knew how long they could touch and tease before passion took over. They finished it the way they might have outside, only better. Liam lay sprawled on his back, Mark still on top of him. Sticky, sweaty, and satisfied.

After another minute Mark peeled himself away, glanced at the clock, and said, "Almost three. I'd better go see what the kid is up to."

"Want me along?"

"Always, but feel free to take a nap. You've earned it." Mark leaned down again, brushing his mouth across Liam's. "So fucking gorgeous."

Liam smiled. "Speak for yourself." He lay there sort-of-watching Mark through the open bathroom door. A quick shower, some beard maintenance. Not bothering to blow-dry his hair, only finger-combing some gel through it. Getting dressed again, making an appreciative comment about the laundry service at the lodge.

Taking the few steps over to close his hand around Liam's ankle. "You're cooled down. Want the blanket?"

"Mm-hmm." He could have pulled it up himself. It was nice having Mark do it. Another opportunity for a kiss. "I love you."

"I love you, too. See you in a bit." Mark picked up his e-reader and left the cabin, smiling to himself on the way to the lodge. The waiting, the anxiety, the bullshit since sweeps: all worth it to have this. He wondered if Liam suspected how nervous he was when they arrived. Those few days of not seeing each other, while Mark was making the trip East to collect Christopher, had knocked him off-balance. It was easy to believe in what they had when they were together. Then being away, determinedly not checking the internet, not knowing if maybe Liam was being hounded by the press. Imagining the questions. Where's Mark, Dr. Byrne? Not working out? Left you already? Afraid to ask, because there was nothing he could do about it anyway, and it might seem insecure to ask. Not that Liam didn't already know he was insecure. If the man wanted a tough guy, a strong silent type who never cried, he wouldn't have come into the kitchen after that song on Thanksgiving. He wouldn't have suggested getting together, wouldn't have called, wouldn't have listened. He made it so easy to trust. Easy to believe.

A text exchange led Mark to the bar, which had a great view. On their first day, he made a point of telling the bar management that he was fine with Christopher hanging out in there. The dining-room people, the front-desk people: everybody knew Chris was with Mark. They all knew who Mark was by day two. Another anxiety he'd been able to dismiss. It was hard, living in the L.A. bubble, not to expect asshattery outside it. But everybody was – at the very least – civil. The only unpleasantness had been the moment with Louis, and Chris solved that. Was still in the process of solving that, maybe, because Louis was sitting with him in the bar and they were talking when Mark came in. "Hi guys, what's up? Oh *hello*." Mark took a long look at the drawing. It was a full-page, full-length portrait of the pilot from the glacier flight, slightly exaggerated as if for a comic book. The guy would love it. Louis made an uncomfortable movement, as if he wanted to close the sketchbook. "No, hang on. That's really good. Where did you learn to draw like that?"

"My grandmother," Louis mumbled.

It was an incomplete answer, but enough. "You grew up close?"

There was a hesitation, as if the boy wasn't sure he should (or could) have this conversation with someone he'd been hate-speeching a few days before. But he was brave. "My sister and I spend the summers with her. We used to. She lives close to my dad."

Oh you poor kid. That answered a lot, too. Another person who he might be losing, because he might have to move, and none of the adults had figured it out. So here he was, knowing only that everything was changing. "You know, a person with talent like that can make a good living in graphics and animation. Keep it up. Chris, if you're good here I'm going to go and read for a while."

"Where's Liam?"

"Nap. That was a long hike."

"Yeah, it was. I'll come find you." The 'when I'm done here' was implied.

"Mr. Valance?"

He turned to look at Louis, eyebrows up with surprise. "Mmm?"

"Why are you being so nice to me?" It almost sounded grouchy.

Mark wasn't fooled by the tone. "Because I'm a grown-up, and you're not. I don't believe in punching down." He watched that sink in. "You're having a rough time. Making it worse wouldn't do anything for me." He gave the kid a small smile as he walked away.

It wasn't a large room, so even though Mark was reading he couldn't help noticing when Louis stood up to go. Chris stayed at the table, doing something on his laptop. Mark checked the time; estimated that Liam might come and find them in an hour or so; returned to his book. He was sufficiently engrossed in 'Mockingjay' that he had to suppress annoyance at hearing his name again. This time it was Jim Turner, the uncle. "Hi Jim. What can I do for you?"

The other man sighed, sat in the chair across from Mark, and said, "You've already done a lot. You and your son kind of saved our trip. I just wanted to say thanks, and Louis told us you were down here."

"Well … you're welcome." He gave it a somewhat questioning tone, because he didn't think that was really

171

all the guy had to say. Waited, decided he was going to have to prompt the next thing, and said, "Was there something else?"

Another sigh, this one communicating discomfort. "The truth is, my brother has made a giant mess and he's not even trying to fix it. My sister-in-law is talking about moving to Florida, and that's going to take those kids away from everything they grew up with. I'm trying to keep things from getting worse. Now, I hardly know you, but it sounds like you try to fix things, so I wondered if you had any advice." It must have cost him to ask; he was flushed and uneasy, not making eye contact. Maybe he thought Mark was going to be a dick about it. Slap the adult around after letting the kid skate.

After a moment Mark said, "If you're serious?" The other man nodded. "First off, get him his own cell phone. No matter where he ends up, he's going to need to stay in touch with people who aren't where he is." Another nod, though with a face that said maybe fourteen was too young to have his own phone. "Christopher's had his own phone since he was ten and started taking the bus alone. Anyway, I think that would help a lot. I can't speak to the mother and sister part of the situation, but it seems like staying in Texas, close to you and his grandmother and in his same school, would be huge for Louis. I don't know if that's possible."

Jim thought about it. Mark waited patiently. After a minute, Jim said, "I'll be honest, I didn't think of that. I was thinking of how to keep the family together. I'll talk to Sandy."

That must be the mom. "Good. I know it's a lot landing on you. There's one other thing, though. The kid has talent. Some support with his art could go a really long way."

"What, those comics he draws?"

"Did you see the drawing of the pilot? People pay good money for stuff like that. He could have a career in graphics and animation. In L.A. for sure, but there are lots of other places around the country. He's going to need computer skills."

"All we have is a cheap PC."

"They're getting less expensive all the time. Maybe his mom could wrap that into the child-support agreement."

Jim made a derisive noise. "Good luck getting anything out of Ellis."

"Well, there are ways. A fundraiser at the church, maybe. Nobody wants another good teenager giving up on life."

"Yeah." Jim nodded again. "Thanks." He got to his feet, offered a hand awkwardly, shook a little too firmly, and went away. Mark did some conscious breathing. He wouldn't have chosen to have that conversation, but maybe it was a good thing. A few minutes later, Christopher came and sat beside him. They smiled at each other and both settled down to read.

Leaving the lodge was a bit anticlimactic, because Liam was already gone. The southbound train came through around noon, so he kissed Mark goodbye, shook Christopher's hand, and got on the shuttle with the Turners a little after eleven. Then Mark had three hours to mooch around and miss his lover before he and Chris got on the shuttle for the northbound train. Once en route to Fairbanks, Christopher dug into his laptop bag, extracted something in a 9x11 manila envelope, and held it out. "This is for you."

Mark took it. Nothing was written on the outside. The flap wasn't sealed. There was one sheet of heavy paper inside. He pulled it out. "Wow! When did he give you this?"

"He kind of didn't. I found it by the room door this morning, like he slid it underneath or something. Figured that meant he didn't want to talk about it, so I didn't say anything when they went down to the shuttle."

Mark studied the drawing. He had every intention of getting it framed. There were traces of pencil lines that must have been erased after the kid inked it. Much like the drawing of the pilot, it was a comic-style full-length portrait. Only this was him and Liam. The Mark figure was in a duster-length coat like Nick Fury in 'Iron Man 2,' upstage hand on his hip. Liam was in a lab coat, arms crossed. They stood angled away from each other, downstage shoulders touching, ready to take on the world. "I love this. I need a coat like that." Chris snorted. "He didn't sign it. If you ever talk, tell him to sign his stuff." Mark dug out his phone, laid the drawing on his lap, took a picture and texted it to Liam without comment.

A reply came in fast: *Holy smokes*

Right?!

Are we going to fight over where to hang that? Cause I want it for my office

I'll get a good photo taken after I get it framed, slap it all over my social media with a credit to the artist. You can have the original

Booyah

LOL See you soon XOX

XOX. Mark waited to see if there was anything else coming through, decided there wasn't, and put away the phone. He'd be home in two point five days, and the next phase of New Life would begin. This getaway had been close to perfect. A break between the initial period of adjustment, time to get used to each other away from the distractions of daily life, time to bond. Time to really let it sink in. He'd thrown himself at Liam; Liam caught him; and now they were moving forward.

Together.

CHAPTER 14

July 2011

Liam dropped his duffel bag on the floor, staring at the bed. "Oh my God."

Mark stepped closer, slid an arm around him from behind, and rested his cheek against Liam's shoulder. "I used to have this upholstered headboard."

Liam wrapped his arm over Mark's, intertwining their fingers. He cleared his throat. "When did you get this one?"

"In March." After he began not only to trust, but to believe. "I saw one with spindles made of iron, but they were so thin. I thought you might like one you could … hold on to."

How in the world had he understood this? They'd barely even spoken about bedroom things. Nothing they'd done so far went beyond that first weekend after sweeps. It was as if they both wanted to ease into it, let their sex life catch up to their emotional life in its own time. Liam was dizzy with lust. He moved their joined hands down to his groin, pressed Mark's palm against his cock, heard him make a hungry sound. Felt the erection against his ass and pushed back against it.

Mark wasn't about to guess what that meant. "What do you want."

Liam closed his eyes. He'd never said this out loud, only tried to communicate it through body language, and wordless noises. "I want you in me."

"Huh? I thought, um." He stalled.

"Everyone does. I blame the patriarchy." What he meant: everyone assumes the bigger guy is the top.

176

Hoping Mark understood. He could live without it, obviously. But he didn't want to, not anymore, not in this room with this man who'd given him the illusion of submission.

Mark was stifling a laugh against Liam's back. He slid his other hand around. Undid the jeans, started pushing them down. Hands inside, on Liam's body, as he took over the undressing part of the operation. They were in each other's way. Separating enough to get their clothes off, then Mark was pulling the covers down. Opening the drawer of the nightstand, taking a few things out. They weren't speaking. Liam was kneeling on the bed, exploring the sturdy turned-wood spindles of the headboard. He didn't even know if 'spindle' was the correct word. Horizontal, not vertical, stabilized by a trio of wrought-iron uprights. Along the length were various rounded shapes, some fitting the palm of his hand so well he might have been measured for it. Some were full, almost spherical. He could wrap his fingers around, and there'd be no torque on his wrists. The thing might have been designed for a man to hold onto. Or to be tied to. Mark behind him again, mouth on his spine. Then: "I need to tell you I've never done this before. I'm assuming you have."

"A few times. More often the other way." Because people expected it, and he didn't want to disappoint. It wasn't that he hated doing it, not at all. Especially with his partner in Minneapolis, who liked it face to face. That made it special. One of many reasons leaving that man hurt. Maybe he and Mark could do it that way someday.

"Talk me through it? I've … had it done to me."

Liam didn't like the sound of that. He turned around, got hold of Mark, made eye contact. "Did someone force you?"

177

God, he didn't want to talk about this. Didn't want to admit it. He glanced away. "Not exactly?" He didn't say no, after all. Didn't say get off me, stop, don't do that.

Holy shit, this surge of rage, he'd never felt anything like it. "Who? I'll break his fucking neck. Was it that photographer?"

"What? No, not Andy. He, well, he started making some moves but he was paying attention and he said you don't want to do this, let's do something else." Mark took a breath. "It was a long time ago, in New York. I didn't assert myself, that's all."

"Which does not make it your fault. We don't have to do this." Sitting back on his heels now, holding Mark's hands. "You know I love the things we usually do."

"I love that too. But you've trusted me with what you want, and I want to give you that. Someday maybe I'll want something different, and you'll want to give me that." Liam nodded. Mark squeezed his hands. "So let's try it. If it doesn't work for us, well." He shrugged. Smiled. "There are plenty of things that do."

"Okay. I just want to be sure this isn't something that actively grosses you out."

"No no no. I like your ass, you know that." Liam was blushing. Mark was grinning. "Maybe we'll start there, with what I've done before. I know you liked it." He'd gone places – literally – he'd never gone before, following Liam's reactions.

"Jesus, yes." He'd especially liked that Mark initiated that, as part of 'kiss you all over,' which had taken well over a delirious hour. Liam leaned in for a kiss. He would never get tired of kissing. It felt like they both had such a deficit of kisses to make up, not only from the waiting game but from all the years before. So they kissed until they were both panting, fully aroused, and past worrying about who liked what.

Mark got a hand around the back of Liam's thigh, pulling that leg up, stroking suggestively down. "Going to make this easy for me?" He murmured it against Liam's skin, the spot he'd found midway between nipple and underarm. Such silky, delicate skin. Creamy white, framed by the fluff of black hair under his arm and the swath of it on his chest. Licking him here made him twitch and moan.

Liam squirmed at the sensation, a combination of kiss and tickle. He wanted that mouth all over him. Angled his body, starting to turn. Mark's mouth followed onto his side, then down his flank, to the top of his hip. Another spot there that Liam didn't even know was erogenous until Mark found it. He bent that leg again, an invitation. *Get in my ass*. Pushing his cock into the mattress with a grunt as Mark moved in, spreading his legs more because he wanted that tongue. Oh Christ it felt good. "So good," he mumbled. After a while, a hand. Wet fingers, Mark must have licked them. Teasing with that hand as he stretched over Liam to the nightstand, getting the lube. Then a more intentional touch. "Mmm. God, yes, like that." Would he have to say anything else? Not yet, no, God, not at all. Mark's tongue again, licking lightly, penetrating. Liam whimpered. Mark's teeth on his ass, a growl as if he liked hearing that sound. Then a finger went in and Liam buried his face in the pillow to stifle a curse.

Mark had to remind himself to breathe. The sounds Liam was making were driving him crazy. Moans, the pitch ratcheting up. Pushing back against Mark's hand. Actually humping the bed, fucking himself both ways. He really wanted this, and things felt loose. Slick with lube, Mark's fingers slid in and out easily. No assumptions, though. He couldn't forget the feeling of entry, rough even with a condom. Uncomfortable was a mild word. But then, that guy hadn't done all this with his mouth, with his hand. Maybe it was bad for Mark because the guy didn't care if it was good. "Is this good, sweetheart?"

"Mmm. Yes. I could. But you."

Mark filled in the blanks: I could come like this but I want you. "Comfortable?" No verbal answer, only a shift. Liam folding his arms under his chest, digging into the bed with his knees, getting his hips up. Wide open and waiting. Mark couldn't believe how abandoned he was. It was an incredible turn-on, as if he wasn't hard enough already. He reached over for a condom. Suited up, slicked himself. Put one hand down beside Liam's chest. Bent to get his mouth on Liam's spine again, felt that whole gorgeous body jerk, and started to engage. Guiding himself, pausing at resistance. Comprehending Liam's sound of encouragement, trusting him, pushing through it.

"Fuuuuck, oh God, ungh *yes*."

"Jesus *Christ*." A breathless laugh from underneath him. Mark wasn't prepared for how this felt. He didn't know how long he could last. Had to somehow not lose his mind. Both hands down. He was still sinking in, deeper, rocking his hips because he couldn't not move. And there was Liam again, nearly a chant, fuck fuck fuck fuck fuck. It might have been funny if it wasn't so clearly 'this is the best thing ever don't stop don't ever stop.' Then a sharp, ecstatic sound. "That's good?" What did he do? What was different? Was it this?

"Holy FUCK!"

Mark lost it. Harder, faster, more. Liam was shoving up against him, back flexing, groaning. And then he came. No doubt about it. A contraction around Mark's cock, a spasm, a helpless cry. Too much. Mark's climax surged through him like a tsunami. "Oh God." The words falling from his mouth on a gasp. He wasn't sure if any of that pulse was Liam or if it was all him. Held on until he was sure they were both done. His mouth was on Liam's shoulder. Oh damn, his teeth. He made an apologetic sound, pulling away, feeling another of those almost-silent laughs. Disengaging. What an unbelievably different experience from being inside a woman. He propped himself on his quivering arms for long enough to press a kiss to that bruised shoulder, then collapsed on his back. "That was."

"Mmm?"

"Amazing. Good for you?"

"Mmm."

How he could hear a smile in that, he didn't know. He turned his head to watch Liam roll slowly onto his back. Face flushed, creased by the pillow. Eyes sleepy. "You look satisfied."

"Uh-huh."

"Only one thing could have made that better."

Liam was still having trouble making words. "Mmm?"

"If we could have kissed."

"We could."

"That works?"

"Yeah." Finally, his brain was in gear. "Haven't you ever looked at porn?" Mark laughed. Liam patted him randomly. "Yeah, it works."

"I could get my hand on you, too."

Unbelievably, Liam's cock twitched. "Oh God, stop."

"Maybe you could hold onto the rails."

"*Stop*." They were both laughing.

"Make you a deal."

"What."

"Let's shower, and then you can change the sheets while I put together some dinner." Mark made a 'so sue me' face at Liam's puzzled look. "I like to sleep on fresh sheets."

"Good thing you have your own laundry machines." Mark laughed again. Liam sat up slowly, feeling well-used. Loose, a little squishy, and happy. He half-crawled off the bed, making it to his feet about the same time Mark did.

The funny thing, Liam decided, was that their homes were so much alike. The townhouse was three times the size of his apartment, but they'd done similar things with kitchen, office, and bedroom. Aside from that mind-blowing headboard. Having two full bathrooms was a ridiculous luxury. And next month, that would be all the time. That was mind-blowing, too. He'd given notice to the management company at his apartment building. Booked movers, put the word out at work and at the gym to try and get rid of his bed, his sectional, and his desk. None of those were the kind of furniture worth putting in storage, much less trying to squeeze into an already-fully-furnished space. The shelves could go in the garage, which was the one part of Mark's home that wasn't perfectly organized. He said he'd be delighted if Liam took charge of that.

They spent that weekend skimming through Emmy screeners in between rounds in bed. (Or out of bed.) More of that the following nights, when Liam came back to the townhouse from work instead of going home. They did not discuss the fact that Mark's erstwhile employers were promoting him for a supporting-actor award. That went along with promotion for Jenny, for the writing team, and for the show itself.

Nothing really awful had happened with the media. There were a few comments from people in the industry. Nobody seemed really angry. As much as a couple of the tabloids would have liked to dig up some serious dirt, nobody had any. Mark's publicist responded to anything that needed response, which was mostly confirming what other people said or providing clarifying details. Social media was a different story, but Mark followed his publicist's advice there, too. He didn't respond to anything critical, didn't make excuses, didn't bring anyone else into it. And if anyone veered toward hate speech, they were blocked.

The media couldn't really come for Liam; his misadventures were so far in the past, and so minor. The guy he'd been out with the previous September managed to get himself on TV for a minute, but nobody important took him seriously. Business associates and former colleagues all said supportive things, and if this was as bad as it ever got they would count themselves lucky.

Mark's agent was cautiously hopeful. If the nominations happened, there were good odds that Mark would get some fresh inquiries. If any of the nominations paid off with an award, he definitely would. Otherwise they might have to wait for pilot season, when a lot of actors could pick up work on short notice to get those 'buy this series' sample episodes made. He tried to conceal his anxiety on Wednesday night.

Liam, as usual, saw through it. "You don't need to worry. You're going to be fine even if none of those nominations come through."

"I hate being so dependent on other people." That could be heard a lot of ways, some of which Mark hadn't intended.

Liam didn't take it personally. "We all do, honey, and we all are." He ejected the last disc, turned off the TV, and stood up. "Let's go to bed and see if I can really knock you out." The prescription sleeping pills were long gone. The insomnia wasn't. Liam had learned a few tricks since May, though. When he woke up, Mark was still asleep. A quiet trip to the bathroom, then downstairs to wake up the computer, taking a moment to indulge a warm feeling because his lover had shared the password immediately, same as Liam. Finding the news story, staring at the screen as disbelief turned into a grin. He left the page up while he went to make coffee. He was sitting at the kitchen island, already done with breakfast, dressed and ready for work when Mark wandered in.

"I can't believe I slept so long." He came for a kiss before heading over to the coffeemaker. "You wouldn't have left without saying goodbye, would you?"

"Not a chance." Liam was smiling into his mug, trying not to give the game away. Except why not? "We have to go out for dinner tonight."

"Okay." Mark was pleased. Then he turned around, mug in hand, and got very suspicious. "What?"

"You might want to take a look at the news. There's a story on screen."

Mark blinked. "You're kidding."

"Go see for yourself." Liam watched him go, counting down.

A minute later, from the office: "Holy *shit*!"

Liam laughed. "Congratulations, honey."

Mark came tearing out of the office, grabbed Liam and kissed him hard, said "I love you," and disappeared again. Liam got himself ready to leave. He smiled all the way into Beverly Hills.

Later that morning he had enough time free to call Robert and tell him what was going on. "Got a minute?"

"Sure, yeah. We haven't seen you guys for a few weeks. Everything good?"

"Well, I'm moving at the end of the month, I think I might have mentioned that –"

"Yeah, about six times."

"And Mark has been nominated for an Emmy."

"The fuck!"

"I know!"

"That's great!"

"I know! We have to go out for dinner tonight. Any chance you and Jade could join?"

"Should be able to. I'll send him a text in a minute. Where and when?"

"I was thinking Ocean Prime, not before seven."

"Nice. If they're all booked up there's always Callender's."

"Seriously?"

"Hey, we like pie."

"I'll let you know as soon as I have something pinned down." Liam disconnected, looked up the number for his first choice, and felt no shame about saying, "Emmy nominee Mark Valance would like to know if you have a table for four this evening after seven." Amazingly enough, they did. A few minutes later, all the essential people had been informed. Liam put his phone away and went to take care of business. If he was going to get home to change clothes and then join the others on time, he had to be efficient.

They hadn't met up in person since before Alaska, so there was a lot to talk about even without the Emmy thing. After an initial round of hugs, a brief and intense period of attention paid to the menus was followed by Jade telling a story about his friend Shaya's ongoing and completely unromantic affair with WWE star Jonathan Morris. "So," he summed up, "if and when he decides to become a movie star full-time, I don't know what the hell she's going to do. She's like, once every other week is about as much as I can take."

Liam said, "I can imagine if you spend a night with that guy, you feel it for a while." Jade nodded, eyes wide. Mark laughed into his glass. Liam nudged him. "So what's the latest on Emily? We haven't heard from her since right after we got back."

"Moving next month," Robert said. "We have a new assistant training with her now. He's, eh." A shrug. "He's all right. We should do a thing at our place before she goes." A second later four phones were on the table. They were still coordinating things with Emily when the entrée plates arrived.

Once the date for the going-away party was set and they were all halfway through their meals, Jade said, "Robert's going to be my model again in September."

"Like last time?" Liam had seen the fundraiser drag pageant on YouTube the previous year. "I want to get there in person."

"We should definitely go," Mark said. "What's the theme?"

"Bond girls," Robert and Jade said together. "We're doing Pussy Galore," Robert added gleefully. "And hey."

Liam and Mark both said, "What?"

"Whoever drew that thing on Mark's website, I want him to draw me in costume."

"Uh, okay? He's a fourteen-year-old from Texas," Mark said. "And I'm not a hundred percent sure he could cope with a drag subject, but I'll certainly do my best to find out."

"There was a little bit of a skirmish," Liam said. He told the Alaska Teenagers story while they finished their meal.

Jade drank some wine. "Wow, that poor kid. And good job, Christopher."

"For real. He's great." Liam smiled at Mark. "Did you talk to him today?"

"I did." Mark looked around the table. "Could not have been more surprised. I can't help feeling it might be all the people who vote throwing me a bone to take with me on the way out."

"Well." Robert glanced at Jade, leaned back in his seat, and stared at Mark. "What if it is?"

Mark shook his head. "No idea. My agent was like, hot damn, but it's still a complete toss-up whether anything new comes in for me. Or at least, anything I'd want to do. And I'm still kind of," he hesitated, searching for the correct word. "Tired? I don't really feel up to diving back into that yet. I want to focus on Liam, and getting into a groove."

"Which works for me," Liam said, smiling. "I want to take our time with everything. If we had the rest of this year to settle into being together, get used to it, I'd love that."

"Plus we need to work on payback." Mark was looking at Jade. "My huge, enormous, bottomless IOU."

187

"Oh, forget about it. Totally worth it. I've known you a long time but I didn't really know you that well till all this started. All I knew about Liam was that Robert liked him best out of all the guys he dated –"

"Except you," Robert clarified.

"Except me, and we've got a lot in common. The four of us. This feels like," he paused for a moment, "well, it's kind of embarrassing to say this. But it feels like one of those friendships you have growing up, where you know everything about each other and you're in the same place. Only we're all heading into our second act, and it's great to have friends who know us *now*." A murmur of agreement. "Which reminds me. My friend Allen up in San Francisco and his wife are negotiating a divorce. He's going to marry his boyfriend as soon as it's legal in California."

"There are going to be a whole lot of weddings when that happens," Robert said, eyeing the diamond ring Jade was wearing.

Mark and Liam glanced at each other again. They weren't talking about that yet. Maybe after the Emmys, when Mark had a better idea what his career options were going to be. He steered them into a detour. "Have you two already started planning your honeymoon?"

"Debating," Robert said. "Between the two of us there's about a thousand places we'd like to go that we've never been."

"We haven't even figured out where to get married yet!" Jade saw their server coming. "Anybody want dessert?" Nobody did, but they weren't ready to go home. Everybody ordered coffee.

They sat around talking for almost another hour. When the check was finally dealt with, Liam made a move to go. "Some of us have office hours tomorrow," he said. "And I have to go back to my place tonight." He pushed back his chair and stood up.

"With me for the weekend, though, right?"

"Right." Liam leaned down to give Mark a kiss. "You be careful when you leave. Make sure your driver is right there."

"I will. Love you."

"Love you too." A quick caress, petting Mark's hair, then Liam shook hands with Robert and Jade. "See you soon."

"Soon," they echoed, and all watched him go. "He really is a hunk," Robert said.

"Hey." Jade gave it an offended spin, then turned to Mark and made a 'can you believe that' face.

"Well, he is," Mark said smugly. "*My* hunk." He listened to the other men laugh, thought *my friends, thank God*, and suddenly had an inspiration. "Hey, Jade. That thing, that picture Robert wants. What if there was one like that for every model in the show? Would those make money in the silent auction?"

"Jesus, yes. Why, do you think the guy would do them? You said he was a teenager."

"A teenager who needs money to buy a good graphics setup if he's going to have a real chance at an art career. Can you send me your contact for the fundraiser? And I'll ask Christopher if he's in touch with this kid." His phone beeped. "That's my driver gently reminding me he's about to go into overtime. This was great, guys. We'll see you soon."

CHAPTER 15

The next day, Mark had another ten thousand phone calls and messages, including one from Sherry Martinez at Pop Quiz. After disposing of all the others (mostly via his publicist and agent), he called her back. "Hi Sherry, thanks for your message."

"Mr. Valance! Thank you for calling. I was so pleased about the nomination, congratulations."

"Thanks, that was a really nice surprise."

"So can I record this call?"

"Sure, go ahead."

"Thank you so much, recording on. I wanted to ask how you're feeling about the future now?"

"Well, to be honest, I'm still trying not to think about it too much. After the awards will probably be a better time. At the moment I'm talking to my shrink, talking to Liam, talking to my friends and family. I have a lot of, how to say this." He paused for a moment. "There are people I've known all along who've had certain ideas about me. I've been presenting myself in a certain way, which the whole world now knows was not an honest way. People may or may not want to know the real Mark Valance, and it's going to take some time to work through all that. We're talking about a lot of people here."

"I hadn't thought about that, but of course. Wow. Is it super stressful? Worse than the other way?"

"Worse than hiding the truth? No. But it's still pretty stressful. I keep feeling like I need to apologize."

"Uh, okay. Even though it was actually nobody's business?"

190

He stifled a laugh. "It was some people's business. But the thing is, nobody likes being lied to. And I can't expect people to process that overnight. So that's very much on my mind, and I'm looking for ways to stay busy that are constructive that are not, you know, looking for a job."

"I've talked to enough other performers to know it's all about finding the next job. What are you looking into?"

"Well, actually, I'm writing a screenplay. I started one over the winter when I wasn't seeing Liam. We turned it into this correspondence, it was good cover for writing letters."

"Aww."

Mark smiled. "Yeah. Anyway it's about a doctor, which I knew nothing about, so he was my consultant. I've read a few hundred screenplays over the years, I think I have the structure down pretty well, but I keep fiddling with it. It's way too long."

"You could always turn it into a book," she suggested.

He stared at the phone for a few seconds. "I never thought of that." But why not? Why not take all the background material that didn't belong in a script, and … okay, he'd come back to this idea later.

Sherry was saying, "In fact, if you enjoy writing, you should write a memoir." She sounded excited now. "I'll bet there's people like me who are entertainment junkies who would love that. The inside scoop from a really different angle."

"Meaning, from someone who isn't looking back from the end of an illustrious career," he said. His tone was a bit dry. "You really think people would read that?" Now a bit skeptical.

191

"I totally do," she said. "There are a lot of people in the world who have big dreams but who haven't made it. Who will never make it. Maybe a story like that, facing up to what it takes to make it and why that is, or isn't, worth doing … well, I would read the hell out of it. Especially if you got some people to talk to you about their side of things."

"Other people who've come out?"

"Or people who didn't until they stopped working, or people who were always out. There must be some great images from projects you've worked on. I've been learning all about how to clear photos and stuff. Anyway, this is really none of my business, I will not mention any of that, let's move on. Who will you be wearing to the Emmy awards?"

He laughed. "Probably Kenji Matsumoto. He dressed Emily Lincoln all last winter."

"Ooh, yes! And will Liam go with you?"

"He most definitely will. By the way, Emily will be moving out of L.A. pretty soon. We're all going to miss her."

"I'd love to talk to her."

"I'll pass that on. And now I have to get on the phone to my son, but it's been a pleasure."

"Thank you so much, Mr. Valance. All the best to you." They disconnected. Mark sat still for a few minutes, thinking about the screenplay, and about his story, and about whether that really was what he wanted to do next. If nothing else, it would be a great exercise. He'd have even more to talk to Chris about. No need to make himself a note, there was no chance he'd forget this. And before he did anything else, he had to call this person at the Los Angeles LGBT Center.

That call answered one important question. The call to Christopher answered a few more. An hour later, Mark was at the computer writing a letter. It was going to be a surprise, and not necessarily a welcome one. He tried to make it as businesslike as possible while also still being cordial.

Dear Mr. Turner,

You're probably aware your nephew Louis is in touch with my son Christopher, which is how I have your address. Some friends of mine are involved with a fundraiser for the Los Angeles LGBT Center. Part of the event is a drag pageant with the theme 'Bond Girls.' If the very idea grosses you out, please feel free to throw this away and forget I ever mentioned it, but we have a proposal for a way Louis could make some money for his graphics computer and it's related to this event.

These friends have seen the artwork Louis did in June, of me and Dr. Byrne. One of them mentioned that he wanted a drawing of himself in his character for the pageant. Someone suggested we could have drawings of each of the models, and auction them off. As I mentioned, people will pay good money for artwork like that, especially if they think they're getting in on the beginning of an artist's career. We could display the drawing of me and Liam as a teaser.

The proposal is that I would commission a dozen drawings, based on photographs taken at the event in September. My lawyer could prepare a contract, which Louis' legal guardian would need to execute. I'm not sure if that would be you or one of his parents. The basic terms would be $200 per original drawing, all rights remaining with the artist (meaning nobody could publish or reproduce them without his permission). We'd need the drawings delivered within a month of whenever we get the images to him, properly packaged and shipped via FedEx.

If you want to look at last year's pageant (the theme was 'Fabulous Ladies of Literature'), the whole thing is online at the LGBT Center's YouTube channel. The models were designed by members of a local costume and makeup artists' union. It's very PG-rated.

I'd be happy to speak with you if you have any questions. And by the way, thanks for helping Louis get his phone. Chris is enjoying having a friend in Texas.

Best regards,

Mark Valance

He blew out a breath, read the letter about ten more times, tweaked a word here and there. Added his phone number and email address. Then he printed it out and signed it, got it ready to mail. The guy might not even tell Louis about it. Mark had cautioned Chris not to mention it, just in case.

He could have gone into detail about how work for hire was the way artists made a living, and it wasn't always going to be an artist's first choice of material, but that would have been too much. If the Turners decided to go for it, Louis would have his first professional gig. From there, who knew? Maybe he'd want to do book covers. A murder mystery set in a prep school might do great with a comic-style cover. *Settle down*, he told himself, smiling. All this inspiration shouldn't be wasted. He pulled up the doctor screenplay and dug in.

The going-away party for Emily would have been intolerable if they weren't there together. Liam didn't even have to ask Mark to know he felt the same. They caught each other's eye about a dozen times in the first hour. At a certain point they landed in the kitchen, needing a private moment as much as ever. Mark followed Liam in, saw him leaning against the counter waiting, and stepped into his arms. "It's wild, isn't it? This time last year, I didn't even know her. I didn't know you, or Robert. My whole life has changed."

Liam kissed his forehead. "Mine too. Last summer was not the best summer of my life. This one is much better." Mark laughed softly. Liam made a move suggesting a proper kiss; they did that for a minute. Then he eased back. "If I hadn't come in here at Thanksgiving, none of this would have happened, would it?"

Mark gazed at him for a few seconds. "I'd like to think I would still have gone public. But I might not have. I needed a reason to. If you hadn't come in at that moment I would have pulled myself together and eventually gone home thinking, well the tall guy was awfully good-looking but keep your focus. The show probably would have killed me earlier in the season, I would have spent the next few months getting some new job, and who knows. I might not even have stayed in Los Angeles."

"And I would have gone looking for somebody else to try again with. I'm so glad I didn't have to. I was not going to do better than you." Another light kiss. Mark was smiling. "Why does that make you smile."

"Because that's what I always think. I could not do better than you. You never thought about calling your guy in Minneapolis? He might be tired of the weather."

Liam laughed. "He grew up there. No, that wasn't a relationship I could have gone back to. We'd just about exhausted our possibilities. Not like Emily and her librarian."

"Shauna. Speaking of, let's go back out there. She's probably wondering what's wrong with us."

"No I'm not," Emily said from right outside the kitchen doorway. "But I've got the maps out and we're talking about what I have to see on the way north."

So they went back out to the living room, where three state maps were spread out on the coffee table. Everybody gathered around to debate while Emily looked things up on her phone. None of them had ever driven to Sacramento, much less into eastern Washington. "Jeez, that's a long way," Jade said after mapping a possible route.

"Through a whole lot of nothing," Robert said. "I mean, I'm sure it's very scenic."

Emily snickered. "You are not outdoorsy guys, I know. Liam and Mark should be more useful here."

"Uh, to be honest I've never been east of Bend in Oregon," Liam said. "I went to Crater Lake once."

Mark was apologetic too. "I've never been up that way at all. I've been to Seattle a couple of times, but that's it."

"Not even Portland?" Emily was scandalized. "I've been to Portland."

"Why did you go to Portland?"

"Because flights were on sale and why not. Well, the four of you are no good to me. My car passed its physical and it's not like I have a job waiting for me, so I'll cruise on up there however I want," she said, and began folding up the maps.

"Text me every day you're on the road," Mark said. "I want to know you're safe."

"Aww. Okay. And you all have to come visit sometime. Shauna's house is on the west side of town, there's a museum close by, and a riverfront park not far away."

"You're excited." Mark was smiling at her. "It's going to be really different."

"So very different." She scooted back to curl up on the couch. "Living in an actual house with an actual yard will be different. Getting snow in the winter. It's much more white there, and frickin' tiny compared to L.A., and there's the whole job thing to work out. But Shauna says she knows it might take a while for me to find the right job and I shouldn't worry about it." She nudged Mark. "Kind of like your situation."

"Kind of."

"Still glad you did it?"

"Are you kidding me?" He glanced at Liam. "I'd do it all over again." Looked back at Emily. "And I will never stop being grateful to you, right along with these guys. The thought of trying to get through that on our own is, well, it's a nightmare."

She patted his shoulder. "All I really did was cost you a ton of money and call your driver once. For that I have a lifetime's worth of stories about my big Hollywood year. I have already warned Shauna there will be an Emmys party."

Mark gazed at her affectionately. "The odds are very much against me winning."

"Don't care. I'll be tuned in from the start of the red-carpet broadcast, waiting to see you and Liam so I can squeal. And the whole time I'm going to be doing the Joan Rivers thing on all the dresses, which by the way Shauna told me to bring all of mine. No idea why. We may be having our own drag pageant someday. Fifty shades of Emily." All the men laughed. "God, I'm going to miss you." She hugged Mark, then got up and hugged Robert, then Jade, and finally Liam. "All of you in a row please, I need a picture. Nobody up in East Wash is going to believe I hung out with men this good-looking unless I have evidence." She lined them up against the wall, took a few pictures, and then had them all crowd around her for a selfie or three. They pretended not to notice she was a bit shiny-eyed.

On the way home Liam said, "We really should visit up there sometime. Maybe with Christopher? You haven't been to Glacier. It's not exactly close to Spokane but then it's not close to anything else, either."

"Road trip?" Mark was smiling. "I would love that. Fly into Spokane, see the girls, drive over to the park and back. There's a park you and I need to see by ourselves, though."

"Oh yeah? Which one?"

"Hawaii Volcanos."

Liam made an interested sound. He'd thought of that for a possible honeymoon trip. Now he wondered if Mark had the same thing in mind. He wondered if he'd know when the time was right to ask.

September 2011

Mark hadn't been so nervous about attending an awards show since his very first time. He and Liam were soberly dressed in tuxedos, walking down the red carpet

198

hand in hand. Half of him was thrilled; the other half felt like he had a target on his back. He wasn't even sure where that was coming from. His shrink would probably say it was an artifact of being closeted. Being afraid of something that could (might, probably wouldn't) happen. Even the nastiest comments about him since May hadn't been violent. He just felt so exposed.

"How are you doing?" Liam asked when they were still a few steps away from the first cluster of press.

Mark squeezed his hand. "Scared to death. I'm fine. It's nothing."

Liam squeezed back. "It's not nothing, but you're fine. We're fine." And they were fine. The questions weren't hostile, they didn't linger, and when they got inside there were people to talk to. People congratulating Mark, saying nice things about his work. Of course everyone was on their best behavior today. Everyone said they were pleased to meet Liam. He felt oversized and out of place, but the tuxedo was good armor. All he had to do was stand up straight and stay close to Mark.

Of the show's three nominations, his category was the first up. He truly didn't expect to win, so he wasn't terribly disappointed when he didn't. He applauded with everyone else, a warm smile on his face, and accepted a consolation kiss from Liam that actually meant more than any stupid trophy. Later in the evening, it was Jenny's category; he was genuinely invested in this one. Liam was holding his hand again; he was leaning forward in his seat as the presenter opened the envelope. Then he was bouncing to his feet, yelling "Yes!" Much to the amusement of the people around him, including Liam, who stood up to applaud Jenny too. They sat down again as she got to the podium.

"Well, wow," she said. "I have so many people to thank. You know this is my first time up here, and we always assume it's the last so there's a really strong temptation to mention everybody we ever knew, but I'll make it quick. First, thank you to my wonderful husband Matt. You make so many things possible for me. I love you. Next, the team at 'Ocean View,' all the talent in front of and behind the cameras." She named a few specific people. "And a special thanks to my friend and colleague Mark Valance, who helped me get here. Thanks to all the voters. I'm truly honored." She was ushered offstage.

Liam leaned over to nudge Mark with his shoulder. "That was nice."

"Yes, it was." The clip accompanying the nomination summary had been from the proposal episode. He was glad that was the last one TV viewers would see. The clip they played for his category was from earlier in the season. He blew out a breath. "Now I can relax."

"I'll make sure you relax later." Liam gave that a suggestive spin, turned his head to meet Mark's amused glance, and then settled down to pretending to care about the rest of the event.

Mark had invitations to a couple of post-event parties, but he didn't really want to go. He managed to track down Jenny and give her a hug, tell her how pleased he was, and shake her husband's hand. Then he and Liam made their way to the valet area and waited for their car.

"I could get used to this," Liam admitted as they were driven to Brentwood.

"It's nice not dealing with traffic, isn't it? I never had my own car in New York, and I never stopped hating having to drive so much to get anywhere in L.A." His phone vibrated again; it had been going off all evening. He dug it out of his pocket. Among the many new texts was one from Emily, who must have been following the results online. He read that one, snickered, and turned it around so Liam could see.

I waited till now because I thought the TV cameras shouldn't pick you up texting during the show. East Wash consensus is GODDAMMIT and also that other guy is a no-talent hack

Liam laughed. "It's a good thing she didn't send that during the show. Oh whoops here comes something else."

Other consensus is Mark Valance had the best-looking date

"Super true." Mark texted back *That was true last winter too*

Aww!! That was literally everybody in the room just now

I guess you're having fun up there

So much fun. Shauna is awesome. We have a Pride Pride and she is Mama Lion

Can't wait to meet her. What happens at the end of an East Wash Emmys Party?

Like I know? Fill you in later. OXO

OXO to you too. Mark waited a minute to see if Emily was going to write anything else, then put his phone away again. He and Liam were still leaning toward each other. He glanced up to make eye contact. "I really, truly loved being with you tonight. How bored were you?"

Liam stretched over enough to get a kiss, then sat back. "Not bored. It's way more interesting to be there live."

"In the good old days they did these things in a fancy restaurant or a hotel ballroom, and everybody sat around drinking while they handed out trophies. Well, I'm glad we got to do it at least once. You know, there's something else I've been meaning to do at least once."

"What's that?"

"Tell you when we get home." He didn't actually have to tell Liam, though. All he had to do was drop the fur-lined handcuffs on the bed.

CHAPTER 16

A couple weeks later they were out in their tuxedos again for the Los Angeles LGBT Center fundraiser. The main event room was packed, with bar-height two-tops set around the perimeter, a field of larger tables, and low café tables for two as a first row around the catwalk. Liam and Mark claimed their table in the back, then went to check out the auction display. It was two long tables set end-to-end, covered with copies of Ian Fleming books (ranging from current paperbacks to first editions), autographed memorabilia, and reproductions of James Bond movie props. On the wall behind the display was a row of four framed movie posters flanking a blown-up copy of Louis Turner's drawing of them. Liam stared at it. "Holy, wait a minute. Did you know about that?"

"Wow. No. I mean, I knew they were going to put it somewhere as a teaser. God, you really do look like a superhero."

They both kind of did. Liam couldn't deny he got a big kick out of it. He studied the table again. There were bid sheets for the twelve custom drawings laid out alongside the sheets for everything else. Their tickets for the night included a copy of the 2012 calendar that would be issued with photos of each of the models. Liam was pretty sure he wouldn't mind having any of those drawings on top of that. He was also sure he wanted Robert and Jade to have the Pussy Galore artwork. He wrote down a bid for each of the drawings, making a mental note to swing by regularly to top whoever else bid for Pussy.

They hadn't seen Jade yet; he was still in the adjacent breakout room helping Robert get ready. Mark wanted to work the room for a while. He knew plenty of people there. Liam wandered around with him, meeting and greeting. It was weird (though not unpleasant) being celebrity-adjacent like this. After a while the background music was dialed down and the emcee started reminding people to bid. The pageant would start in fifteen minutes. One more swing by the table to update Liam's bid, and they were back at their table. A server was there a few seconds later to make sure they had a beverage to go with the pageant. Of course there were James Bond-themed cocktails on the menu: Vesper, Americano, Old Fashioned. Mark and Liam both chose the Black Velvet, thinking that Guinness stout plus champagne was something they wouldn't come across just anywhere.

Mark said, "Did you notice they've got a Bond playlist too? Even the stuff that isn't from the movies sounds like it should be."

Liam hadn't really noticed, except when he recognized one of the movie themes. "Wonder what they're going to play when the models walk. I'll bet it's the classic theme." He was right. It was a remix, but definitely a version of the original theme. The first model out was Honey Ryder; the last would be Miranda Frost. The crowd was going wild. After Robert's walk, Liam leaned over to Mark and said, "This is even better than last year."

"They all get to be sexy this year."

"For real." They joined in the applause, asked for a pair of Americanos for their second drink, and waited for the next thing to happen. Liam kept an eye on the swag table; he had to update his bid three times before all the models and their stylists came out to mingle.

Shaya was there with May Day; Jade and Robert were right behind them. The last person out of the breakout room was Andy Martin. "Oh, he did the photography again this year."

"And this is your chance to meet him." Mark had mixed feelings about that. He and Andy weren't close friends; they'd stayed in touch in a casual way, but hadn't seen each other for five years. Plus he was the last guy Mark had been with before Liam. And he'd told Mark to do what Mark had finally done, which was blatantly for another guy. Would he be pissed off? Well, Mark would deal with that later. Right now they had to catch their friends. "You look amazing," he told Robert, looking up. With those high-heeled boots on, the guy was even taller than Liam.

"These are four-inch heels," Robert said, glancing down at his foot with an air of disbelief. "Last year they were three inches and I thought I was going to face-plant the whole time."

Jade shook his head. "At first, maybe. You got good at it fast."

"Thanks, baby. So I have to get over to the swag table and get my bid in!"

Liam said, "No you don't. I'm bidding on your artwork. Finally a good way for us to say thank-you for all the support." People were crowding the auction table; he narrowed his eyes. "In fact, I'm going over there to lurk."

Robert made a WTF face. "Liam! You don't have to do that."

Liam was already a few steps away; he smiled at Robert over his shoulder. "Yes I do."

"Resistance is futile," Mark said. "So let me hear your thoughts on the wig."

"I hate the wig so much. But letting my hair get this long so Jade could style the real thing was not gonna happen."

Mark was grinning. "Between the heels and the hair, which do you hate more?"

"Definitely the hair! It was like you in that 'Chicago' thing back in the day, though. No way to pull it off without the hair."

"For me it was the heels that were a challenge. I've been wearing wigs forever because red hair, well, let's say it isn't always in fashion."

Jade made a dismissive sound. "Yours is gorgeous. There are some varieties of red hair that can be, let's say, unfortunate." All three of them snickered. "I'm going to make the rounds and see what everybody else did."

"I'm going to go and pose for pictures." Robert went to lurk around the swag table with Liam.

"And I guess I'll hang out," Mark said to Jade, and headed back to their table. He could have gone over to the swag table too, but he thought Liam would enjoy having a few minutes with Robert. And it was a mob scene over there anyway. He was halfway-watching the crowd, halfway-listening to the music when he heard his name and looked over. "Andy. I was hoping I'd get a chance to talk to you."

"Mind if I join you for a few?"

"No, please. Liam is sitting on the bid sheet for the thing he wants, he won't be back till they close the auctions."

"They had a ton of good shit this year." Andy waved to a server. "God, thank you for coming over, can I get a Black Velvet and a bottle of water? Thanks. Anything for you, Mark?"

"Water here, too, thanks." When the server left he studied Andy for a moment. "Do these events give you flashbacks?"

Andy cracked up. "All those guys in the dressing room bitching about the heels and the hair? For real. So how's it been? I mean your personal stuff. I've been dying of curiosity but I didn't want to tack that onto the discussion about the artwork."

"Yeah, I know. Honestly? It's great. I'm so glad I did this."

"You did it the hard way."

Mark shook his head. "It was the only way I could see to improve my chances of a good outcome on the career side. I might have done it different if Liam wasn't willing to do it with me. So to speak." He watched Andy laugh. "I really hit the wall last Thanksgiving. Jade and Robert asked me over, and Liam was there, and something about the situation just tipped me over the edge. All this time I've thought, someday I should, but the fear always beat the frustration." He half-shrugged, smiling. "The things I was most afraid of haven't happened. Still don't know about my future employability, but I have some time before that's a real concern."

"Well, I'm glad you finally did it. Also for the record the beard was pretty hot, but I like the clean-shaven look better. You have a nice mouth." It sounded suggestive. Mark shook his head, smiling. "Okay, nothing ventured. Your gentleman friend seems to be all in."

"Jesus, yes. I know he wants to meet you. I told him about you."

Andy's eyebrows went up. "You did?!"

"Mm-hmm. The day after we met."

207

"Fuck, Mark. When you decide to talk you really don't mess around, do you." The server came back with drinks while Mark was laughing. Andy thanked her again and guzzled some of his Black Velvet, made a yummy sound, hid a small belch behind his hand. "Why?"

"It was part of a long conversation. I wanted to tell him the last time I was with somebody, and then it only seemed fair to tell him who, and why it was you."

"Wow." Andy thought about that for a few seconds. "Why *was* I the last one? That's a hell of a long time."

"Well." Mark drank some water. "The truth is, there was a lot right about you, and you were really great to me, and I was really pissed off with myself for not being ready. Not being willing to take the chance. There were lines I couldn't cross with you. I am grateful you drew those lines," he clarified. "Because I might have tried to make it into some kind of undercover thing, which would have been bad for both of us."

"Yeah. No bueno. And then when you were finally ready you met him, so," Andy shrugged. "Missed my chance."

He was smiling, but there was a tinge of regret. Mark leaned in a little. "There hasn't been anyone?"

"Oh, sure. But it's been a lot of almost and not quite and not now. Eh." He swallowed some more of the cocktail. "So you've taken a joint vacation, he's met your kid, you've met his family?" Mark nodded. "And you've been to the Emmys. What's next?"

"Keep settling in. Keep getting used to it. Neither of us has lived with anyone for a long time."

"God, if I ever get to that point, it's been *ages*. The last time I lived with somebody it was a girl." Mark laughed again. Andy started telling stories about living in West Hollywood with his friend Dana.

Over by the swag table, Liam kept one eye on his bid sheet and one eye on Mark. The auction clock was ticking down. He was going to be forking over a good chunk of change for the artwork, but it was only right that Robert and Jade got their Pussy Galore. The thought made him smile even though he was a bit nervous about Mark. Or about Mark plus Andy Martin. He told himself it was silly to be jealous. The son of a bitch was just really sexy, and he had history with Mark, and now that Mark was out of the closet things could be different. It was impossible to tell, from here, whether Mark was interested. He was an actor, and he was used to concealing his interest. *Stop it, he loves you.* Whatever Andy was talking about was funny. Mark glanced his way, and because Liam was staring at him they made eye contact. Mark smiled. He said something to Andy, still looking at Liam. Andy twisted around, spotted Liam, said something to Mark. They shook hands. And then the photographer was on his way across the room. *Oh fuck.* Liam tried to look as though he had no bad thoughts about anyone ever.

"Dr. Byrne."

"Mr. Martin." They shook hands. Liam tried on a smile. "Call me Liam."

"Thanks, I will, and I'm Andy. Mr. Martin always makes me look around for my dad. Mark told me you're after one of the original drawings."

"Yeah, I'm going to get Pussy Galore for Robert and Jade. A thank-you present. We owe them a lot."

"That's what he said. So this kid is quite a talent. When Mark emailed me about it I was like, really? But then I checked out the drawing on his website and thought, okay. What did you think of him?"

"The kid? Confused, sad, frustrated. But definitely talented. Up in Alaska he drew a portrait of a tour pilot that belongs on a movie poster."

"It's good he's using art to help get him through that. I've always felt so lucky that my parents stayed together."

"Jesus, me too."

"So," Andy lowered his voice a little. "Mark told me he told you we had a fling back in the day. You don't need to worry about that. I'm not going to be coming for him just because he's out in the world. He's happy with you."

Liam didn't know what to say for a second. He swallowed. "I, uh, thanks. Did he tell you I cyber-stalked you?"

Andy laughed. "No, he didn't."

"Well, I watched 'All That Jazz,' and I was thinking okay, no wonder." Andy laughed again. Liam was smiling now too. "Oh hang on." He lunged for the bid sheet. "Sneaky bastard." The emcee was doing a countdown. Liam was half-aware that Andy was taking a picture of him writing in the last bid, physically warding off the other person bidding, both of them laughing. Then the auction was over. "Ha! Suck it. Okay." He turned back to Andy. "Thanks for coming over to talk to me. I was watching the two of you and getting a little wound up."

"Be sure and tell him that," Andy said, smiling. "I think he'd find it flattering that you were jealous." He offered his hand again; Liam shook it. "See you."

"See you," Liam echoed, and watched him go. Watched him fetch up beside one of the models, instantly beginning to flirt. Liam headed back over to Mark. "Got that drawing."

"Good work. Right up to the last second, wasn't it?"

"There was a lot of action on all of them, you should tell Louis."

"I'll tell Chris and let him pass it on. So," he paused, "everything okay?"

"Everything's good. I love you."

"I love you, too. Give me a kiss." They did that. It was a thrill every time.

October 2011

Two months into living together, they were finding their groove. The daily routine was running smoothly and their sex life was great. Mark stopped worrying about being the perfect housewife. Liam stopped worrying about taking up too much space in the townhouse. His work schedule let them both use the kitchen, gym, and office without getting in each other's way. They were seeing friends regularly. Going out to dinner at least once a week. The press still poked around here and there, but there was never anything particularly annoying. The only problem was, Mark still hadn't decided what to do with the rest of his life.

"Is it a problem?" he asked one Sunday morning, when they were lying in bed post-coitally contemplating the day.

Liam turned his head, which was the only part of his body he wanted to move at the moment. "Is what a problem?"

"That I still don't know what I want to do."

"Is that accurate, though? You've been working on that screenplay. If the questions you ask me are any indication, you've been doing a fuck-ton of research for it."

Mark thought about that for a minute. Liam didn't know he was now working on a book version too. For some reason he felt shy about saying so, which was ridiculous. He could say anything to Liam. "You have a point. I guess research is something I always did as part of a job. The truth is, I started turning it into a book."

"No shit! That's great. How's it going?"

"It's amazingly easier than writing a screenplay," he confessed, and felt Liam's silent laughter. "I don't have to obsess about how would they film this, I can just tell the story."

"Well, it sounds like being a writer is your job for a while. Would it help to talk to somebody else who's made a career switch? I keep going back to that, you know." He turned onto his side, propped his head on his hand, and gazed at his lover. One of these days he was going to ask one of those questions. He didn't want to do it while Mark was in this limbo, though. Didn't want to risk it sounding like he thought Mark was going to be his dependent. They were splitting expenses, and that was its own special negotiation. Mark was giving him a 'what' look; Liam dragged his thoughts back on track. "What would I do if I couldn't be a doctor, I mean. I have no Plan B. Never did."

Mark blinked. "Wow. I never thought of that." He turned as well, getting comfortable for what might be a longer conversation than they usually had in bed. "Are there options? You could teach, right?"

"Mmm. Possibly. Go into some clinical research kind of thing. But like if I couldn't use my hands the same way, if I lost the fine motor control, I couldn't even give injections. There's some of my job I could still do. Consulting, exams, and analysis. I might be more effective in the oncology space than the cosmetics, which is more of where I am now."

"So if you were thinking ahead. Like if you could see into the future and you knew you were going to have to step sideways somewhere along the line. What would you do?" Mark was thinking out loud, not really trying to push Liam into some kind of strategy session. Then he heard himself. "Oh jeez that's kind of, sorry."

Liam wriggled closer and leaned in for a kiss. "No, it's a good question. I'm going on forty-four. It would be great to have twenty more years of the same kind of practice, but I shouldn't assume that's going to be the case." He nuzzled Mark's face, brushing his lips across coppery stubble. "The loans have been paid off for years. For the longest time I was just, you know, not spending that money. Maybe I should spend some of it on learning new tricks."

"You could run studies," Mark suggested. "Be an administrator. Be an executive. Go to work for one of the evil pharmaceutical companies." Liam was laughing under his breath. Mark kissed him again, taking his time with it. "I really love you."

"I really love you, too. Will you marry me?" He heard himself and thought *fuck*. But Mark was smiling, so he doubled down. "Serious question."

"Serious answer. Yes." He squeaked as Liam launched, pressing him down, kissing him. Both of them laughing, with tears in their eyes. Two hours later, when they were finally out of bed, showered, and fed, Mark returned to the original topic of conversation. "The thing is, I do know someone who's made the switch, but I

213

wasn't sure you'd want me talking to him again so soon."

"What? Why?" The penny dropped. "Oh. To be honest, I'd love to meet him again in not such a mob scene. But if you want to talk to him on your own, that's fine too. I'm not jealous." Not now. How could he be jealous when he had all of Mark? That guy only got one weekend. "You should give him a call."

Mark didn't question it. He got up to find his phone, running a hand over Liam's head as he returned to the table, saying nothing about the wiry gray hairs showing up here and there. Sat down, scrolled to the number, pressed 'call' and then put it on speaker. Two rings, and then, "Andy Martin."

"Hi Andy, this is Mark Valance. I wasn't expecting to catch you."

"You wouldn't have if somebody's wedding didn't get cancelled. What's up?"

"Well, you'll be relieved to hear that I'm not going to complicate your life by demanding copies of event photos this time." He had to stop talking because Andy was laughing.

"Uh, good." Andy cleared his throat. "How's Dr. Byrne?"

"He's great. He's sitting right here."

Liam said, "Hi Andy."

"Hi. So what can I do for you."

Mark said, "Long story short, trying to plan my second act, wondering if you had any advice for me. Or maybe just some how I did it kind of stuff."

"Oh, I can talk about myself all day. Why don't you guys come over? Since I unexpectedly have the day off."

Mark and Liam exchanged a glance; a 'why not' face; a shrug. Mark said, "Sure. Want to text me your address? Oh wait, you're not out in the Valley are you?" Liam stifled a snort.

"Jeez, it's been forever, hasn't it? No, I'm at the Brewery now, north of downtown. Yes. Coordinates coming in a minute. Bring food, I was planning to scam some from the caterers, fucking runaway bride." He disconnected without waiting for an answer.

Mark and Liam stared at each other for a few seconds, on the edge of cracking up. "Well," Liam said, "I guess we have a plan for the afternoon."

"I guess so." The text came in as they stood up to go get dressed.

Liam didn't know what to expect from the Brewery. It was one of those places that he sort-of knew existed, but had never even contemplated visiting. "This is a trip," he said as they made their way up a series of staircases and ramps. "How do you – oh, okay." Andy's door was standing open. They stepped through into a mostly-empty, all-white space. The only color came from a shelf of books over the built-in desk spanning the far wall. To one side was a huge multi-paned window; to the other, a loft over enclosed spaces that must be kitchen and bathroom. The only soft furnishing was a big slipcovered couch.

"Hi guys." Andy got up from one of the task chairs by the desk. "The apologetic but emphatic email submitting my cancellation-fee invoice has been sent. I am officially done for the day. What did you bring?"

"A little of everything. This is some space." Mark was looking around. If not for the two big monitors and the books – all about graphics, photography, and art – it would be difficult to guess Andy's profession. He didn't even have any framed work up on the wall. The space was big enough to dance in but there was no sign he ever did. No signs of his previous profession at all. Mark squashed the impulse to ask.

Liam followed Andy into the kitchen and started unpacking deli bags. "Thanks for asking us over. Mark's been talking to a few people here and there but everyone kind of assumes he's going to go back out on the audition round pretty soon."

"And you're not sure you want to do that?" Andy gave Mark a glance. He set three mugs by the coffeemaker and got half-and-half out of the fridge.

"I've been doing some writing," Mark said. "It was initially a justification to correspond with Liam while I was getting off the show, but it's turned into an oversized screenplay and maybe a book." They talked about that while they ate, which started with piling things on plates and taking them over to the couch. Andy sat on one of the task chairs, facing his guests. After finishing his snack, Mark sat back and said, "I want to take it seriously, I guess. There's no deadline, so I keep fiddling with it. And I'm beginning to think I should have done something else with it."

Andy took a sip of coffee and set his mug on the desk "Well, like what?"

"Okay, so." Mark bought some time with coffee. Liam took his empty plate and set it on the desk with the other things. "It's not a romance, but there's a romance in it, because I like movies where the main character has a relationship. I made it a straight relationship because I thought that would be more commercial, and now I'm annoyed with myself because who cares? It's a spec script. There's a very small chance anyone besides us will ever read it, and if by some miracle somebody

216

wanted to produce it they'd have stuff to change anyway."

"So, make it a non-straight relationship." Andy set his plate on the desk and got his mug back, holding it in both hands, smiling. "Like you say. Why not? Who cares? In fact, that might even make someone pick it up. They'll see it's by you, they'll see it's about a doctor, they'll instantly assume you've been inspired by Liam, and they'll be disappointed if you have your doctor in bed with a girl." Liam laughed. Andy shot him an amused look. "Of course if you have him in bed with a guy don't get too descriptive or they'll assume that's what you do in bed. They'll be all, oh! Now we know."

Mark cracked up. "I'll write that scene for our eyes only."

Liam gave him a nudge. "How hard would it be to change that?"

"Oh, not at all. There's nothing stereotypically female about her except the name and the pronouns. I mean, she's a medical professional too. The story didn't call for, like, her trip to the nail salon."

"You do have them going out for dinner. Which is a very gender-neutral activity." Liam liked this idea. It was flattering on a lot of levels that Mark started the project in the first place, that he stuck with it, and that he used so much that Liam told him. If it had a gay romance in it too, he'd be thrilled. "Maybe there'd be another way to get them out of the medical center. I remember you said you wanted to."

"I don't have a good frame of reference for grown-up male-female dating," Mark admitted. "Kerry and I went from college to being married. If you have characters going to the theater or something like we do,

217

even restaurants, that's expensive to shoot. I wouldn't want more than one of those scenes in the script."

Andy suggested, "Some kind of sport? All you need is a couple of guys and a court. Or a golf course. Except, golf." He wrinkled his nose.

Liam was smiling. "Not a fan?"

"I dated this golfer for a minute. Never shut up about it. I was like, mention your five-iron one more time and I will shove it up your ass."

Liam choked back a laugh. "That sounds familiar. What was his name?"

"Bob."

"Bob the golfer." Liam nodded. "Yep."

"Oh shit, Jade dated that guy too." Mark was laughing. "Okay. So maybe my doctor plays tennis. Wait, you don't have any awful tennis dating stories, do you?"

"No," Liam and Andy said simultaneously. Liam added, "I have some awful basketball stories. People tend to think I should play because I'm tall."

"Ugh, no. I hate games involving projectiles, even inflatable ones." Andy put up a hand in a warding-off gesture. "Actually, I hate games, period." Mark laughed again.

"The guy I lived with in Minneapolis played hockey," Liam volunteered. "There were a lot of jokes about who gives a flying puck." Andy and Mark both groaned. Liam got to his feet and started taking plates back to the kitchen. "So why don't you have any of your artwork up on the wall?"

Andy was right behind him. "It's distracting. I shoot a lot of stuff here. When I have a show going, it's wall to wall prints, but the rest of the time I like to keep it clean."

"That's a good segue." Mark came in for a refill of coffee. "How did you decide this was going to be your next act?" He leaned on the counter. So did Liam.

Andy swallowed some coffee and shrugged. "I'm the guy who needs something to do. There's a lot of downtime when you're doing a show. Started taking snapshots behind the scenes, and after a while I thought, I should try to make something out of this. So that's it, really. Digital was a lifesaver."

"And I feel like a dick because I haven't been to any of your shows since the first one." Mark glanced at Liam. "He hung it in this dance studio in WeHo, it was these really spooky nighttime shots of L.A. with one model. Like, no other people. I loved it." Focusing on Andy again. "When's your next one?"

"March, probably. Want me to tip you off when it's opening?"

"Definitely. So." He made a move toward the main room. Time to get down to business.

CHAPTER 17

All three of them trooped over to the couch. This time Andy joined them, curling up in one corner. Mark sat in the middle. He thought for a second, wanting to start with the most important thing. "After the Emmys, I got a lot of inquiries. But everything was so fresh and kind of raw, and I wanted to focus on Liam. I still do. I'm not going to do the part-time lover thing, or the long-distance thing. Now it's been quite a while since I was in front of a camera and," he made an 'eek' face, "the truth is I miss it. But I'm not sure if it's performing I miss, or simply having a job."

"I miss performing," Andy said. "But, you know." He produced an uncomfortable-looking wriggle. "I didn't want to be out there fighting with the other two dozen old guys for the one part –"

"You're not old," Liam said. "You can't be old, we're practically the same age." Mark reached over to pat him.

Andy rolled his eyes. "If you'd've seen me the morning after a performance my last year out, you'd know what I mean. Anyway, and I didn't want to be fighting with the two hundred young guys for a chorus part. It was time, and the only reason I'm talking about it today is I know you get it. Doing 'Chicago' was like pulling off a scab. This is," he hesitated. "I was going to say better but it's really just easier. Someone not liking a particular image I created is not the same as someone not liking me up on stage, and I can do this until I die. So." He shrugged. Looked at Liam. "The thing is, I was a dancer. There was always going to be a last show. I wanted to leave the stage on my terms."

"I understand. We were talking this morning about what's *my* Plan B. I honestly don't have one. But I should be thinking about it, because there are physical limitations for my work, too."

"Of course there are. Listen, can I digress?"

"Jeez, Andy, it's your house."

He made a grand of-course-it-is gesture. "So I sent off those photos and got a confirmation back from the kid. He's been in touch a couple of times."

Mark winced inside. "He's not being a pest, is he?"

"Oh no not at all, it's fine. He asked for some advice about gear." He hooked a thumb over his shoulder to indicate the computer setup. "And I had a thought. This is professional photo guy stuff. It's not what I started with. And that stuff is not state of the art anymore, but I still have it, and it would be good entry-level stuff for the kid."

Mark blinked; turned to make eye contact with Liam, who made a well-why-not face; turned to Andy again. "Are you serious?"

"It's literally just sitting in my storage unit with my display walls, some unsold prints, and one million spiders. You know it's not worth the trouble to sell old computer equipment, or I would have," he added. "But I'd be happy to give it away to someone who would use it. There's all the software, manuals, all that crap."

"You are seriously awesome." Mark thought fast. "If you could package it up and ship it, I'd reimburse you. My kid will be excited. They're talking about Louis doing a cover for his book."

"Well, tell him I want an advance copy. Okay, that's done. Now Mark, what would you do if you had complete control of the career situation?"

221

The question was so abrupt that Mark was caught off guard. Even though it was close to what he'd been asking himself for over a year. "I think," he began, then shook his head. "You know how there are teaching hospitals?" Liam and Andy both nodded. "I think I'd love to work in a teaching theater. Really get back to the stage, to the nuts and bolts of it, helping people learn the mechanics of the environment. Then building a play from the ground up. Who was the writer, when and how and where did they live, why this story. Why these characters, and why these words. I did some Shakespeare every year in New York, for twelve years. The workshops we did were so satisfying. And I haven't gone near it since." Liam closed a hand on Mark's shoulder, shook him gently.

"I don't know anything about Shakespeare. The closest I ever got was 'Kiss Me, Kate.' But there's a ton of it here in L.A." Andy made a self-mocking face. "I mean, I only know because my friends Dana and Rory are always trying to get me to go with them."

"Maybe I should talk to those people," Mark said, smiling. "Dig into what's going on. Pick up a job here and there to make a little money, and then do Shakespeare."

"Sounds good to me." Liam patted his shoulder. "I seem to remember reading a play about somebody named Henry, back in high school. So you don't have to worry about me saying, jeez, not that again." Mark laughed. They wrapped up the conversation not long after that, feeling that they had more to talk about between them but maybe it was time to let Andy have his space back. On the way home, Liam said, "Was that helpful? I felt like it was helpful."

"Oh, definitely. Part of it is, I guess, giving myself permission to miss it. But figuring out exactly what I

222

miss, that's going to be key. I really appreciate your support."

Liam glanced over from the driver's seat, then back at the road. "We probably need to talk about money again. Since you mention support. I don't want you thinking you have to go out and take a job."

Mark heard the emphasis on 'have to' and suppressed a sigh. "I know you don't. I've got, it's, you know I've had so much help. My parents were propping me up until I was twenty-six."

"So? I racked up debt. Nobody does it alone."

"Okay, but you paid off all that debt by yourself."

Because I had nothing else to do with my money, Liam thought and didn't say. Him not having much of a life for fourteen years was not the point. "Do you feel like you should have paid your parents back, or something?"

"Yes." Mark heard the reflexive response. "No." Liam huffed out a laugh. Mark threw up his hands. "I don't know. They said I didn't need to. I know I didn't need to, they make a ton of money. When I bought the townhouse my dad was pleased. He said that was exactly what I should be doing with my money. They didn't let Kerry pay them back, either. She quit mentioning it after Christopher was born."

"You know the only reason I have disposable income is I didn't buy a house," Liam pointed out. "You have the house, I have the income. It's a good balance. And you know you're going to get something eventually. The right project will come along. So I'm not going to insist that you join the group health plan. You can stick with your fancy-pants union plan." He heard an amused sound. More seriously, he added, "If it

223

were me, I'd assume more work is in the pipeline. Even if it takes a while."

"I might unload my publicist, though." Mark had been thinking of that for nearly a year, too. "I feel slightly guilty about it but the real reason I needed her doesn't exist anymore."

"Then save yourself a buck and say goodbye."

"Yeah." They were quiet the rest of the way. Mark was mostly thinking about how this marriage was going to be so very different from his first. In so many wonderful ways.

Liam noticed the smile after he turned off the car. "You look like you stopped worrying for a minute there."

Mark leaned over and kissed him. "I started thinking about our wedding."

"Oh." Liam smiled against his mouth. "That's nice."

"Let's get inside, get a drink, get on the phone and tell our people."

"All of them?"

"Absolutely." Of course, before they could do that, they had to think about all the things, because people were going to have all the questions. It didn't take long to decide on having the actual wedding in December in New York, followed by a January honeymoon on the Big Island. In between, they'd go down to San Diego to party with Liam's family. And after getting home, they'd have a party here in Los Angeles. Mark suggested putting his mother in charge of organizing their ceremony; Liam was perfectly fine with that. He suggested he could take care of booking the honeymoon; Mark was perfectly fine with that. An hour of brainstorming later, they were on the phone.

When they were finally done talking, both phones went on their chargers and Liam said, "Whew. That was really fun, but I'm exhausted."

"You're probably hungry. It's hours since we ate."

"That's an excellent point."

Mark stood up, stretching his back. "Why don't you find us a bottle to open and I'll see what I can throw together. And hey."

"Hmm?"

Mark leaned over the couch and kissed his fiancé. "I love you. I'm unspeakably happy about marrying you."

Liam smiled up at him. "All of that. I'm so glad I was right in front of you when you hit the wall."

"God, me too." Mark kissed him again, straightening up with reluctance. "I never want to stop kissing you." He shook himself and left the den, heading for the kitchen.

Liam watched him go, thinking about kissing Mark some more after dinner. Or, more accurately, about cleaning up the kitchen and then going directly to bed.

November 2011

For a man who was technically unemployed, Mark spent an awful lot of time conferencing with people. It seemed like every week, there was something going on. This producer, that director, a screenwriter, a reporter. He was doing a lot on social media, especially Twitter. There was an ongoing conversation about what was happening on Broadway, in the West End, and (to a lesser extent) in Los Angeles. Liam was aware of it, without being involved. He knew Mark was working on the doctor projects. But the stack of scripts in the home office kept growing.

He wanted Mark to embrace all the opportunities that might come his way. But he was terrified, because one of those opportunities was bound to take him away. And now that he could be who he was, how could he be content with this tame, domestic routine? Why should he be? He wasn't even forty.

Liam kept his fears to himself. They'd only known each other for a year, had truly been together less than six months. It was too soon to start worrying. He was positive that Mark sincerely loved him, that they would get married as planned, that living together would continue to be this sweet and comfortable thing. He had to remind himself that Mark liked being married, that he wanted to be married, and that Liam's past relationship failures had nothing to do with their situation. It would all work out. It was just that he really hadn't expected so much to be happening on the career front, after so little time. Then he had to remind himself that nothing actually was happening. It was all talk, and that pile of scripts.

So much started from that concert in March. It hadn't been a big event, only Mark and a pianist, at Herb Alpert's place. It wasn't a huge crowd; full, but not packed. An appreciative audience, but not a standing ovation. The whole thing was on YouTube now. At first only two songs were uploaded, but Mark's lawyer cleared all the others after the Emmy nomination. And Liam knew too much about the business now. He had to wonder, if he'd known this much last year, would he have called? Would he have dared to believe that someone like Mark could be satisfied with someone like him? All that talent, all that ambition: he had to want more. It was a strain trying to keep all that bottled up.

226

Trying to trust, and believe, and see what happened next. At the same time, trying to get every bit of love that he possibly could, in case this was all he ever got.

They were planning to go to Robert and Jade's again for Thanksgiving. It would be the same guest list, except for Emily, still happily unemployed in Spokane. Could have gone there; could have gone to New York; could have gone to San Diego. Instead they were going back to the beginning, and (in his most insecure moments) Liam hoped it wasn't simply a bookend to their relationship.

Especially after he saw the letter from England. He didn't snoop in the home office, he really didn't, but it was lying there on the desk. Which he remembered thinking was oddly uncluttered, after the fact, when he was in the home gym trying to work off some of his anxiety.

And he broke. They were done eating, lingering at the kitchen island as they often did. Mark seemed preoccupied, and Liam only meant to ask if everything was all right. Instead he said, "Are you going to London?"

Mark looked up, startled. "What? No. Why did you think I might be going to London?"

"I saw that letter. I wasn't." He stopped talking. There was no point claiming he wasn't trying to see what Mark was up to. Obviously he was, and now he was asking. He closed his eyes. "I'm sorry."

"Sweetheart." Mark touched his hand, watched how he flinched away, eyes still closed. Grasped that hand and held it. "Sweetheart." Softer. "I'm not going to London. Or to New York, or Toronto, or even San Francisco. I don't want to go anywhere unless it's with you."

"You shouldn't say no to things like that."

Mark couldn't read the tone. "Do you want me to say yes?"

"No." Liam instantly rejected the slight emphasis on 'want.' He opened his eyes. "I want you here with me. But that was huge. Even I know that was huge."

"Yes, and it was a minimum eighteen-month commitment a whole day of travel away." Mark wasn't sure what else he should say. He'd never dreamed Liam thought Mark might leave. Hadn't they both said, don't leave? After a moment he thought *I have to break it down*. "Yes, all right. There was a moment when I thought, do I want to. Huge new musical, everyone in the world knows the story, they're using a lot of the same music, it's going to be an absolute smash, except maybe it isn't. So many things can go wrong with any kind of show. The expectations will be sky high. Liam, they only contacted me because I have some buzz and there was that video. You must have seen that."

Liam nodded. It was right there in the first paragraph, 'we saw you do 'Pure Imagination' and we want you to come and be a part of this.' Meaning they wanted Mark to play Willy Wonka, and who would pass that up? "You seriously don't want to do it?"

"I don't."

It sounded so definitive. "How is this going to be enough for you?" Again, not at all what he meant to say, and it came out in a rush.

Mark was bitterly regretting his cavalier approach to the scripts, strewn all over the office. Obviously Liam had spent the past two months seeing all that material come in and counting the days till Mark said yes to something. "Liam. Do you remember when I said I'm choosing love?" A silent nod, eyes averted. "Can you possibly think I've had anything close to enough of you? Of being with you? After what we had to go through to get here?"

"But you thought your career would be over."

Now he was almost angry. "Oh, so it was the flip side of eighteen years ago. Instead of definitely career versus maybe love, I had maybe career and definitely love. And being a person who hedges my bets I came down on the side with better odds? Liam, *everything* was a maybe last year. You could have changed your mind at any time. God knows I expected you to."

"You what?"

Mark didn't hear him. "And if I didn't want you more than my career I had six months to tell you so. Six months to say, you know what, I'm sorry. Going back to New York to be with my family and start over on Broadway. I don't *want* to start over. Maybe someday I'll get some kind of offer I'll accept, but the thing that'll make it acceptable is that it will be *here*. I haven't said yes to anything, I've recycled all that crap. The only reason I even kept that letter was so I'd have something to back up the stories I'll tell about it someday. Liam, for fuck's sake let's get away from this mess." He stood up, clinging to Liam's hand. Couldn't have cared less about cleaning up from dinner.

Liam got to his feet, still stuck on, "You expected me to change my mind?"

"Why wouldn't you?" Mark turned to face him. "You knew me for two days, during which I made scenes and promised you six months of heartache and loneliness. Presented you with evidence of a lifetime of deception. Asked you to be faithful to me while I was running around town with somebody else."

"You didn't ask me for that." Liam put his arms around Mark, not at all surprised to find he was shaking. "I'm so sorry. I didn't mean to upset you."

"I didn't mean to upset you either." Slightly muffled against Liam's shoulder. "I was curious, that's all. With those scripts. To see what people thought I could do. There are so many things I haven't done. But none of it's important. *You're* important. You're everything."

"We need to be in bed right now."

"Yes, we do." So they went to bed, not to make love but to hold each other, and kiss, and murmur reassurances.

CHAPTER 18

After a while Liam fell asleep. Mark didn't. He lay there in their quiet room, unable to quiet his mind. Might as well get up. Out of bed – he never worried about waking Liam up; nothing short of a 6.5 earthquake would – and back down the stairs to the kitchen. Clearing up, washing up, brain churning. He was obviously not getting this right. He didn't know how to do it. Being with Liam was not like being with Kerry. They were still figuring out their roles. And of course when he lived with Kerry, he was working. He'd had a reason to be out of the house, be with other people, be engaged with the world. Now he barely went anywhere by himself, never saw anyone except their few mutual friends, and was all too aware how few those were. All the people he used to work with were only Twitter contacts now.

He swiped the back of his arm over his face, furious to be crying again. So what if it was only normal, as his shrink claimed. His shrink who did work that was important, who had a job that would never go away because there were always going to be fucked-up people like Mark. A job like Liam's, doing something that people needed, not pointless bullshit like a TV show. *What am I going to do.*

"Mark?"

Oh shit. He was doing that thing again, leaning on the counter again, losing his grip again. If he tried to talk he was going to scream.

"Mark, what's going on? Are you okay?" He clearly wasn't okay. His breathing was all wrong, too fast, too shallow. He wouldn't turn to look at Liam,

231

whose concern ratcheted up fast. Oh fuck, he was crying too, these awful hiccupping gasping sobs. Liam felt like a monster. This had to be his fault. "Come on, honey, talk to me." Jesus, it was getting worse. Liam got his arm around Mark, eased him down to the floor. It wasn't difficult; Mark's legs folded like wet spaghetti. "Get your head down, honey. You're hyperventilating. Slow down. Deep breath. One, two, three, four. Hold it, two, three, four. Now exhale, two, three, four. Again, in, nice and slow. Hold it there. I love you. Exhale, nice and slow. There you go. One more time. Honey, I'm so sorry."

Both of them were on their knees, Mark's body resting against Liam's, sheltered and supported. Liam's hand on the side of his face, brushing through his hair, as that low voice rumbled reassurance. Mark got enough distance from feeling like he was about to die to realize he was face-down across Liam's lap. Liam was curled over him protectively. *I have to say something.* Mark didn't know what to say. Didn't know how to admit how lost he was, because that would make Liam feel like he was doing something wrong, and he wasn't. But he had to say something, because Liam thought he was doing something wrong right now, or he wouldn't keep saying he was sorry. "I don't know what to do." His voice sounded (and felt) raw. "I don't know who I am anymore."

Liam was so out of his depth. He wanted to say 'you're mine' but that wasn't about Mark; it was about him. And that wasn't enough of an identity for someone like Mark, anyway. If he couldn't be a doctor anymore, how would he feel? How would he cope? He'd never even thought about it, not the emotional side. What if he were in an accident, or had a stroke, and couldn't use his hands the same way? He should think about these things. Make a plan. Oh, shit, that was what Mark was trying to do with the scripts and all that stuff, and Liam made him feel like he was in the wrong. "You are Mark Valance, same as ever," he said softly. "Better than ever, because now you don't have to lie. You're an actor, a singer, a dancer, a writer. You're a good father. You're a smart and talented guy who will figure out the next act. Give yourself a minute. Let me take care of you. I need a plan, too. We're still not even used to living together. We have so much to learn. I want to help you, and I need you to help me. Tell me what you need." He stopped talking, because he wasn't sure this was doing any good at all. At least Mark felt like he was calm now. Liam didn't move. Wouldn't move until Mark did. "I am not leaving," he said. "No matter how much of a mess we are."

Mark huffed out a breath that was some fraction of a laugh. "I'm not either. You're stuck with me and this mess."

"That's what I want. I'm going to marry you." Another quiet moment. "Are we ready to get up off the floor?"

"Mmm. I'm sorry." Mark got a hand out from under himself, put it on the floor, pushed himself up off of Liam.

"Don't be sorry. Don't ever be afraid to feel what you're feeling." They were untangled, but still on the floor. Liam got to his feet with a wince. "Speaking of feeling, I think I need to stretch more." He put a hand down. Mark accepted the help standing up, then took a step into Liam's waiting arms. They stood there for another minute. Liam patted Mark's back. "Come on honey. Think you can sleep now?"

"Mm-hmm."

"Let's talk tomorrow night, after dinner. I want you to tell me about those scripts, and why they weren't things you wanted to go out for. Okay?"

"Okay."

Mark spent some time the next day thinking back through the past year of sessions with his shrink. There must have been advice. Suggestions. Ideas. It was never anything concrete, like 'start a podcast' or 'go to church.' But there was more to it than simply talking to the guy about his feelings. He was sick of talking about his feelings, anyway. Sick of thinking about himself as this problem to be solved. He didn't want to be a problem for Liam. He wanted to be the person who solved problems. "Huh," he said out loud. That was a new thought. What problems did Liam have, that Mark could help solve? Did he have any? The fact was, Mark didn't know, because he'd been so solipsistically obsessed with his own shit the whole time they'd known each other. It was definitely time – past time – to start asking Liam what he needed to make *his* life better.

On one level, Mark understood that it was. Liam wanted to live with someone; they were living together. He wanted to be married; they were going to get married. He wanted an enthusiastic lover, and he definitely had one; they were great in bed. But he probably also wanted a lover who wasn't a pile of neuroses. It was time to try some new things, because the old things were not getting Mark over that last hump of 'who am I now.' If he wanted to know who he was, he needed to start taking action. And, "Holy shit." Again out loud.

Who he was would be a function of what he did. It always had been, he realized. He used to be a closeted gay man who worked as an actor. Now he was an out gay man who was – at least – a writer. A self-employed writer, meaning he could write any damn thing he wanted, on his own schedule. He could be as deep or as shallow as he wanted. He could do research for months in advance or he could make stuff up and fix it later. He could create every character, visualize every setting, design every costume and stage every show – whether a show was a play on a fictional stage, or a crisis in a fictional operating room. Good grief, he had so much *power*. Was this why Chris wanted to write? Because as a super-smart teenager he had ideas he couldn't act on in real life? It was a question worth asking. Mark could give his son some insight on how that limitation did not apply only to the young.

For now, though, he was going to read through the script notes he'd kept so he would make sense when he talked to Liam tonight. Then he was going to organize all the random story ideas he'd had, and set up a schedule to work on the doctor things until they were one hundred percent finished. He'd block out time to read, and to watch things, and to go out. Maybe he needed a dance class. Well, obviously, he needed a dance class. Even if he never worked on stage again, dancing was fun. Good exercise, social, fun. He was going to start noodling around with a memoir, too. Even if he never tried to sell it, the process would help him organize his thoughts about things he'd done that he wouldn't do again, and about things he hadn't done that he might be able to do now.

Apparently all he needed to kick into a new gear was a breakdown in the kitchen. That seemed to be his thing. Maybe the memoir should be called 'The Kitchen Sink.' He snorted out a laugh and went to get started.

Everything seemed normal before work, but Liam was still inclined to worry a little. He didn't want to be checking in on Mark all the time; they were partners and equals, both competent adults. Mark knew he could come to Liam with his concerns. If he chose not to, Liam had to believe it was because he wanted to deal with things on his own. Not because he thought Liam couldn't help. Or wouldn't try to. There might be a way to make him feel less whatever about it, though. Less uneasy, or embarrassed, as if talking about insecurities were a sign of weakness. Liam might not have been so great about doing that himself. Tripping over that letter might have been the first time he really showed his own insecurity.

He let the topic simmer while he attended to business. There was plenty of it; the celebrity connection (even with someone who was not a huge star and might never be) was a giant visibility boost for the practice. Liam, his partner Marcie, and their physician assistant were fully booked every day. The aestheticians always had been, and now they were both full-time. Wei came in Tuesday through Saturday, Tara worked Monday through Friday. Everybody had been so busy for so long that the partners decided to close the office for the entire four-day Thanksgiving weekend. People needed a break.

He'd have to sit down and talk to Marcie about travel plans, too. They were used to covering for each other, but he was going to be away for a week in December and two weeks in January. Plus there was the summer trip to Glacier National Park. Marcie surely had her own vacation plans. It might be worth finding another local M.D. who could be on call for them, or even join the practice as an associate. They could start looking, anyway. Couldn't expect to find the exactly-right person immediately. Liam wrote up the idea in an email and sent it off to Marcie. Then he heard his phone buzz, and pulled it out of his messenger bag. *Hi sweetheart I'm having a very constructive day. Kitchen meltdown apparently = breakthrough. Love you a lot XOX*

Liam smiled. He loved getting messages in the middle of the day. Loved having someone who sent messages, someone to go home to. He could deal with the occasional meltdown if it came with all the great stuff. He sent back *Glad to hear it (all of it). I love you a lot too. See you around 6:30 XOX*

Liam got home from work to the aroma of dinner in the oven, but no sign of Mark. He dropped his messenger bag on the kitchen island. "Hi honey, I'm home," he called on his way upstairs to the bedroom. "Oh." Mark was stretched out naked on the bed. "An appetizer?"

Mark laughed under his breath. "Or an all you can eat buffet." He watched Liam strip. "Jesus, you're gorgeous."

"Speak for yourself." Liam got on the bed, crawled over Mark, leaned down to kiss him, one knee between his legs. Mark ran his hands up Liam's arms, down his flanks, to his hips. Around in front, playing with the erection springing to his touch. "Mmm. What are you in the mood for this evening."

"I was thinking about kissing you all over."

Yes please. "That sounds nice."

"And then maybe you'd like to hang onto the rails while I do something else."

Oh Jesus yes. "Like what?"

237

Mark bent his knee, wrapped one hand around the back of Liam's neck, planted the other one on his ribs and rolled them over. "Whatever you want." Mouth against Liam's, holding eye contact. "Anything you want." He licked into Liam's mouth.

"In me. Like this." With the height difference, it took a little bit of adjustment for them to kiss when they did it face to face. Mark usually ended up with his mouth on Liam's chest somewhere, or his neck, or on a shoulder. It was all good, because they could see each other. Liam was so turned on he almost didn't want to wait for the kissing-all-over part. But he loved that part. "I want your mouth."

"You're going to get it." Mark kissed him again. Hard, sloppy, toothy. Then he went on another tour of Liam's body. Licking, nibbling, kissing. Taking his own sweet time with his front, everywhere except his cock. Making him roll over again. There was that little patch of soft hair, black peach fuzz, at the small of his back. The top of his cleft, licking there was always a sure winner. The super-sensitive spot at the iliac crest. The insides of his ankles, the wildly erogenous backs of his knees, and that creamy skin between nipple and underarm. Delicious, and Liam was going crazy. Mark listened to the sound effects, put a hand on the front of his hip, and pushed him over. His cock was flushed and sticky. "How much do you want me."

"Ungh. So much." He couldn't resist getting his mouth on that cock. Only for a few seconds, long enough for Liam to buck up with a gasp. "Jesus!"

Mark gave an evil little laugh. Liam tugged on his hair. "Mmph." Mark let go, crawled over to the nightstand, and got what they needed. He had to dry himself off with the sheet before rolling on the condom. Then he went to work on Liam with the lube, watching his face as his eyes drifted shut. As he reached for the rails, blindly wriggling into a comfortable position. Mark loved what that did for his torso. The guy was fucking *built*. "My superhero."

"Uh-huh." It was half a laugh.

"How much do I love you."

Liam opened his eyes. "So much."

"You know it." Mark started to engage. "God *damn*." A breathless laugh from Liam, turning into a moan as Mark rocked his hips, in and in and *in*. He knew exactly how to do this now. Exactly when to hold still, deep inside, and when to move so he hit Liam's g-spot. One slow stroke and then *ungh*, right there, rewarded with that sound and the look on Liam's face, the pressure of Liam's heels up on his back. Alternating, taking his time again, they both loved this part. But it couldn't go on too long, or they'd peak too fast once they finally let go. Mark wanted to come, and he wanted to see Liam come. Wanted to feel it. Moving faster, hearing the pitch of Liam's sounds ratcheting up. Feeling the wetness between them, Liam's cock drooling onto his belly. Sometimes he'd go without Mark ever touching him there. Today Mark wanted to drag that climax out of him, wanted to feel it as he was peaking himself. He shifted his weight, braced on one arm, and reached for Liam.

"Oh holy Jesus fucking hell I can't no oh my God Mark *yes*." Bucking wildly, spilling over Mark's fingers. And Mark shoving in hard, that contraction setting him off. He had to let go, had to catch his weight on both hands. Made some kind of loud, wordless sound. Held still, feeling the waves of his climax ebb. Liam purred, legs sliding down.

"So good," Mark murmured. He disengaged, shifted up, kissed Liam. Felt him let go of the rails, wrapping his arms over Mark's back. They lay there for a minute or two, catching their breath.

Liam ran his fingers through Mark's hair. Finer than his, silky to the touch, even his beard (when he let it grow out). Still no signs of gray, unlike Liam's. He was going to be beautiful forever. "I get insecure too," he said softly, out of nowhere. "You've probably noticed. All those things that didn't work out. When I'm rational I know it's never less than fifty percent circumstances plus twenty-five percent the other guy, but it's still something that didn't work. Then I go to the what if his circumstances change again thing. And then I go to how we met, and how desperate we both were, and I get very unstable."

Mark pressed a kiss to his chest. "You're never unstable. That's one of the reasons I loved you right away. You're like Kerry. Someone who'll have my back no matter what, even if someday we're mad at each other and not understanding each other." They gazed at each other for a few seconds. "I didn't walk away from her, you know. We fought through a couple of rough years, till we both knew exactly what staying together would be like. How much it would suck for both of us. She finally said you're right, it doesn't work anymore. We took Christopher to her parents' house the day we filed the papers. Then we went home and got drunk together and just cried for a while." He almost cried again, remembering. Swallowed hard, blinked, took a breath.

"I cried when I left the guy in Minneapolis."

"Did he?"

"No. He was all, have a nice life."

"Fucker," Mark muttered. Liam stifled a laugh. "Well, I'll bet he's sorry now." Liam snorted. "I'll bet he's fat and losing his hair." Liam laughed out loud. "Says me with the dodgy hairline."

"Your hairline is fine. Everything about you is fine." Liam changed position, enough for a kiss. "I love you."

"I love you too. Hey."

"What?"

"I want you to tell me if there's something troubling you. I want to help solve whatever problems you might have. I don't want to be a problem for you, I want to be part of the solution. And I have a lot of time to think. Most of the time my brain works pretty well."

Liam gazed at him for a moment. "Okay."

"Ready to eat?"

"Yes please." They peeled themselves apart, organized their limbs, scrambled off the bed. A quick shower, into their robes, and downstairs for dinner. A sweet routine, though still so new and wonderful that it didn't feel like routine. Maybe it never would. They'd both lived without it for so long.

With food on the table, Liam started telling Mark about the Almost Too Successful situation at the office. All through dinner they tossed around different scenarios – an associate, another physician assistant, a nurse practitioner – to cover the increased demand. All of the potential solutions were expensive. Getting unsustainably big was also a concern. Eventually the demand would settle into a new normal, which might be perfectly manageable with the staff they had. Liam also wanted to maintain a balance between the profitable cosmetic treatments and genuine medical dermatology. He and Marcie had a good track record for keeping their patients healthy.

No decisions were reached, of course. Mark was only serving as a sounding board. But he appreciated playing that role. "This was interesting," he said as they were clearing the table. "I honestly never gave a thought to how a doctor's office operated until you and I started writing those letters."

Liam set the plates in the sink. "It's been good for me. You know how it is. Anything you've done for a while, you stop thinking about how you do it. Or why, sometimes. But I haven't had any serious dark night of the soul events. I've been really lucky." He leaned against the counter, watching Mark load the dishwasher.

"How's that."

"I don't lose patients very often. I mean, they don't die on me, not of something I might have helped with. A couple have died of unrelated issues. I lost one to melanoma."

"That must have been rough, though." Mark wiped his hands. "I've lost co-workers to this or that. It's not the same thing."

"No. So are you going to tell me some things?"

"I am. Let's take a little whisky in the office."

"A whisky kind of night, huh." Liam was smiling. He fixed the drinks and followed his fiancé down the hall.

Mark was perched on the desk, a document open on the computer screen beside him. "I wrote up some notes on all the scripts Brian has sent me since May. We've been talking pretty often, and he knew I wasn't likely to say yes to any of the TV or movie stuff that was open. He was a little pissed about the musical."

"Would have been a nice commission for him, huh."

"It would have been. But I told him at the start, the whole point of this was to have a life with you, and your life is here. So mine is going to be here too. If that show ever tours and they need a Willy Wonka for a local stage, I'd be all over it. Not in London." He gestured at the task chair. "Feel free to sit and scroll through that. I ended up making a chart out of it."

Liam sat, sipped his whisky, scrolled through the chart. "Huh."

"Yeah."

"A guest role, that's like a little part in one episode, right?"

"Usually."

"So there's this category of things like the last thing you played. And then there's Random Gay Guy."

Mark grinned. "Yeah. A character whose sexuality is completely irrelevant, but the show runners think a gay guy, meaning stereotypically camp or bitchy or both, will boost the episode's diversity quotient. It's like the Random Black Guy, or girl. They count on the actor to bring all the characterization, because I guarantee you it's not in the script."

Liam nodded. "And then there's Villains. You don't want to play a villain?"

"I'd love to, actually, but not a single-episode villain. I'd like to be one of those bad guys who causes trouble for a whole season, or in a movie. Something I could really sink my teeth into, and be seen in. I don't want to pick up a week of work that results in six to eight minutes of screen time after which the average viewer will remember that the murderer or embezzler had red hair. I want a role that affects the outcome." He could see that Liam understood. "It may be a while till something like that lands."

Liam sat back, looked up at him, smiled. "You know we'll be fine."

"I know." Mark shut down the computer, tugged Liam out of the chair, walked him around to the couch, and pulled him down for a cuddle. He felt so relaxed, so contented. It probably wouldn't last – he'd spent a lot of years training himself to be anxious – but for tonight he felt great. "I'll always want to be involved with some kind of creative effort, but I've realized I don't need to be onstage right now. I do want to stay a part of the theater community, so I'll probably be dragging you to every possible thing we can see."

"Gee, honey, I don't know how much going out on the town with my gorgeous guy I can take." Liam tried his hardest to make that sound dry.

Mark bit his earlobe, not too hard. "Otherwise, writing feels rewarding right now, so I'm going to concentrate on that until it doesn't. But the very most important thing is us. We're getting married."

Liam held him a bit tighter. "Yes we are. It's going to be a great year."

"Even better than last year." Mark wriggled a little, enough to get in position for a kiss. They did that for a few minutes before he put enough distance between them to make eye contact. "That reporter asked me if I had any regrets about giving up my career."

"And do you?" It was soft. Might have sounded hesitant. This was the question that could make or break them.

They stared at each other for a few seconds, long enough for Mark's certainty to sink in. He could see it happen: the tiniest relaxation of the skin around his fiancé's beautiful eyes. "Not a single one. I'll never regret it. I haven't given up anything that really

244

mattered." Brushing a hand over Liam's cheek, down that strong neck. "Everything that matters is right here."

THE END

If you enjoyed GIVING IT UP, please consider leaving a positive rating or review. It really helps! Thanks for reading.

Want more? Robert and Jade's story is **A LITTLE TURN**. Discover this world of romance at
www.thelastories.com

*****

About the Author

Alexandra Caluen lives in a small purple house with her husband, a bottle of Laphroaig, a lot of books, and nine pairs of ballroom shoes. She works in patent law and has enough hair for three people.